Karen E. Olson is a long-time journalist. She lives in Connecticut with her husband and daughter.

Visit the author's website at:
www.kareneolson.com

SECONDHAND SMOKE

Reporter Annie Seymour investigates a suspicious fire in a neighborhood-favorite Italian restaurant. A body is found in the rubble, the restaurant owner is missing and the FBI is involved. Annie begins to realise that she's an outsider in her own neighborhood, searching for a way in. She is forced to question some of the very people who watched her grow up, from opinionated Italian mothers to a retired Mafia godfather with active mob connections. And at every turn, Annie keeps bumping into heartthrob P.I. Vinny DeLucia — a mixed-up romance that only makes her task even more difficult.

KAREN E. OLSON

SECONDHAND SMOKE

Complete and Unabridged

ULVERSCROFT
Leicester

First published in Great Britain in 2006 by
Little, Brown Book Group Limited, London

First Large Print Edition
published 2007
by arrangement with
Little, Brown Book Group Limited, London

The moral right of the author has been asserted

This book is a work of fiction. Names, characters, places, and incidents are the product of the author's imagination or are used fictitiously. Any resemblance to actual events, locales, or persons, living or dead, is coincidental.

British Library CIP Data

Olson, Karen E.
    Secondhand smoke.—Large print ed.—
Ulverscroft large print series: mystery
1. Women journalists —Fiction 2. Fire investigation
—Fiction 3. New Haven (Conn.)—Fiction
4. Detective and mystery stories 5. Large type books
I. Title
813.6 [F]

ISBN 978–1–84617–823–8

Published by
F. A. Thorpe (Publishing)
Anstey, Leicestershire

Set by Words & Graphics Ltd.
Anstey, Leicestershire
Printed and bound in Great Britain by
T. J. International Ltd., Padstow, Cornwall

This book is printed on acid-free paper

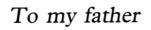

To my father

ACKNOWLEDGMENTS

My father's memories of growing up Swedish and Lutheran in New Haven's Italian and Catholic neighborhoods were the seeds for this book — Wooster Street, raising chickens in his backyard in the Annex, and going to confession with his Catholic friends.

My husband, Chris Hoffman, played a very big role in the development of this story. His knowledge of the Mafia in general and his research into the history of the New Haven Mafia and the city's Italian-American community were invaluable.

My writer's group — Liz Cipollina, Roberta Isleib, Chris Falcone, Angelo Pompano, and Cindy Warm — gave their usual insightful critiques, which helped me mold the plot and characters even further.

The public relations department at the Tropicana resort in Atlantic City was more than helpful when answering myriad questions about their special chickens.

My daughter Julia's support — even though she knows she can't read this until she's much older — warms my heart.

My agent, Jack Scovil, continues to be a

staunch cheerleader, and I'm grateful for his guidance and sense of humor.

It is such a joy to work with everyone at Mysterious Press/Warner Books, among them Susan Richman and Harvey-Jane Kowal, and especially Les Pockell and Kristen Weber, whose encouragement and wisdom helped me push the envelope to make this book even better.

1

I smelled smoke. My feet hit the floor before my eyes opened, my nose leading me into the kitchen. I flicked the switch next to the refrigerator, and the light above the stove blinded me for a second before I saw all the dials were on 'off.' I turned toward the living room, walked around the counter, my eyes searching every nook and cranny until I saw the red glow outside, catty-corner from my brownstone on Wooster Square.

Jesus. I moved to the window and stared. The flames danced between the skeletal limbs of the trees. In my half-sleep state, it was hypnotizing. Until the first siren pierced the air. Shit, I'd go deaf if I stood here. When I moved, my reflection caught my eye — I was naked, standing at my window with the lights on. The clock on the wall read 6:00 A.M. The last time I was awoken at such an ungodly hour, I'd had a dead girl to deal with.

At least I wasn't hung over this time.

I could go back to sleep and pretend I hadn't noticed. But the chorus of sirens below kept getting louder; it would be easier just to drag my ass out there and see what was on fire.

As I got dressed in the bedroom, I glanced outside again and noticed it was snowing. I could see it in the streetlight below my window. And it was coming down pretty hard. Nothing worse than a fucking snowstorm at 6:00 A.M. on Thanksgiving Day.

I found my boots in the back of the closet and rummaged around in a drawer for a pair of gloves. One look in the mirror told me my bedhead was out of control. A hat was definitely called for. I finally found one stuck in the sleeve of my winter coat. A notebook in my pocket, a couple of mechanical pencils, and I was ready.

Yeah, right.

I let myself out the front door of my brownstone, one of my neighbors behind me.

'Annie . . . ' I heard Amber Pfeiffer's breathy voice. 'Annie, wait up.'

I turned to see her mousy brown hair sticking up on the back of her head. She needed a hat worse than I did.

'What's going on?' she asked.

'That's what I'm going to find out,' I said, not even trying to keep the irritation out of my voice. I'd met her and my upstairs neighbor Walter a couple of months ago. They had proved completely useless as they watched me getting mugged, and I hadn't forgotten it.

And speak of the devil, here was Walter, who bore an uncanny resemblance to a pit bull, coming down the stairs with a cup of coffee. 'Something's on fire,' he said, proving that perhaps he was at least as smart as a pit bull. He barely glanced at me — we'd never bonded — and smiled at Amber, pulling a ski cap down over his crew cut with one hand and offering to get her a cup, too.

Amber declined, and I skirted around her during the distraction, trying to get a head start on them. But they stayed on my heels, and as we got closer, I saw that most of the neighborhood had turned out as well. Who gives a shit about a little snow when there's a raging fire down the street?

I tried to ignore Amber's patter, something about how I must know a lot about fires since I report about them for the newspaper, as I gingerly crossed the street, squinting through the snow and smoke to see what was on fire.

It was Prego. Probably the best Italian restaurant in the entire city, in my personal opinion. I couldn't get enough of their lobster ravioli. Washed down with a fine glass of Chianti, it was a perfect meal.

I slipped on the slick sidewalk and fell on my ass.

'Shit.'

'Good to see you, too,' said a familiar voice, and I looked up into Vinny DeLucia's eyes. I hadn't seen him for about two months, but I wasn't surprised to see him here, since his apartment was just a block away in the other direction on the square. I had imagined that when I saw him again, I might have the upper hand. And here I was with a wet butt, looking anything but attractive.

He held out his hand, and I grabbed it, pulling myself up. 'Long time no see,' I said. I glanced around, but Amber and Walter had finally gone off on their own and were talking to someone else now, several feet away.

Vinny's eyes lingered on mine, and he smiled that sexy smile that turned me into Jell-O. 'You look good.'

'Fucking liar,' I said, brushing the slush off my jeans.

Vinny chuckled, his resemblance to Frank Sinatra once again throwing me off guard. 'I forgot how charming you are.'

I felt a tingle that I hadn't felt in a long time, but there was something in the way. 'How's your fiancée?' I asked.

The smile disappeared, and he shrugged but didn't say anything.

So that was the way it was. I was disappointed, since he'd told me his feelings

4

for her had waned. If his kisses were any indication, well, they had been in big trouble. But maybe they'd worked it out. Which sucked for me, since I still harbored unconsummated feelings for him.

I couldn't spend valuable time thinking about this. 'I have to find out what's going on with the fire, okay?'

I moved past him, deeper into the smoke and to the corner of the square, but I could still feel his eyes on me.

I sidled up to the small wrought-iron fence that circled the square, but I couldn't get any closer because of all the commotion. Flashing lights blinded me as firefighters' silhouettes moved as if in a silent movie, the shouts and loud truck engines their music. The one-story white wooden building squatted on a little plot between two three-story architecturally historic gems. The only things keeping the houses from catching fire were two fairly wide driveways on either side of the restaurant and two walls of water cascading from hoses held by the firefighters.

Prego had never flaunted its reputation, rather quietly understated it with a small oval sign by the front door that announced its identity in black and gold. The sign was illuminated by the streetlamp with a sort of halo effect as flames leaped ferociously from the windows around it.

It was a goddamn shame.

I grabbed the sleeve of one of the firemen as he moved in front of me, and I stared into his sooty face for a moment before recognizing him.

'Al, it's me, Annie. Is the chief around?' I shouted over the din.

His heavy glove pointed a few feet away. 'Thanks!' I shouted again, but I didn't think he heard me.

Len Freelander had been fire chief for exactly one week. The last time I'd seen him was at his swearing-in ceremony. He'd looked dapper in his dress uniform, his hair tucked neatly under his cap, his hands in white gloves. This morning, despite the snow, sweat poured out from under his hat; his hands were red and chapped from the freezing water, his yellow jacket practically black from the smoke.

'Any idea how this started?' I shouted.

He stared at me as if I were from Mars.

'Annie Seymour? The *Herald*?' I reminded him.

His eyes flickered with recognition. 'Oh, yeah.' He shook his head. 'No, no, we can't make any speculations at this point.'

We heard a shout, and Len started

6

running. My own adrenaline was pumping, so I ran after him.

'I'm bringing the guys out. The structure's not sound,' I heard a fireman tell him as we got closer to the restaurant. And after a pause: 'There's a body in there. We can't get it out.'

I felt an arm around my waist, pulling me back.

'Let go of me!'

'You can't go any farther.' It was that fireman, Al.

'But what about a body? There's someone in there?'

He pulled me across the street, back to the square, and left me alone without answering my questions. No surprise there.

I watched as four silhouettes emerged from the building; they weren't running, but they moved efficiently toward the trucks.

'What's going on?' Vinny was back at my side.

'Sounds like they found a body.'

'Inside?'

'Yeah.'

'There wouldn't be anyone in there this morning.'

'Don't they make their own bread? They do that pretty early.'

Vinny shook his head. 'When was the last

time you ate at Prego?'

'I dunno. Six months ago?' So Prego was a little out of my price range. I could indulge only a couple of times a year.

'Their baker died a month ago, and Sal hasn't been able to find anyone he likes to replace him, so he's been getting bread at Benini's on Grand Avenue.' He paused. 'And anyway, Sal doesn't open on Thanksgiving.'

Vinny's parents owned a pizza place on Wooster Street, just a couple of blocks away, so it wasn't a shocker that he would know all that. And because I pride myself on being antisocial in the neighborhood, it wasn't a shocker that I wouldn't be privy to any goings-on outside my own little cocoon up the street.

'I hope it's not Sal — the body, I mean,' I said, thinking about the cheerful man with the hooked nose who gave my father his first job as a dishwasher way back when. If it was Sal Amato, my dad would be crushed. I didn't want to be the one who would have to call him in Vegas and tell him.

The look on Vinny's face told me he'd been wondering the same thing and dreading it, too. But before I could say anything, I heard a voice behind me. 'Have you found out how it started?'

Dick Whitfield was like the cockroach that

wouldn't go live in the little motel under my sink.

'Why the fuck are you here?'

Vinny's eyebrows shot up into his forehead, and I rolled my eyes at him. It's just too hard to try to explain to anyone that Dick needed to be kept in his place if I wanted to get any real work done. He was still a rookie reporter, even if he had proven himself a little useful the last time we'd worked together. Marty Thompson, the city editor, had wisely kept him away from me for the last month. But here he was again, breathing down my neck in my neck of the woods.

Dick looked like he was going to back down, but then: 'Hey, we can work on something together again.'

Vinny didn't turn away from me fast enough. I saw the smile, and I was going to remember it.

'Why don't you go home,' I started to say, when an explosion crashed through the thick, icy air.

2

Part of the roof had caved in. The firefighters looked like they'd frozen in that moment, staring at the burning building as the red lights from the trucks flashed in synchrony like a strobe. I looked around me at all the neighbors huddling together, watching the scene as if it were on TV and not in their own backyards. A scream resonated somewhere off to my right.

Sal's wife, Immaculata, the rollers in her gray hair bouncing off the top of her head, her pink chenille bathrobe trailing behind her as her slippers sank into the slush, was stopped by a fireman before she could get to what was left of the restaurant. Her face was contorted with fear, and even from where I stood, I could see tears freezing to her cheeks.

'Who's that?' Dick asked no one in particular.

I was glad I wasn't the only one who ignored him. Everyone else there knew Sal and Mac Amato — they grew up in the neighborhood, they got married at the church around the corner, they raised their son there, they ran their business. They knew everyone's name, and everyone knew them. Dick had no place here.

I heard Vinny telling Dick maybe he should let me handle this right now. I stepped back toward the street. I never liked covering fires; people lost stuff — their possessions, their memories, their family. But this is what I do; it's the only thing I know I'm really good at, so I made my legs take me into the middle of it, where I knew I'd get my story.

'Was there anyone in there?' I asked Len Freelander, who was shaking his head, muttering to himself.

'There was a body.'

I already knew that, but now I had it on the record. 'Only one?'

'Yes.' I could see he was relieved.

'Was it Sal, you know, the body?'

Len sighed. 'I don't know. With any luck, we can still get it out of there in one piece. But it's just too dangerous to let anyone go in now, until the fire's out completely and the structure's secure.'

He walked away from me, and I went back to my spot near the square. Dick was talking to some of the people who'd gathered. At least he was doing something other than bothering me, but this meant he was getting in on the story, and Marty might let him stay on it with me.

Vinny was standing by himself, staring at what was left of Prego.

'Was it Sal in there?' he asked me as I approached.

I shook my head. 'They don't know.'

His mouth tightened into a grim line. Vinny DeLucia was a private investigator and had played a big role in finding the guy who'd embezzled money from a slew of prominent city folk back in September. My mother, who'd hired him, vouched for his professional talents. As for me, I could vouch only for the way he both annoyed me and turned me on at the same time. I suppose he would call it a talent. I called it a goddamn pain in my ass.

I glanced over at Mac, and two women with scarves obscuring their faces were on either side of her, literally holding her up while Len Freelander held her hands. I could see his mouth moving, and then hers, the pain etched into her forehead.

'I have to go try to talk to Mac,' I said, mostly to myself, but I felt Vinny's hand on my arm.

'She's not in a state to talk right now,' he said firmly.

I didn't really want to deal with her now, either, and I was very aware that my ass was numb because the slush that soaked through my jeans and underpants had frozen. I was a fucking Popsicle. So it was easy to pretend I was more sympathetic than I really was, even though my editor would undoubtedly tell me that the story is more important than whether I'd actually feel something when I sat down.

I nodded. 'Okay. I need to change my clothes. But when I come back, I have to talk to her.'

'Thanks, Annie.' Vinny's voice was low and gruff, and I looked more closely at him. He was watching Mac, and I saw in that second that she meant something more to him than just being one of the little Italian ladies on the block.

His eyes swung back to me before I could look away. Caught.

'She's my godmother,' he said quietly.

I shifted a little, uncertain what to say. Sorry your godmother's probably a widow? It would be just as bad as laughing at a funeral. Which I did once, but I didn't actually know the corpse. And it was just a chuckle, really.

But I felt like I needed to offer up something. 'It'll be okay,' was the best I could do, a little white lie, and before I could do any real damage, I climbed over the short iron fence and headed toward my brownstone.

I'm not sure he even heard me.

13

Okay, so I left Dick to do all the dirty work. But I would be back, after I got myself thawed out.

It would take at least three showers before my hair would be smoke-free. My underpants came off with the jeans, leaving a huge red mark in the middle of my pasty white butt. I threw them both and the hat in a large trash bag; it wouldn't be worth trying to salvage them. The stench would always be there.

But I was in a bind. It was the only pair of jeans that fit me at the moment, and that hat was the only one I owned. I needed to take a serious look at my wardrobe situation.

I pulled on a sweatshirt and a pair of yoga pants — not that I had anything to do with yoga. I have an aversion to anything that requires me to pretend I'm a pretzel, and I'm about as flexible as a stick. But yoga pants are comfortable, and I go with comfort every time.

I glanced out the window and saw some lingering smoke, but it looked like the fire was finally out. Even from here, I could make out Dick's figure as he darted around. I forgot what it was like to be that enthusiastic — oh, wow, a fire, a real fire. At this point in my career, I took a lot of shortcuts, shortcuts I

14

knew I could get away with because I'd seen mostly everything already. A twinge of guilt hit me in the gut. I sat down, surprised. I hadn't felt that in a long time.

I suppose I should've felt guilty more often. Guilty that I didn't give a shit about Dick Whitfield and his enthusiasm, guilty that I made fun of him for his eagerness. I still got that rush from the job when something big was going down. But most days I hated it, the redundancy of it. Listen to scanner, go to accident/fire/some sort of crime scene, write down what I can, talk to cops who won't talk to me, go back to the office, put it into my computer, see the spelling error in the headline or the copy the next day, and cringe over a fucking three-inch brief.

I should be getting back out there. But it was warm in my apartment, and I had coffee, no thanks to Walter the Pit Bull.

My thoughts strayed to the body in the restaurant. This was big news. Sal Amato commanded a lot of respect in the neighborhood. It would be a huge funeral. My father would even come out from Vegas, and I couldn't remember the last time he was in Connecticut. My mother wouldn't care much about this. She never fit in here, that's why she lives across town, with her people.

I never thought too much about my

15

parents' cultural differences, what with Mom being Jewish and Dad being Italian. My mother tried taking me to temple when I was in elementary school. But I spent too much time with my dad's friends' kids, and they were all Italian and Catholic. My mother finally gave it up when I was about ten and the priest called to find out why I was going to confession if I was Jewish. I ended up at a Catholic high school because the city schools were so questionable. I think Dad was secretly pleased about that. I went to his alma mater, St. Anthony's. Which was the first place I remember noticing Vinny, even though he must have been around before that. But I didn't have anything to do with him because he was so geeky and president of the chess club. I wasn't exactly Miss Popular, either, but I had standards.

This was way too much ruminating for one day. It tired me out, and it was still pretty damn early in the morning. I'd need another cup of coffee just to get myself out the door. But what to wear? I stared down at my sweats. Too tempting. I rustled through my drawers and closet until I found a pair of heavy knit pants I'd bought at some point and never wore. Because they were knit, I figured that I'd bought them at a 'heavy' point in my life. Which I still seemed to be in.

They clung slightly to my thighs, but a long sweater disguised that.

The *What Not to Wear* stylists would have a field day with me.

I wrapped myself up in my smoke-scented coat and pulled on my gloves. The cold hit me in the face, and I regretted leaving the hat behind.

'Back so soon?' Vinny held out his hand in front of me so I couldn't walk past him. 'They do think it's Sal in there. Mac says he got up about four. She said he always goes to the restaurant when he can't sleep. He works on the books, figures out what he needs to order for the day, that sort of thing.'

I sighed. 'Shit.'

Vinny nodded. 'Yeah, I know.'

'I have to go talk to these guys.' I indicated the firefighters, who had become more still, like the rest of us. The cops were also there, and I had to talk to them, too. Dick was still getting quotes from neighbors. The old-timers could talk anyone's ear off, so he'd be a while.

Vinny backed off and headed toward his parents, whom I could see were trying to console an inconsolable Mac. She was a far cry right now from the woman who gave me ice cream every time my dad brought me around to the restaurant. That woman always had a bright smile and a twinkle in her eye. This woman's mouth sagged with her grief, her eyes almost lifeless.

There was another woman with them, and when Vinny approached, she looked up at him and touched his cheek, an intimate gesture. It was Rosie, his fiancée.

Vinny and Rosie had been together for five years. Vinny had told me how close Rosie was with his family and how she ended up with a ring on her finger because she pressured him into it and he thought it was the 'right' thing to do. Typical.

I turned around as the job pushed me forward.

I found Len Freelander again.

'Is it Sal?' I asked.

Len shook his head. 'We can't get the body out yet, it's still too dangerous to try. And even when we get it out, we might not get a positive ID right off the bat because the body could've gotten pulverized when the roof collapsed.'

Not a pretty picture, but realistic.

Len was nodding. 'But it looks like it's probably Sal. Mac said . . . ' His voice trailed off.

No one wanted to believe it.

'You're up early.' Another country heard from. Tom Behr and I had called it quits at the same time I became interested in Vinny. Of course Tom, being a police detective, figured it out well before I did. But there was still a little spark between us, more than just a friendly cop-reporter thing. I didn't like knowing I was attracted to two guys at the same time. The really stupid thing was that I wasn't sleeping with either of them.

'When do you guys think you'll go in and get the body out?'

Tom shook his head. 'I have no idea. Len says it's still too dangerous.'

Old news. Give me something new. 'I know Mac says she thinks it's Sal. What do you think?'

Tom shrugged. 'Beats me. Could be. It's gotta be someone, and it's his restaurant and he wasn't home. When he wasn't home, he was at the restaurant. One and one is always two.'

'So can I quote you as saying you suspect it's Sal Amato?'

'Go ahead. Sure. What's wrong with you?'

'What's wrong with me?'

'You're so, well, professional. You don't have to be so formal with me. It's okay.'

'Sure. Okay. Yeah.' I can be so eloquent sometimes.

Len Freelander approached us, but he was concentrating on Tom.

'We can go in.'

Tom's face changed, and he took a deep breath as he started toward the charred building.

This was going to take a long time, and I could barely move my fingers. Dick was talking to Mac now, but before I could interrupt them, a short, elderly man sidled up next to me.

'Where are the chickens?' He chewed on his lip, and as I looked closer, I could see it was a bad habit for him. His gray hair stuck up on its ends, and the creases in his face showed that he'd lived hard.

But before I could ask him what he was talking about, his eyes grew wide and he started backing up, his voice at a high pitch as he wailed, 'They're dead, aren't they. He killed them, too, didn't he.'

3

The little man scurried off into the crowd of neighbors, and I started after him but felt a hand on my arm, pulling me back.

'What the hell are you doing?' It was Tom — he was pissed — and I realized I was stuck to the crime scene tape.

Yellow is not my color.

'Did you see him?' I asked, pulling the tape off the front of my coat. 'The little guy' — I pointed in the direction he'd run — 'he asked about chickens.'

Tom frowned, but he didn't say anything.

'He asked if the chickens are dead,' I continued, but Tom's face didn't change.

'I didn't see him,' he said after a few seconds, and I knew if there was any fowl situation going on, he certainly wasn't going to tell me about it.

'I thought you were going in there,' I said, indicating the restaurant and eager to change the subject.

'Had to get something. You can't get this close to the building,' he said as he turned and walked away from me. I think I heard him muttering something like 'crazy.' Hell, I'd been called worse.

It was time to talk to Mac. I moved closer to her, where she was, unfortunately, already talking to Dick.

' . . . always worried about the restaurant. I told him to leave it be. He needs time off, he isn't getting any younger.' Mac was in shock; it hadn't sunk in. Dick was taking down every word.

I reached over and touched Mac's shoulder. 'You okay?' I asked softly.

Dick's head snapped back up so fast, he probably got whiplash. He stared at me as if I were a stranger. Okay, so this was a side of me that rarely showed its face in the newsroom.

'You have to be careful what you put in that newspaper of yours,' Mac said harshly.

I nodded. 'I know. Don't worry about that.'

Dick's eyes were so wide, I thought they'd pop out of his head.

'Are you sure Sal was in the restaurant, Mac?' I asked.

She pulled her arms around her chest and hugged tightly. Someone had given her a coat, and she wore big boots that were obviously not her own.

'Are you sure?' I asked again.

Mac's eyes bored into mine. 'He's gone, Annie. I feel it.' She patted her chest. 'He's here now, only here.'

My faith was long gone, if I'd ever had any, but I believed in hers. I turned to Dick and murmured, 'Let's leave her alone now.' I took his arm firmly, seeing he was about to protest, and pulled him away.

'I know these people,' I said before he could speak. 'She's a friend of my father's. We can't do anything until that body is identified officially and Mac can bury her husband properly.'

'I've got lots of quotes.'

'That's nice.' Vinny was coming toward us, distracting me from the matter at hand, which was to get Dick out of there. 'Maybe you should go to the office and start typing up your notes, and I'll be there in a little while and we can put this together. I know they'll want it for the front page.'

I'd have to get a picture of Sal, but that shouldn't be a problem.

I watched Dick skulk back to his car.

'You're still treating that kid like shit,' Vinny said.

'It's none of your business,' I said flatly.

He put his hand on my shoulder, but I knew that only because I could see it there. My coat was pretty puffy.

'Are you going to be able to write this okay?'

He knew I was close to Sal and Mac, or at least I had been in the past. I didn't want to hand this story over carte blanche to good old Dick, but I didn't relish the thought of having to cover this one.

'I'll be fine.' I wouldn't look at him, knowing he'd see my doubts there. I glanced over at Mac, ankle-deep in snow. 'Do you think you could get her back into her house, get her warmed up?'

'I tried, but she won't budge.'

'It's good your mother is with her.'

'They've always been close.'

I didn't like it that all of this was news to me. Where the hell had I been all these years? I'd been living in their midst and knew nothing.

'Oh, by the way, did you see that weird little guy I was talking to?' I asked.

Vinny nodded. 'I don't know him, but I've seen him around. He fishes through the Dumpsters behind my parents' restaurant.'

'That explains it, then. He asked me if the chickens were dead, if they were killed, too.' I chuckled. 'He probably got released too early from the VA hospital.'

Something crossed Vinny's face that I couldn't read, but then he cocked his head toward his mother and Mac. 'I have to go see how they're doing.' His lips brushed my cheek, burning it with his heat despite the cold.

* * *

I volunteered to work Thanksgiving because I didn't want to have dinner with my mother. Not that I didn't want to spend time with my mother on a national holiday, but I really didn't want to spend it with her boyfriend, Bill Bennett, my boss, the publisher of the *New Haven Herald*.

Their relationship was lasting longer than I'd wanted it to. I'd hoped that within a couple of weeks Bill Bennett would see the side of my mother that I saw most of the time and decide she just wasn't worth the work. No such luck. They had already been on a three-day cruise to the Bahamas and were planning a trip to Paris in the spring. Not exactly something a couple would do if a breakup is pending.

I had heard less from my mother and more from Bill Bennett in the past couple of months. Bennett apologized for threatening my job in September, but only after I apologized for accusing him, albeit in a roundabout way, of stealing from his employees' pension fund. Since then, he'd been my buddy, my pal. And was fucking up my life in the newsroom bigtime.

'Thought you'd be breaking bread with the publisher today, Seymour.' Henry Owens was

25

the metro editor who had gotten the short stick and, thus, holiday duty.

'I've got the fire covered,' I told Henry, ignoring him. I handed him a picture of Sal, which I'd gotten from Mac's sister before I left the scene.

Henry waved it off. 'We're not publishing that until we've got it confirmed.'

'Oh, Christ, Henry, you've got the story on a fucking platter. Take it.'

He shook his head. 'You've gone off half-cocked before. There's no official ID on the body. Dick says no one will say it on the record.'

Dick's status had been growing with the departure of two more senior reporters in the past month. I'd hoped Marty would give him the education beat or social services. But Dick had a weird talent of stumbling onto a story, and it wasn't always in the same place. So Marty and the other powers that be decided to give him more free rein to see what he could come up with.

'Tom Behr said it on the record,' I said, keeping my temper down. 'He says one and one always make two.'

'You've been doing this long enough to know that isn't always the case.'

'I've got it from the cops, Henry. Can we just move on?'

There was more to my relationship with Henry than I'm saying. Several years ago, when the paper was still owned by a family that liked Christmas parties and didn't think them a drain on the profits, and after many trips to the holiday punch bowl, Henry and I found ourselves in the then publisher's office, locking lips. We were young and stupid and still embarrassed about it because we didn't like each other then much more than we liked each other now. Thus, our rather tense relationship.

I pulled off my coat and stormed over to my desk. The red light was blinking on my phone, and when I checked the message, my mother's voice echoed through my ear.

'I heard about Prego. I'll call Mac this afternoon. And I'll save some leftovers for you, in case you want to stop by after work.'

I didn't think I'd have time to stop by. I glanced at the clock. It was 10:00 A.M., plenty of time to find something to do later on. Like watch *Survivor*. It was stupid, but those people made me look interesting.

Dick hopped over to my desk. Really.

'I typed up the comments from the neighbors,' he said.

'Thanks.'

'You know, you were really nice to those people out there.'

I sighed. 'Listen, Dick, I grew up with those people. Why wouldn't I be nice?'

He shrugged, smoothing his flyaway hair with his hand. 'You're not nice to anyone.'

My phone rang, and I was glad for the interruption. 'Newsroom.'

'Annie, I just heard. What's the official word?' My dad's deep baritone rumbled soothingly into my ear, and he sounded as if he were in the next room rather than across the country. I forgot that I'd been angry as I closed my eyes and let his voice wash over me, relaxing me, sort of like my own personal, nonprescription Xanax.

I told him everything I knew, which wasn't very much. 'It's not going to be much of a holiday for Mac,' I said.

He was quiet for a minute. It had been half a year since I'd seen him, and every time he called, it reminded me how much I missed him. I knew through the grapevine that he was a real bastard to work for, which was one reason I kept turning down his offer of a PR job at his casino. I didn't want to have my bubble burst. Even though he wasn't my biological father, he was the only father I'd ever known.

'There won't be an autopsy until at least tomorrow, maybe even Monday,' I continued. 'And they have to do that before they release

28

the body to the funeral home.'

My father made a snorting noise. 'Christ, can't they leave the old man alone? Why do they have to cut him up?'

'They need an official cause of death.' I didn't want to tell him about the roof caving in and the possible destruction of what was left of Sal, but I knew he'd find out anyway, and better it came from me.

'Fuck,' he said softly when I finished.

My colorful language runs in the family. 'My thoughts exactly,' I said.

'Keep me posted, okay?'

I knew he'd hear from more people than me. He'd probably gotten fifteen phone calls since the fire this morning. 'Sure.'

'How's your mother?'

'Still dating my boss.'

He chuckled. 'Think she's doing it to piss you off?'

'It crossed my mind. Of course, she'd never admit it.'

'Have you seen Vinny?'

He'd asked me this same question every time we talked, but this time, now that I knew Vinny's relationship with Mac, its meaning was different. 'Yeah, he was there this morning.'

'Doing okay? His mom's okay?'

'Guess he's okay, can't say about her.' I'd

met Vinny's mother only once. 'First time I see Vinny in two months and I fell on my ass in the snow right in front of him.'

My father's big laugh resonated over the phone line. 'I guess he's still with the fiancée?'

'Yeah. She was there, too.'

'Give him a little more time. He's a good kid.'

That 'kid' was almost forty, like me. I didn't say anything. I knew my dad liked Vinny and wanted to see us together. I didn't have the heart to tell him it was probably a lost cause.

'So it's snowing,' he said in response to my silence.

'Like a bitch.'

'Drive safely.'

I heard the dial tone and put the receiver back in its cradle. When the Indians built the Foxwoods and then the Mohegan Sun casinos, I'd hoped my dad would leave his general manager job at the Sun Casino in Vegas and come back here to work. But he said he didn't want to deal with the winters, he loved the desert, and anyway, Suzette, his longtime girlfriend, would kill him if he uprooted her.

I had just started putting Dick's quotes into my story when the scanners started screaming.

'Hey, Henry,' I said, looking in his direction, 'there's a bad accident at State and Grand. I'll finish this up when I get back.'

In most newsrooms, there are no walls. No cubicles. There are aisles between desks, and if you stand up, you might see the sports department at one end of the room and the features department at the other. Sometimes there are dividers between departments, but at the *New Haven Herald*, we're all out in the open — nothing is sacred, not our conversations or our bagged lunches or our bodily noises. I doubted I could work any other way.

Henry glanced up from *The New York Times* and nodded as he sipped his coffee. 'Think it's bad enough to get a photographer out there?'

I nodded. 'Yeah.' But he didn't move.

Dick did, though. In a second, he was next to me.

'I'll go, Annie, if you want to finish up that fire story.'

I looked at him out of the corner of my eye. 'Now why would you want to do that?'

He shrugged. 'It's a holiday, and you've got a big story.'

'So what? As far as I know, you're not even on the schedule for today. Why don't you go home and have dinner with your family?'

Dick shrugged. 'Dinner's not until three.'

'Go home, Dick. Really. You need a life. Don't become me.' What was I saying? That fire must have burned my brain.

I grabbed my coat and my bag. 'Go home,' I repeated as he just stood there, staring at me like a zombie. 'Jesus, Dick, you're freaking me out.'

'Dick, stop freaking Annie out,' Henry called from his desk. 'Annie, get your ass over to that accident.'

He didn't have to tell me twice.

4

The snow hadn't let up, and I could barely see past the hood of my car. I was beginning to regret going out. With the way it was snowing, one false move of my Honda and the scanner would be announcing my demise at any moment. I should've walked over. It would've been faster and safer.

I made my way down State Street, past the Knights of Columbus museum, which had a faded tapestry depicting Pope John Paul II — he'd been pretty popular here, and the museum was featuring some sort of traveling exhibit about him.

I skidded past a few buildings, a couple of empty lots, and through the little hole the wipers had made in my windshield, I could make out the mass of steel that used to be a car. Had to be a fatal. No one could survive that. I carefully pulled over to the side of the road, parked, and walked up the street.

'Haven't seen anything like that on a city street in a long time,' one of the cops was saying when I approached the scene. 'The truck that hit him had to have been going at least eighty.'

I could smell the smoke that hung in the air from Prego, just a few blocks away. The car had been sitting at the light, and someone smashed the shit out of it, pushing it into a Jersey barrier along the side of the road that was supposed to be protecting cars from bridge construction next to the State Street train station.

'Where's the truck?'

The cops turned to stare at me.

Tony Martino's mouth broke into a grin. 'Look what the cat dragged in.'

Okay, so my hair was sopping wet from the snow, not to mention my puffy coat, which shouldn't be exposed to too much moisture or it starts looking like something died on me.

'Where's the truck?' I asked again, ignoring him.

Tony pointed up the street and I squinted, making out a Ford pickup, the front end totaled. 'Anyone survive this?'

'Lucky fuckin' bastard,' Tony said, indicating the driver of the pickup, who was leaning against his truck, surrounded by cops and paramedics.

I pointed toward the mangled car, the whine of the Jaws of Life echoing through the air as two firemen worked on it. 'What about that guy?'

Tony snorted. 'Another lucky bastard.

Must have nine lives.' He turned back to his partner.

I wasn't going to get anything else out of Tony, so I moved across the street to get a better vantage point of the cops interrogating the pickup driver. He looked familiar, but I couldn't make out his features since he kept his hands up near his face, massaging his cheeks, running his palms through his hair. But suddenly he straightened up and looked across the street, right at me.

Jesus, it was Pete Amato. Sal's son.

Before I could react, someone slammed into me, pushing me forward.

'What the fuck . . . ' I looked over to see Wesley Bell, his camera hung over his neck, his usually neatly combed hair flying in the snow.

'Sorry, Annie. Slipped.' I looked down at his feet and saw the penny loafers that shouldn't be out in such weather.

Wesley Bell was the antiphotographer. While most of our staff wore jeans and made sure they had boots in their car trunks, Wesley's outfits included paisley ties and slacks. It was impractical, but it didn't matter in the long run. When Wesley looked through his camera lens, something wonderful happened, something miraculous. He saw pictures that no one else saw, and they were goddamn award-winning pieces of art.

'Is he dead?' Wesley asked, his face obscured by the camera.

'A miracle he isn't.'

'Saw you over at the fire.'

I hadn't seen him, but Wesley had an uncanny ability to be invisible.

'Got some pretty good shots, I think.'

He didn't understand his own power. My eyes strayed back to Pete Amato. 'Gotta find out what happened.'

I left him there, knowing he'd get his shot. He'd been at the paper only a year, but he gave me a little hope that journalism hadn't used up its own nine lives just yet.

'You can't get any closer, Annie.' This time it was a cop that stopped me, about five feet from Pete.

'Was he driving the truck?' I indicated Pete.

The cop, Ronald Berger, nodded. 'He said he heard about his dad and was on his way to his mother's. Said some guy was on his ass, and when he tried to speed up to get away from him, the road was too slick, he just slid into the car.'

That wasn't what I'd heard Tony say on the other side of the street, but I wrote it down anyway. Maybe it really was what happened, but from the look of the other car, I wasn't so sure.

'So where's the guy who was following him?' I asked.

'Said he took off when he hit the car.' Ronald snorted. 'Said it was a Cadillac. One of those new ones with the big grille. Guy probably thought he was in a goddamn SUV.'

Ronald moved a couple of steps, and I caught Pete's eye.

'Hey, Pete, you okay?' My voice came out way too loud, and everyone looked up.

He nodded. 'Annie, can you go tell my mom that I'll be there as soon as I can? Don't tell her about the accident.'

'Sure.' That would be the last thing Mac would need right now.

I surveyed the accident scene again, asked the cops a few more questions, what time did it happen, how long would it take to get the victim out of the car, which hospital were they taking him to, all the standard things. I didn't want to be out there too much longer — the snow was still coming down pretty hard, and I was going to have to scrape my car windows again.

'Are you writing Pete up?' I asked Ronald.

'Yeah. I hate to do it, considering what happened to his father and all, but he's at fault.'

'What's the charge?'

'Reckless driving.' He paused, his eyes

traveling down the road to the other car. 'Hopefully, that guy'll be okay. If not, Pete could be in a lot more trouble.'

I had to get out of there while I still could. 'Can you fax me the report when you get back?'

Ronald nodded. While it was hard getting police reports in a timely manner, Ronald knew that Pete and Sal would want all the facts straight since it would be in the paper anyway.

'Thanks.' I shuffled back to my car, looking around for Wesley, but he was already gone.

My car moved slowly down State and over the bridge to Water Street. I circled around to Wooster Street and aimed the Honda toward the square.

A crowd stood outside Sal and Mac's two-story house a block from Prego. I eased the car along the sidewalk and parked.

'Need an update?'

For someone I hadn't seen in a while, I certainly was getting my fill of Vinny this morning.

I pulled him in the opposite direction of the neighbors. 'Pete Amato was in a bad accident.' I saw the look on Vinny's face and said quickly, 'He's fine, but the other guy, well, he may or may not be.'

'Shit,' Vinny said quietly.

'I have to tell Mac he's on his way, but he doesn't want me to tell her about the accident.'

Vinny brushed a strand of wet hair off his forehead. 'I'll take care of it. I can say he called me because he couldn't get through to her. Her phone's been ringing constantly all morning. She might wonder why he would get in touch with you.'

I hadn't thought of that. 'Okay.'

I looked up toward the remains of the restaurant. Firefighters and cops moved back and forth, getting their jobs done. The TV vans had all arrived, late for the party as usual but pretending they'd been there all along. The satellite dishes swung high above us, and for a moment I wondered if any of them had ever come crashing down on top of some poor, unsuspecting reporter.

Tom saw me and beckoned. 'Thanks, Vinny,' I said, not looking back as I walked away from him.

'What's up?' I asked as I neared the scene.

Tom took my arm and steered me down the block.

'Shit, Tom, my feet aren't even touching the ground,' I said.

He finally stopped, closer to my apartment building than to Prego. 'What do you know about Sal Amato?'

I narrowed my eyes at him. 'What are you talking about?'

'Does he have a vacation home somewhere, does he have another woman somewhere, anything like that?'

'Jesus, Tom, what the fuck are you talking about?'

'Annie, I know you grew up with these people, you know everyone, and that's why I'm asking you before stirring up anything with anyone else. If you know anything, you have to tell me.'

I tried to read his face but couldn't.

'I don't know what you're looking for, Tom. You've got to be straight with me. What are you asking this for?'

Tom glanced over at the restaurant and then down at the pack of neighbors before looking back at me. 'The FBI's here.'

I glanced back at Prego, searching for a telltale jacket with the large 'FBI' on the back, but didn't see one.

Tom shook his head. 'They're inside.'

'Jesus. What the hell for?' This was definitely out of the ordinary.

Tom took a deep breath. 'Sal Amato wasn't killed in that fire. It was a woman's body we fished out of there, not a man's.'

5

Once he realized I didn't have a clue about Sal Amato's private life, and unwilling to give me any more information, Tom left me standing on the sidewalk, his words swirling around in my head. A woman? And what was the FBI doing here?

As I was asking myself these questions, I spotted Jeff Parker, the head of New Haven's FBI division, ducking under the yellow crime scene tape and walking toward a very nondescript brown car just a few yards away. I gave myself a fifty-fifty shot that he'd tell me anything.

'Hi, Jeff,' I said as I approached him, careful not to slip again.

He blinked a couple of times. 'Oh, hi, Annie,' he said casually, as if we were at a cocktail party instead of a fire scene.

'So why is the FBI investigating a fire at Prego?' I asked, pulling my notebook out of my purse.

Jeff Parker smiled condescendingly. He was over a head taller than me, with shocking red hair and a maze of freckles covering his face. His jacket was open despite the cold,

41

revealing a slim physique that probably saw more than a few hours at the gym. 'Now, Annie, why do you think I'd tell you that?'

The FBI was even more closemouthed than the city cops, but I had to try. It was my goddamn job. 'Because even if you don't say anything, it'll still be in the paper that you were here, and then everyone will be speculating and no one will talk to you.' Not that they'd talk in this neighborhood anyway.

This was a place that didn't take kindly to anyone nosing around, especially the FBI, since business may not always be what it appears. I hate to stereotype, but it is a very old Italian neighborhood that hasn't changed much over the years, despite the fancy trellis over Wooster Street proclaiming it New Haven's 'Little Italy,' like anyone who knows anything about New Haven didn't know that already.

Jeff's smile didn't waver. Apparently he wasn't concerned, or he was just stupid. 'You'll find out soon enough,' he said, unlocking the trunk of the car and pulling out a small case.

'So you're investigating something. Is it the woman who was found in there?'

He pushed past me. 'I can't tell you,' he said gruffly.

I watched him for a few seconds as he went

back under the yellow tape, but a movement to my left distracted me.

A white Lincoln Town Car with tinted windows sidled up against the curb and sat idling. The passenger door opened, and a woman with a short brown bob and wearing a camel hair coat got out. She leaned into the car and an elderly man stepped out, holding on to her arm, his back a little hunched, his white hair slicked back. He pulled his wool coat closer around him, and the woman cupped his elbow, helping him along the sidewalk, toward Mac and Sal's house. I could see the resemblance between them in their profiles.

He looked familiar, but I couldn't place him. And why the hell didn't the driver get out? The car just sat there, exhaust filling the air, wafting toward me. If I didn't move soon, I'd end up like one of Dr. Kevorkian's patients.

'What're you doing?'

Tom's voice startled me. 'Shit, you scared the crap out of me.'

'It's Dominic Gaudio,' Tom said, indicating the man now going up Sal's front steps. 'And his daughter.'

Jesus. Dominic Gaudio was a fucking legend. He'd been indicted more times than I could count on both hands, but nothing ever stuck. Gambling, racketeering, money laundering — no one could prove anything.

'They say he's got Alzheimer's now,' Tom was saying. 'I think it's just another scam.'

Dominic Gaudio disappeared into the house, his daughter behind him. 'Why would someone pretend to have Alzheimer's?' I asked. 'That's too cynical, even for you.'

Tom ignored me. 'So did you get anything out of Parker?'

'You just want to know because you don't know anything either,' I said. It was well known that the city cops and the FBI never told each other anything.

'Okay, fine, don't tell me.' He scowled and turned away, but I reached out and grabbed the corner of his jacket.

'Wait a minute,' I said. It worked. Go figure. Tom stopped and faced me.

'Do you have an ID of the body in the restaurant yet?' I asked.

'No ID yet.' He paused a second. 'The body was pretty burnt.'

I took a deep breath and let go of him. 'It must have been someone connected to the restaurant, right?'

From the look he was giving me, I knew he wasn't going to say a damn thing about it. 'I have to go to the Amatos,' he said.

'Have you told Mac yet that it's not Sal?'

He blinked a couple of times, and I could see that he hadn't and that he was about to. I shrugged, like I didn't care, and he turned toward the white house with the gingerbread porch.

I waited until he was safely inside before heading there myself. The reporter in me wanted to be there when he told Mac, even though the daughter of Joe Giametti wanted to be as far away as possible when he lowered the boom.

I slogged through the slush and followed a couple of women carrying large covered baskets up the steps to the house. One of them was Vinny's mother, Mary DeLucia. To anyone who didn't grow up here, it would look as if she didn't even see me. But to my trained eye, she never took her eyes off me.

A woman wearing a light blue jacket, her hair completely hidden by a flowered scarf, tapped me on the shoulder so I'd let her pass. An aluminum-foiled tray balanced neatly on her forearm.

I moved from the foyer into the living room, glancing around. The whole neighborhood had turned out. They were my father's friends, people who had places in my childhood memories, but I hadn't seen too much of them in the last twenty years or so while I was busy keeping to myself and

45

establishing my career. I was Joey Giametti's 'reporter daughter.' Dad thought it was funny, but we both knew it distanced me from the neighborhood even though I lived in the middle of it.

I didn't see Mac, so I started toward the dining room. A man with a shock of white hair blocked the doorway.

'Hey, Uncle Louie.' I smiled. 'Long time no see.'

'When's that father of yours moving back here? We miss him.' Uncle Louie and my dad had worked together at Prego when they were teenagers.

Someone pulled on my arm, and I saw the kind gray eyes of my longtime baby-sitter, Auntie Kay. I grinned as she leaned in to kiss my cheek.

'I hope you're not up to no good here,' she said in her raspy voice. 'Your father'll have to have words with you.'

'He always has words with me,' I said. 'How are you?' I started feeling guilty. I couldn't remember the last time I'd seen her, and she'd always been there for me when I was a kid.

She shrugged. 'The emphysema isn't good, but I hold my own.'

'I'll come by sometime,' I said, but she chuckled as she shook her head.

'You always say that.' She gave my arm a little squeeze. 'I know you want to, though,' she said as she moved past me into the kitchen.

My childhood was jumping up and biting me on the ass.

The minute I smelled the garlic and tomato sauce coming from the kitchen, I forgot about feeling guilty. Death in most neighborhoods called for food, and lots of it. It was lunchtime, my stomach growled, and I picked up a plate.

Reporters don't usually eat at things like this, but I knew what I'd be missing if I didn't, and I wasn't about to miss any of it.

I spotted Tom across the table. He was staring at my plate. 'You have to get your own,' I hissed at him, his mouth watering almost as much as mine.

'She's always hungry.' Vinny's voice came from somewhere to my left; I was too busy piling on some ziti and antipasto to look up.

'She'll eat anything.' Tom didn't have to say that the way he did, and I temporarily forgot the plate in my hand as I gave him a dirty look. Vinny was smirking, and it was almost as if they were forming some sort of alliance.

That wouldn't do.

I popped an olive in my mouth and eyed Vinny. His resemblance to Frank Sinatra hit

47

me again. Not the old, fat Frank who couldn't remember the words to his songs, but Frank from the 1950s, like when he was in *High Society* with Grace Kelly and had some pretty smooth moves. Yeah, that was Vinny, smooth as silk.

'Now, boys, let's not get nasty,' I said.

I could see both of them itching to say something, but to their credit, they just shook their heads and tried not to laugh.

'What's going on?' Vinny asked Tom as I took a bite of bread stuffed with spinach.

'Routine questioning.' His look told me not to say anything. He motioned toward Mac, who was in the corner talking quietly with Dominic Gaudio and his daughter. 'Need to get a timeline.'

'What for? Sal's dead, can you give her a day?'

Tom didn't say anything, and I could see Vinny's thoughts moving faster than a fucking hamster on a wheel.

'There's something you're not saying,' Vinny finally said. He turned to me, his eyes boring into my soul. Fortunately, my mouth was full and I couldn't say anything, but that didn't mean much.

'You know, don't you. Come on, Annie, what gives?'

I shook my head.

'Vinny, what's going on?' It was Rosie, coming from the kitchen, carrying the coffeepot.

Vinny took it from her and put it on the table. 'Nothing,' he said, but I saw he wouldn't meet her eyes, which fell on me as I swallowed, suddenly nauseated. I put down the plate.

'You again,' Rosie said simply.

'Hi,' I managed to spit out.

She glowered at me, then turned to Vinny. 'I thought this was over. And to bring her here, now, when your family needs you.' Her tone was sharp, and I knew she wasn't thinking about Vinny's 'family.'

'You young people need to take this outside.' The woman in the flowered scarf was back. I peered more closely at her and recognized her as Uncle Louie's wife, Aunt Sophia.

I wasn't related by blood to any of these people, but calling them 'Uncle' or 'Aunt' was just something we did in the neighborhood. And I was being sucked right back into it without even realizing it.

'Oh, Rosie, dear, you're such a help.' Aunt Sophia turned to Vinny. 'The wedding's in May, isn't it?' Her twittering laugh echoed through my head. She knew damn well when the wedding was. I could feel a migraine starting.

Tom, sensing this was not something he wanted to get in the middle of, moved quickly past us and toward Mac. Damn. I tried to follow him, but Aunt Sophia's hand held my arm in a vise grip. All these old ladies could scare the shit out of me when I was a kid, and they still had the same effect.

'It's nice to see you're back with that nice police officer,' Aunt Sophia said, but with an edge in her voice that told me I'd better steer clear of Vinny DeLucia or else.

'We're not back together,' I told Aunt Sophia, wanting to clear up any misconceptions, but at that moment, Dominic Gaudio and his daughter swept past me and through the living room and out the front door.

I wanted to follow them. Call it instinct, but something told me that Dominic Gaudio would know why the FBI was checking out Prego.

But then I saw Tom escort Mac down the hall and out of sight. He was going to do it now; he was going to tell her and then quiz her about where Sal might be.

Aunt Sophia's grip got stronger, but she spoke to Vinny. 'Come around this weekend, and I'll make supper. We should talk about the wedding.'

But before he could say anything, a scream echoed through the house.

6

Oh, Christ,' I muttered, breaking away, Vinny on my heels.

Tom was standing by the window, Mac was sprawled across the bed, facedown. Her support hose peeked out from under the black crepe dress. Vinny pushed past me to Mac and held her hand, looking up at Tom.

'What the hell did you do to her?'

Tom's face was hard. 'Nothing. I told her her husband did not die in that fire.'

Vinny's face contorted with confusion. 'What?'

Tom shook his head. 'It wasn't Sal in the restaurant. The body was a female.'

Mac's back heaved with her sobs, but she finally lifted herself onto her elbow and looked up at the three of us.

'If he's not dead,' she said, sobbing, 'I'll kill him for putting me through this.'

Mac waved her hand at the people who had gathered just outside the door. Rosie was in the front and started whispering. They shuffled away and the door shut, but not before I saw Rosie's eyebrows arch at Vinny, mentally asking him what was going on. He shook his head, and she frowned at him, but then she disappeared, too.

Mac shifted on the bed and adjusted her dress, her hand covering the top buttons near her neck, as if something might show. Vinny gave her a tissue and she blew her nose, blinking a couple of times. Finally, she spoke.

'You must excuse me,' she said, looking first at Vinny, then at Tom. Her eyes made their way to me and stopped. 'Annie, you be a good girl.'

I knew what that meant: You write one word about this and you may find yourself in a situation you might not enjoy. I nodded.

'So I assume you don't know where your husband is?' Tom asked. I recognized his 'official' voice.

'I have no idea. First you tell me that he's dead, and now you tell me he's alive. What am I supposed to think?' Mac asked.

Tom sat on the bed next to her, and she inched over a little to make room, even though I could see Tom was treading on thin ice. He should've stayed where he was, but it was too late now.

'Is there a reason why your husband might want to disappear?' Tom asked.

Mac frowned. 'My husband is an upstanding citizen. He has no reason to hide.'

'Then where is he?'

Vinny moved away from the bed and came over to stand next to me at the window. His eyes lingered on mine for a second, and I felt myself flush.

Mac's face was flushed for a different reason. 'I don't know where he could be. The car's in the driveway, so he didn't drive anywhere.' Was she lying or just pissed that Tom would ask her that? I couldn't tell. I glanced at Vinny, who was trying to figure it out, too.

The door flung open, startling us, and Pete Amato fell toward his mother, his face twisted with rage.

'What do you think you're doing? Get the hell out of here, all of you,' he shouted as he cradled his mother's head against his chest.

'Oh, Petey,' I heard Mac mutter, 'they say your father's alive. He didn't die in the fire.'

Pete frowned, and I felt Vinny's hand take mine out of my pocket and lead me out the door. Tom was trying to ask Pete a question, but what it was or whether he got an answer, I'll never know because Vinny didn't stop in the living room but led me out the front door and back into the snow.

He stopped at the bottom of the steps.

'What the hell was that all about?' he demanded.

I shrugged. 'What was what? Tom wanted

to tell her it wasn't Sal. And he needs to find out who it was and where Sal might be.' I knew Vinny wasn't stupid; that wasn't what he was looking for.

I turned around and started to walk away but felt Vinny's hand on my arm.

'I'm sorry. But Mac's a friend.'

I sighed. 'I know. She's my friend, too, remember? I guess I thought it might make her happy to find out Sal's alive, but . . . ' My voice trailed off.

'Yeah, something's not right, but why don't you let Tom find out about it?'

'What about my story? I need this.' I felt the anger rising. Vinny had been such a cheerleader for my crusading journalist a few months ago, but then again, he wanted my help at the time and was feeding my ego.

'You'll get it when you need to,' he said, his eyes searching my face as he moved closer to me, close enough to kiss me.

I found myself leaning toward him, but then Vinny pulled back, asking, 'What the hell's going on over there?'

He pointed toward the restaurant, and I could see the FBI guys trying to be discreet in their matching jackets and slacks.

'It's the FBI.'

Vinny stared at me. 'I can see that. What are they doing?'

I shook my head. 'I don't know.'

'Shit,' he said quietly. 'I have to go back in.'

'Can I tag along?'

Vinny smiled condescendingly, and it pissed me off. 'That's not a good idea. No one will talk to you right now, you know that.'

I did know that, but I had to try.

I followed him all the way up to the door, where his mother and Aunt Sophia appeared. Vinny shrugged his shoulders at me as if to say, *Told you so,* as they let him squeeze past but blocked me from entering.

'Don't you think you've caused enough trouble today?' Mrs. DeLucia asked.

'I didn't do anything,' I began, but Aunt Sophia put up her hand to silence me.

'There's a lot to sort out here.' She was about a head shorter than me and rather birdlike, but her voice was like steel. 'You can come back tomorrow.'

The door closed before I could say anything else, and I knew nothing would get me back inside.

My car was parked near my brownstone catty-corner to where I was. The snow was starting to taper off, and I heard a plow somewhere in the distance. It wasn't until I was halfway to my car that the white Town Car pulled up beside me.

A window rolled down in the back, and I

could make out a profile. Dominic Gaudio.

'Miss Giametti?' I smiled on reflex. It had been a long time since someone called me 'Miss Giametti' — I had taken my ex-husband's name, and even though we divorced after being married about a nanosecond, I never changed it back.

The door opened, and a hand extended from the black hole inside. My heart quickened, and I caught my breath, but curiosity overtook any fears, and I folded myself down and climbed into the car. Dominic Gaudio was alone in the back; his daughter was in front, next to the driver.

Age spots dotted his face, but his smile was bright and his eyes clear, indicating his intelligence. Tom was right. There was nothing wrong with this man.

He took my hands in his, and I could feel his warmth through my gloves. 'You look like your mother,' he said simply.

No one had ever told me that — it simply wasn't true — and I began to be suspicious.

'It's the eyes,' he continued. 'Beautiful eyes.'

Okay, so I wasn't going to call the cops.

'Be careful what you write, Miss Giametti. Things are not what they seem.' His voice was light, despite his words. Sort of like Yoda, dispensing wisdom instead of an obvious threat.

'I get the facts, sir,' I said respectfully. This was not a guy I could fuck around with. I wondered if he knew the body in the restaurant wasn't Sal, if that's what he was trying to say.

'Make sure you get all of them before you do anything else.' His voice was barely above a whisper, shades of Marlon Brando as Don Corleone, but without the cotton in his jaw. 'And please give my regards to your father.' He shifted in his seat, and I knew I was being dismissed.

I climbed back out and watched the door close after me. The Town Car moved past me, turning right on Chapel before disappearing down the street.

★   ★   ★

Somehow I managed to make it back to the paper in one piece. The trucks had done a half-ass job plowing, little bits of sand and salt peppering the way but not doing a helluva lot for traction.

The whole way back, I ran Dominic Gaudio's words over and over in my head. I knew the guy was a mobster, but I couldn't help it: I liked him, even though I'd spent barely five minutes with him.

When I got inside the building, I made my

way to the newsroom, threw my bag on my desk, and landed hard on my chair. Dick Whitfield was at his computer next to me, tap-tap-tapping with one finger on the keyboard.

Before I could even log on to my computer, I heard Henry calling my name.

'I hope you've got a good story. Wesley's been back for an hour, and he's got some great shots. Of the fire and the accident.'

No shit. Wesley would have a good shot of Dick's ass.

'Yeah, I've got some good stuff. Just need to make a call first.' I picked up my phone and dialed Paula Conrad, my friend and source at the FBI. If Jeff Parker wasn't going to tell me anything, I might be able to get something at least off the record from Paula that I could work with.

Paula was having dinner with her parents in Westport, and I knew she wouldn't mind getting a call on her cell phone interrupting her visit. She was probably undergoing major interrogation from her mother about her personal life, which was about as exciting as mine.

'Oh, thank you for calling me.' Paula's voice resonated in my ear, and I heard her say, 'I have to take this, please excuse me.' A few more seconds and I heard a muffled, 'Oh,

God, it's worse than ever. I even had to make up a boyfriend, just to get her off my back. I hope you don't mind, I borrowed Tom.'

'He's not mine to borrow anymore, so go ahead.' I paused. 'I have a question.' I fiddled with a pencil.

'Work related?'

'Prego burned down this morning.'

'What?'

'Prego, the restaurant across the square from my place. Problem is, the owner is missing and there was a body in the rubble. A woman. Not sure who. But here's the thing: Jeff Parker showed up. Do you know anything about that?'

She was quiet. Too quiet.

'Okay, Paula, what's up?'

'I'm sorry, Annie, I really can't tell you.'

'Are you working on this?'

'They didn't call me, if that's what you're asking. Although I wish they had.'

It was getting more and more mysterious. 'Can't you tell me anything? They've been out there most of the morning.'

'Jesus, and they didn't call me? They knew how to reach me.' I was getting pissed at Paula for not telling me, and she was pissed at her fellow suits for not letting her in on the game.

'I gotta go,' I heard her say, and the line went dead.

This wasn't good. Paula always told me something, and if she wasn't telling me anything on this, then there was something really big going down.

I'd never heard anything concrete about Sal Amato except the usual rumors that he was mobbed up. That's what everyone said about everyone in the neighborhood. But if Dominic Gaudio was showing up to pay respects, it seemed more likely than not. Maybe Sal was in trouble. One person probably knew the whole story, and I reached for the phone again.

'I'm sorry, Annie, but your father left an hour ago.' Suzette's voice was a little squeaky. I wondered how my father could stand it.

'Where'd he go?'

'He's on his way to Connecticut. Didn't he call you?'

There was no voice mail message on either my cell phone or my work phone. He knew I was working. Oh, shit, he'd probably called my mother, thinking I'd be there later on in the day. I wasn't about to make her my third call. I had enough to deal with.

'Do you know when he's supposed to get in?' I asked.

'I don't know, honey, but you know Joe,

he'll call you.' She hung up.

I sat staring at my phone for a few minutes.

'What's up?' Dick's voice invaded my space.

I shook my head. 'Nothing. My dad's coming to town.'

'For Thanksgiving?'

It's too bad looks really can't kill.

Biting my tongue, I got up, found my way to the cafeteria, and pondered the calories in either a Twix or a Baby Ruth. I shouldn't have volunteered to work on a holiday. I should've stayed home and made myself a bowl of soup and told my mother I was working. But I would've gone to the fire even if I wasn't and ended up here anyway.

I decided on a Twix and hoped Dick would be gone when I got back.

No such luck.

'You really have to start being nice. I saw you out there, you can be nice.'

I made a face at him as I chewed. Oh, Christ, I shouldn't have let him see me like that. Now I was going to be held up to a higher standard, and that sucked.

I knocked out the story about the accident in about twenty minutes. Ronald, as promised, had faxed the report already, so it was pretty routine. When I was done, I sent it to Henry's queue for editing and pulled up the story about Prego and started filling in the blanks. I got so into it, I didn't even notice Henry and Dick standing behind me, reading every word.

'Annie, do you know what you've got here?'

I looked up at Henry and snorted. 'A fucking page one story?'

Henry actually smiled. 'This is the fucking lead story. It lets me off the hook, too. I was looking at the annual Thanksgiving dinner down at the homeless shelter with the sad but hopeful story of a family trying to pull themselves out of a hole.'

Glad I could be of some help.

'So you don't know why the FBI is there?' Henry squinted at my screen.

I shook my head. 'No. Jeff Parker wouldn't tell me. I even called my source, and if she won't tell me, then no one will.'

Henry scratched his chin. 'We don't know who the woman is?'

'Tom Behr said she hadn't been ID'd yet.' I'd been running through possibilities, however, the best one being LeeAnn Hayward, Sal's hostess at the restaurant. I knew LeeAnn was more like family than an employee, but I wasn't willing to share without being absolutely sure. No one had even mentioned her name, and it dawned on me now that I hadn't seen her at Mac's, which was unusual under these circumstances.

Henry was nodding. 'Okay, we can get that later. Wesley's got some good shots. I wonder if he got any of the FBI guys.' He started moving toward the photo lab. 'If anyone's got the FBI guys in a picture, it'll be Wesley . . . ' His voice faded as he got farther away.

Dick was fumbling with his notebook filled with his chicken scratches. 'Wait a minute, Annie, I think I've got something. When I was talking to the neighbors, Jeff Parker came up and started asking questions.'

'You talked to Jeff, too?'

'No, not directly, but he started asking the old ladies stuff about Sal Amato, weird stuff like where were Sal's chickens, were they killed in the fire, too.'

Chickens? What was it that old guy had asked me about chickens?

'What did they say?'

'They said they didn't know what he was talking about, but one woman got this look on her face, like she knew, but she wouldn't say. Then he went over to talk to the firemen.'

I took a deep breath. 'Please tell me, Dick, that you asked him what it was all about.'

Dick bit his lip and gave me a sheepish look. Shit. I'd have to follow up on it in the morning.

We had a pretty good story, regardless. When we were finished with it and Henry was happy, I was exhausted. Up at six, and now it was after dinner. I had warm thoughts about my bed as I drove home, the snow sparkling in the streetlights along the way.

My apartment was dark and cold. It looked as though both my neighbors were out, probably with family or friends, finishing up the turkey and stuffing and cranberry sauce. I could still go to my mother's, but after considering it briefly, I knew I couldn't deal with it. I turned up the heat and put the yoga pants back on. I slapped together a ham-and-cheese sandwich, grabbed a beer out of the fridge, and started channel surfing.

I woke up about an hour later on the couch, turned off the tube, and padded into the bathroom. The door buzzer scared the shit out of me as I was brushing my teeth.

I looked out the window, down to the steps below. A tall man in a gray overcoat stood on the stoop. He looked up at me, and I buzzed him in.

My father gave me a big bear hug the second he came through the door.

'I'm sorry I didn't call first,' he said as I handed him a beer.

I pulled my feet up under me on the couch, and he settled into my rocker. I studied his face. Although I'd seen him only about six months ago, he was a little grayer and there were more lines in his face.

'Everything okay, Dad?'

He shrugged. 'Long trip.'

'Did you stop and see Mac?'

'Came here first.' He ran his hand through his hair; I didn't like seeing how he was aging. And before I could tell him about Sal, he surprised me by saying, 'I'm thinking about retiring.'

'Really?'

'Everything's changing, the technology, the owners, it's not easy running a casino these days. Foxwoods has everyone stumped. How can those Indians be raking in all that dough in the middle of fucking nowhere in Connecticut?'

I smiled. 'You could come back and work there.'

He shook his head. 'No thanks. I can't come back here.' He didn't elaborate, and from the look on his face, it probably had something to do with my mother.

'So where would you go?' Where does someone retire to after Vegas? Florida would be way too humid, California way too yuppie.

'Thinking about Utah.'

'Ugh, all those happy Mormons? What do you want to do, marry a few women and make more babies?'

He laughed. 'Suzette's enough for me, and you're plenty enough daughter.' He paused for a second. 'Thinking about building a cabin in the mountains.'

I chuckled. 'That doesn't sound like you. What do you need, to go into hiding or something?' His face changed, and it took me by surprise. 'I was just joking, or do you really need to go into hiding?'

He shook his head. 'You've been a crime reporter too long.'

Which reminded me . . .

'Did Sal Amato need to go into hiding?'

He frowned at me. 'What?'

'Sal's not dead, Dad. It wasn't his body in the restaurant, and the FBI was there, sticking their noses into the scene. No one knows where Sal is.'

'The FBI?' He got up, walked over to the window, and looked out over the square, toward Prego. 'Oh, shit.'

'One of the local FBI guys was asking about chickens. Does that make any sense to you?'

Dad straightened his back a little and stretched his neck before turning around. 'What the hell do chickens have to do with Sal?' But I could see something in his eyes that made me wonder if Sal did indeed have some sort of poultry problem that the FBI would be concerned about. But I had to drop it, at least for now. I knew if I pressed, Dad would clam up and I'd never get anything out of him.

'Whose body was in the restaurant?' he asked.

I shrugged. 'All I know is it was a woman. Tom said there was no ID yet. Probably tomorrow. I didn't see Lee Ann Hayward anywhere today. I hope it wasn't her.'

Dad sat down and rubbed his face with his palms. 'Me too,' he said flatly.

'You look tired. You should probably get some sleep. Where are you staying?'

'Omni Hotel downtown.'

I chuckled. 'That sounds nice.'

'I know the manager.' He knew everyone.

Dad got up and kissed me on the top of the head. 'I'll come by in the morning, take you to breakfast.'

From my window, I watched him walk down the sidewalk and climb into a car. I glanced toward Prego but couldn't see it in the dark. I shut the lights out and went to bed.

7

He could've told me he was going to bring Vinny along.

'Look who I ran into,' Dad said as I came down the steps and nearly lost my balance slipping on some black ice. I gripped the railing, uncertain whether to tell Dad that Vinny had a habit of lurking around my apartment and it wasn't too hard to run into him. At least that's the way it had been two months ago, and it was looking like that was the direction we were headed in again.

Vinny grinned at me, and I tried to look like I didn't give a shit. I'm not sure I pulled it off, because he put his arm around me, no mean feat because I was again wearing my puffy coat; it was goddamn cold outside.

'Let's go to the diner.' My father didn't act like he lived in the desert. His coat was unbuttoned, his hair flying in the frosty breeze, his cheeks ruddy. He grinned at me. 'I miss this weather,' he said.

Vinny and I huddled together to keep warm; at least that's what I told myself. I missed that hat, but I'd improvised with a thick scarf I'd found shoved behind some stuff on the shelf in my hall closet. Between the big coat and the scarf, I looked like one of those Middle Eastern women in the bee-keeper outfits.

The diner wasn't too far away, but I felt like a fucking snowman by the time we got there.

'Joey!' The waitress had to be about my dad's age, wisps of obviously dyed red hair falling out of the knot on top of her head.

My dad leaned over and kissed her cheek. 'Alma, always good to see you. Alma, this is my daughter, Annie, and Vinny DeLucia.' My father indicated us with a wave of his hand.

Alma smiled, nodded. 'I know Vinny, of course. Nice to meet you, Annie,' she said. 'Coffee all around?'

My father's eyes twinkled at her. 'Thanks.'

We took off our coats and sat down.

'Alma and I went to high school together,' my father said as he pulled a copy of the paper off the table next to us. He nodded at me. 'Good story.'

Sal's face stared up at me from the front page.

Alma came back and poured the coffee. Her eyes lingered on my father for a few seconds before she left.

'Did you talk to Mac yet?' I asked my father.

'I was over there this morning. So was Vinny.'

'You might as well hear it from me. Mac's hired me,' Vinny said.

I frowned. 'For what?'

'To find Sal.'

I had a sneaking suspicion that if Sal wasn't around, it was because he didn't want to be.

'I can't drag him back kicking and screaming, that's for sure. But Mac wants me to make sure he's okay.'

'She's paying you to find him?' I asked.

Vinny actually blushed. 'I told her I didn't want her money, but, well, you know.'

I did know. Mac was proud and didn't want a handout from anyone. I also knew that Vinny would find a way to keep her from paying him. 'What does the FBI want him for?'

Vinny shrugged. 'Mac says she doesn't know.'

'Do you think she does?'

'Beats me.' He stared into his coffee cup, making me think he definitely had an opinion on this, and it was annoying me that he wasn't sharing.

I looked from him to my father. 'Do either of you know?'

Vinny took a long drink from his cup, and my father flagged down Alma with a broad smile. These two knew a helluva lot more than I did, I would bank on it. We all ordered eggs and toast before my father looked at me again.

'You'll find out soon, I'm sure. You're too good a reporter.'

'Why don't you make my life easier and tell me now, and I can just get it confirmed.' And I thought it was bad when I had a cop boyfriend who wouldn't tell me anything.

'Have you talked to your mother?'

I could play this game, too. 'Have you?'

Dad grinned, his brown eyes flashing with amusement, and I could see what my mother and Suzette and Alma and probably a million other women had seen in him. 'I thought maybe you could tell her I'm in town.'

'Only if you tell me about Sal.'

He sighed. 'Maybe I don't know anything. Have you considered that?'

'No.'

'Why not?'

I shrugged. I just hadn't.

'I can tell you that I think I know who the woman was who died in the fire.' Vinny's voice surprised us.

'LeeAnn Hayward?' I asked, and it was Vinny's turn to be surprised.

'How the hell do you know?' he asked.

So I was right. 'Educated guess,' I said.

Vinny nodded. 'Mickey came around last night to the restaurant looking for LeeAnn. He didn't know about the fire, because he was in Boston for the holiday. He said LeeAnn left the night before, they had a big fight.'

Mickey and LeeAnn Hayward had been fighting since they met fifteen years ago, when Sal hired LeeAnn as his hostess and Mickey as his head chef. From what I'd heard, it was instant heat between them, and Sal had to reprimand them more than once for screwing around, literally, in the supply closet. But when they weren't screwing, they were fighting, and sometimes it got pretty messy. Mickey had given LeeAnn a black eye at one point, but only after she'd stabbed him with his favorite knife. That was my first story as cop reporter. You never forget your first story on any beat, and that one was a doozy. Apparently Mickey thought LeeAnn was fucking one of the dishwashers, and LeeAnn thought Mickey was fucking one of the waitresses. I couldn't put that in my story, but Mickey had gotten twenty-five stitches and LeeAnn went to a battered women's shelter for a night.

The next day they were in the supply closet again. Sal almost had a heart attack trying to keep them from killing each other, one way or another.

'So LeeAnn's missing?' It made sense, then, that perhaps she was the body in the restaurant. I'd never warmed up to her, we were really only acquaintances, but I certainly hadn't wanted any sort of harm to come to her.

Vinny nodded. The waitress came with our breakfast, and we were all quiet for a few minutes while we ate and digested this new information. 'It would make sense if it was LeeAnn, but then, if she came home early, why wasn't she at home, why did she go to the restaurant?' I asked after a few bites of toast.

'Who knows. There could've been a million reasons for her to go there,' Vinny said.

We pondered that a few seconds before I remembered something, a complete non sequitur.

'You know, I had a little chat with Dominic Gaudio yesterday.' The way they looked at me, you'd have thought I'd said I'd fucked Mick Jagger.

My father stared at me. 'When?' He didn't look as if he were pleased to get this news.

'Oh, he said to say hello. In his car, after he left Mac's.' I paused. 'He said nothing is as it seems. Does that make any sense to either of you?'

Vinny frowned. 'You know LeeAnn Hayward

is Dominic Gaudio's niece, don't you?'

I didn't know that, and he knew it. I scowled at him. 'So? He thought Sal was dead in that restaurant when he went to see Mac.' But as I said that, I wondered again about his words and whether he knew more about what was going on over at Prego.

'Sal hired LeeAnn as a favor to Dom,' my father said. 'She'd been taking care of her mother, who had cancer, and when she died, LeeAnn needed something to do. Sal needed a hostess, and Dom got her in.'

At that moment, the door opened and a tall, mustached man wearing a long black trench coat stepped inside. He and my father exchanged a nod before he sat at the counter.

My father pushed his plate to the middle of the table and drained his coffee cup. 'Excuse me, my appointment is early.' He got up and took the seat next to the man in the coat.

I was in a goddamn Martin Scorsese movie.

Vinny had my coat in his hands, and in seconds I was wearing it and we were outside on the sidewalk.

'What's that all about?' I asked.

Vinny shrugged. 'I have to get going.'

'To find Sal?' I asked sarcastically.

He grinned. 'Smart-ass. Yeah, to find Sal.'

'Why don't you just ask those two' — I

74

tossed my head in the direction of the diner — 'where he is?'

'Aw, that'd be too easy.' He chuckled. 'See you later.'

* * *

I had to walk past Prego on the way to my car. The crime scene tape was flapping in the breeze. Tom stepped out from behind the building as I stood staring at it.

'You always come back to the scene,' he said matter-of-factly, as though he expected me to be there.

'I heard the body was LeeAnn Hayward.' Well, not exactly, but sometimes it was easier to get a confirmation if I presented my speculations as fact.

That surprised him. 'How the hell did you find out?'

'So it's confirmed that it's her?'

'Dental records don't lie.'

'That was fast.'

'Dentist faxed them over about an hour ago, and the medical examiner made a positive ID.'

'Mickey must have been pretty worried. I heard he was looking for her last night.'

'The husband? Oh, yeah, he came to the department.'

'Does he know why she was in the restaurant?'

'She works there.'

'But the restaurant wasn't open, it was before six in the morning.' I could tell he was wondering why she was there, too.

'Want to get a cup of coffee?' Tom was asking. 'It's cold out here.'

'Just had some with my dad.'

Tom frowned. 'Why's your dad here?'

I thought about my father's 'appointment.' 'He came because he thought Sal was dead,' I said. I wanted to believe that.

Tom ran a hand through his blond hair, and he wouldn't look at me. He didn't believe it, either.

A Ford Explorer was coming toward us. As it got closer, it slowed down, and Vinny waved as he passed. I raised my hand, sort of like the Queen Mother.

'What's going on with you two?' Tom asked.

'Nothing,' I said.

'But you want it to.'

I couldn't lie to him, but I didn't want to say it out loud, so I kept my mouth shut. I should learn how to do that more often. But it backfired.

'You know, Annie, the chief's been on my back about you. Anything that's in the paper, he thinks you got it from me.'

I usually did.

'You know, our relationship has changed a lot in the last couple of months,' he continued, and I had a bad feeling about what he was about to say. 'Maybe we should just keep it professional from now on.'

And I wouldn't get shit out of him anymore. That's what he was really telling me. I wasn't stupid. Or maybe I was. Why the hell was I waiting around for a guy who wouldn't make up his goddamn mind when I could have Tom, even though we'd had our own commitment issues?

'I don't think you should call me on my personal cell phone anymore,' Tom was saying. 'Let's cut all the ties.'

I felt a huge swell in my chest, as if this were the first time we were breaking up. But did I want to cry for our lost relationship or because I wouldn't get any more information out of him?

It sucked that I didn't know.

I mumbled something like 'Sure' or 'Fine' and took off.

★ ★ ★

I didn't even hear him behind me until I reached my car and saw his hand come out in front of me, keeping me from opening the door. I turned around quickly, not wanting him to know how much he'd scared me.

'I heard your father's in town. Where is he?'

'Mickey!'

Dark circles accentuated the deep wrinkles under Mickey Hayward's eyes; his long face seemed even longer in his grief. 'Where's your father?' he asked again.

I shrugged. 'We had breakfast at the diner. He might still be there.' The minute I said it, I regretted it, since he might still be there with his 'appointment.'

Mickey started to move away from me, but he couldn't move that fast.

'Hey, Mickey.'

He turned around. 'Yeah?'

'I'm sorry about LeeAnn. You okay?'

He shook his head. 'I just can't fucking believe it.'

'You were in Boston, right?'

Mickey nodded and pulled his black leather jacket closer around his long, lanky body. 'Yeah. Sal gave me Wednesday night off, it's a slow night, right before Thanksgiving. Everyone's getting their turkeys ready. So LeeAnn and me, well, we decided to make it a real holiday.' His face started to contort, and I watched as he pulled himself together again. 'We had a nice dinner, you know, went back to the hotel, you know, that sort of thing.' His lips moved into a smile, remembering, but then he sighed. 'We had a big fight, you know me and LeeAnn, we just can't let ourselves be happy.'

'About?' My voice seemed to startle him, as though he'd forgotten he was talking to someone.

'About what?'

'What did you fight about?' I fought the urge to take out my notebook. I'd spook him if I did that, so I'd just have to keep this going around in my head until I could get my hands on a pen.

'Stupid stuff, you know.' He wouldn't look me in the eye, and something told me it was a lot more specific than he was letting on.

'Stuff at home, stuff at work?' I probed.

He sighed. 'I loved her, you know that, Annie, don't you?'

'Sure.' I wasn't quite sure, but it was good enough for him.

'I'm not sure she loved me that much.'

'Sure she did, Mickey. You guys always had the hots for each other.'

He snorted. 'Her hots were a little cool lately, if you get my drift.'

'So you think she was having an affair?' Nothing like stating the obvious.

'She said she wasn't.'

'Then why didn't you believe her?'

Mickey stared at me a second before answering. He looked like shit. His eyes were bloodshot, and his hair looked like it hadn't been washed in a few days. 'Because I'm an asshole.'

We were quiet for a minute, and he started to turn away again, but I remembered something. 'Hey, Mick,' I said, 'you wouldn't by any chance have a picture of LeeAnn on you, would you? I have to write a story about her, and I'll need a picture.' I could see him thinking about this, and I wasn't sure he was happy about this turn of events. 'It's my job, you know, but because I knew her, well, I can get more personal, tell everyone what she was really like.'

My words softened him, and he reached into the back pocket of his jeans and produced a wallet. He took a small snapshot out of the folds and handed it to me. I stared at it a minute. LeeAnn's face looked up at me, smiling. Her brown hair, with bright highlights framing her face, was pulled back from her forehead, and wisps clung to her cheeks. She was pretty, I had to give her that, even with the East Haven big hair and bright blue eye shadow. 'I'll get this back to you as soon as I can,' I said, and he nodded and turned again.

I watched him walk down the sidewalk, his shoulders hunched over, pulling his coat even closer around him. He was an asshole, everyone knew that, but the man could cook — he made those great raviolis with big chunks of fresh lobster meat — and I also knew he loved LeeAnn in his own way and was probably beating himself up over fighting with her the night before she died. He'd never get another chance with her now.

I forgot to ask him what he wanted to talk to my father about.

8

Marty Thompson was leafing through the newspaper when I threw my bag onto the desk next to him and handed him the picture.

'What's this?' he asked, his mouth full of bagel and cream cheese.

'LeeAnn Hayward. She was the dead body in Prego.'

He almost spat bagel on me, catching it instead in a napkin.

'Gross.' I pulled away from him.

'How'd you get this?'

I shrugged. 'My natural charm.'

'You wish. I hope this is on the record.'

'Straight from Tom Behr's lips.' I didn't like the way Marty smiled, so I added, 'But I'm not sure I'm getting anything else from him ever again.' I brought him up-to-date on my most recent conversation with Tom.

'That's too bad,' Marty said, and I knew he meant it was too bad I wouldn't get extra information from Tom, not that my personal relationship with Tom was most definitely over. He was my friend, but he would always be my editor first.

I started taking off my coat, but felt a chill

and thought better of it. Shrugging back into my sleeves, I asked Marty, who I now noticed was wearing a thick wool sweater over his usual dress shirt and tie, 'What's up with the heat?'

Marty rolled his eyes. 'Or lack thereof, you mean?'

I nodded.

'Air-conditioning kicked in for some reason. Maintenance guys are working on it.'

Which meant we'd probably be icicles by midnight.

I glanced around the newsroom. 'Where's Dick?'

'He took today off. Personal day.'

Dick? Personal day? That was an oxymoron if I ever heard one. 'Does he have a personal life?' I asked before thinking.

'Annie, not everyone is like you. Yes, Dick has a personal life. I also know that he is dating someone.'

Someone actually was dating Dick Whitfield? She couldn't be human. Maybe some sort of alien from *Star Trek*. One of those little furry Tribble things, perhaps. I seemed to remember they liked everyone, even Mr. Spock. Come to think of it, Dick could be sort of Spock-like at times. Like when he took off the lime green ski cap and his hair stuck up over his ears.

I stared at Marty. 'You know you have to tell me now. You started this.'

Marty's lips were twitching, and I knew he was dying to tell me. He might be my boss, but he was still a journalist, and good gossip was good gossip. It didn't matter if it was who was ripping off City Hall or who was fucking whom in the parking lot. We couldn't help ourselves. We had to know, and we had to tell people.

'Cindy Purcell at Channel Nine.'

'You're kidding, right?' Cindy Purcell was one of the second-string reporters at Channel 9 in Hartford. She was fairly new to the state, coming from somewhere in the Midwest. I'd seen her around the office, because Channel 9 rented a corner of our newsroom from which it could broadcast its *Shoreline Report* every day. Channel 9 didn't really give a shit about the shoreline, thus the makeshift 'newsroom,' and they'd put Cindy Purcell here so she could prove herself before they gave her a real shot in Hartford.

'Heard they went to the movies a few nights ago.' Marty was trying to be nonchalant about this, but it wasn't working. He leaned toward me and whispered, 'They saw that new Russell Crowe/Penelope Cruz movie.'

'No shit!' I was avoiding that movie because I heard it was so steamy, I would have to take

84

about seven cold showers afterward if I went alone.

Oh, Christ, Dick Whitfield's love life was better than mine. How pathetic was I?

'What's wrong with her?' I asked, thinking of Cindy Purcell with her feathery blond hair and porcelain white skin. I'd thought at first that she was anemic, but she'd confided to me in the ladies' room one day, without any prompting at all, that she believed the sun was every woman's enemy. Like that was big news. She was a ditz, which would explain why she might actually find Dick Whitfield attractive.

'She seems nice,' Marty said.

'You think that because she's got big breasts. She practically trips over them every time she comes in here.'

'You're just jealous.'

'Of that?' I shook my head. I couldn't stand it any longer. 'I've got work to do. I can't sit around here all day gossiping with you.'

'Hey, that's my line.'

Halfway to my desk, I heard Marty call my name. 'So if it was LeeAnn Hayward in the restaurant, then what's going on with Sal Amato?'

'He's missing.'

'Obviously. Do you have any clues where he is?'

I thought a minute. 'Mac hired Vinny DeLucia to find him.'

'So get your ass over to Vinny's and find out what he knows. We have to find out about that fire, too. What caused it and why LeeAnn Hayward was inside at the time.'

'Let me write up what I've got so far, and then I'll see what else I can find out.' I glanced at the clock. It was only eleven. 'Hell, we've got all day.'

Marty scowled, and I knew he was thinking about how he'd just gotten reamed out by the executive editor for pushing deadline too close to production time. But it wasn't my fault if I couldn't get information faster.

I was typing frantically, trying to ignore my blue fingers, when the phone rang.

'You could've warned me that your father was in town.'

'Hello, Mother.'

'And you never came for turkey yesterday.'

I took a deep breath and let it out slowly. 'I had a busy day. Didn't you see the paper? By the time I finished up here, I just went home and went to bed.'

I heard the heavy sigh that indicated I was a terrible daughter and would never appreciate what a wonderful woman my mother was. 'I have leftovers.'

'Okay, okay, I'll come by after work and

86

have dinner with you.' Another thought gave me a panic attack. 'Bill Bennett's not going to be there, is he? Because I don't know if I can deal with that right now.'

'Bill has a previous engagement, so you don't have to worry about that.' Her voice was curt, and I knew I'd hurt her feelings.

'A previous engagement without you?' I asked before thinking.

'I'll see you later.' The dial tone reverberated in my ear, and I hung up.

I finished putting together what I could about LeeAnn; Mickey's quotes sounded more poignant on the computer screen than they'd been out on the sidewalk.

Even though I'd gotten the positive ID from Tom, I wanted to talk to the medical examiner's office to get more details about the autopsy. But a phone call only revealed that the report wasn't done yet and I'd have to wait.

Maybe Vinny had some news about Sal, but all I got was his voice mail. I didn't leave a message. I had a feeling I'd run across him at some point again.

Len Freelander actually came to the phone.

'I was wondering if you guys had determined the cause of the fire at Prego yet,' I said after reminding the fire chief again who

I was. He apparently had some sort of short-term memory loss when it came to me. God knows why. Everyone usually remembered me, and always for the wrong reasons.

'Not yet, Annie. We'll keep you apprised.' He hung up.

As I sat there, pondering the existence of my fingernails and what my next move would be, Wesley Bell snuck up behind me and scared the crap out of me by saying quite loudly, 'I've got something you might want to see.'

His necktie was crooked, his shirtsleeves rolled up. Wesley Bell actually looked disheveled. He most likely did have something I'd be interested in, so I followed him into the photo lab.

The photo lab isn't what it used to be. It used to be a place that smelled of chemicals as the photographers physically developed film. But that had gone the way of the dinosaurs with the advent of the digital camera. Now the photographers merely downloaded their shots into computers and played around with Photoshop to get them the way they liked.

Wesley Bell led me to one of those computers, and a row of thumbnails danced across the screen. 'What am I looking for?' I asked.

Wesley moved the mouse, clicked on one of the pictures, and it got bigger. He pointed, his long finger jabbing at the screen. 'See here?'

It was one of the pictures from the fire the day before. Len Freelander was in focus in the front, his face drawn with the realization that his weeklong honeymoon period was over. Wesley's finger, however, was off the center of the photograph and touching the face of the little man who had accosted me with questions about chickens.

'Oh, that's that weird old guy,' I said, ready to go back to my desk and do nothing for the moment.

But Wesley wasn't ready for me to do that. 'No, no, Annie, here.' His finger stabbed the screen, and I looked more closely.

It was Sal Amato, in the shadow behind the chicken guy, watching the firemen put out the fire at his restaurant.

9

Holy shit,' I whispered. Sal had been there. I hadn't seen him, and no one else had indicated they'd seen him either. What the hell was he up to?

'That's Sal Amato,' Wesley said, stating the obvious.

I nodded. 'So you didn't notice him there either?'

'I didn't see him until I was going through these, and there he was. I was concentrating on the fire chief last night when I was picking a picture to use in the paper.'

'Can you blow that up?' I asked him. 'You know, as evidence?'

'I can do it in Photoshop, but it probably won't look great.'

'As long as we can recognize him, that's all we need.' I went back to my desk to let Wesley do his computer magic, but I was more confused than ever.

Had he been in the restaurant when the fire broke out? If he had been, then he must have known LeeAnn was in there. A horrifying thought popped into my head. Maybe he'd set the fire. Maybe he'd meant to kill LeeAnn and destroy his restaurant. And maybe that was why he was missing. That led to another thought, and I called the police department.

'Hey, Richie,' I said casually to the dispatcher, 'it's Annie Seymour. Could you do me a favor? Is there any way you could let me know who called 911 about the fire at Prego yesterday?'

'I'm really not supposed to do that.'

'I know, but it's really important.'

'It's always important with you.' He paused. 'What does the detective say?'

'Let's keep him out of it,' I said, trying to keep the irritation out of my voice.

'Really,' he said thoughtfully. 'Okay, well, what about dinner sometime?'

I had never been desperate, and I certainly wasn't going to date Richie just to get 911 information. But I'd been around the block enough to know what might placate him.

'I don't think that's a good idea,' I said. 'There's a new rule here at the paper that we can't date sources' — maybe not new or enforceable, but it got my point across — 'even if I wanted to.' That last bit would leave him wondering whether maybe I did want to date him, thus making it more appealing to him to give me what I was asking for.

'Hold on, okay?'

It seemed to be working. Go figure.

My phone beeped, indicating I was getting another call, but I couldn't hang up on Richie now. Whoever it was would have to leave a message on my voice mail.

'You can't tell anyone who you heard this from,' Richie whispered when he got back on the phone.

'Why are you whispering?'

'I don't understand why no one picked up on this before.' Richie was still whispering, but now he seemed to have forgotten whom he was talking to altogether.

'Picked up on what, Richie?' I prompted.

'The call came in from Prego. I don't know who called it in, I'd have to listen to the tape to find out, but the call definitely was made from the restaurant.'

* * *

I knew I had to call Tom and ask him about the 911 call, but I was as frustrated as my prom date had been because I knew I wasn't going to get jack shit from him.

I dialed before I could think about it any longer.

'Behr.'

'Hi, Tom,' I tried to say casually.

'Annie, I thought I told you I wasn't going

to give you preferential treatment anymore. Which means you can't call my cell phone.'

'You're kidding me, right? Any reporter would use what she or he has, your cell phone number being one of them.'

'I'm going to hang up.'

'Wait a minute. I'm sorry, but I have to ask you something officially, okay, about Prego?'

He didn't hang up, but he didn't say anything, either.

'I heard that the 911 call about the fire came in from the restaurant itself. Do you have any comment on that?'

I heard him catch his breath. 'Christ, Annie, you don't need me at all, do you. Where the hell did you hear that?'

'Sorry, Tom, confidential source. So it's true?'

'Yes, it's true,' he conceded.

'Who made the call? Do you know?'

'Finally something she doesn't know.'

I waited, but he was not forthcoming. So I tried again. 'Can you tell me?'

'No.'

He disconnected the call, but at least I had something official, and I could leave Richie out of it. I sauntered over to Marty's desk.

I like making Marty happy. He's cute when he smiles, and he doesn't do that too often. After I told him what I'd learned, I apologized for not knowing who made the call, but he shook his head. 'That's okay, you'll find out. Just when you start getting burned out, you go on a roll.'

I frowned. Burned out? Me?

'Does anyone else have this?' Marty asked.

I shook my head. 'I'm pretty sure we're the only ones.' I thought for a second. 'But Dick better keep his mouth shut when he's out with Cindy Purcell.'

Marty chewed on his lip thoughtfully. 'I'll take care of that. Let's try to fill in the holes so we can make tomorrow's paper, okay?' He went back to his computer like we didn't have a big fucking story sitting in our laps.

I saluted him. 'Yessir!' I turned on my heel and went back to my desk, where my voice mail light was blinking rapidly at me. Oh, yeah, someone had tried to call me. I dialed my code and listened. But no one spoke. I just heard some static, then the call ended.

I began typing up the stuff about the 911 call — this would have to be a sidebar to the story about LeeAnn — but my stomach interrupted with a loud growl. Kevin Prisley, the City Hall reporter, had come in while I was in the photo lab, and he glanced in my direction as he continued his phone conversation.

It was just about noon, and I had a craving

for a meatball sub from Frank and Mary's Deli on Wooster Street. I also needed to warm up a little, so I slipped out of the newsroom, knowing that if I told anyone I was going out, someone would decide he wanted coffee and I'd end up having to take orders for Dunkin' Donuts.

Wooster Street is a menu in itself. The narrow street is home to the best pizza places anywhere: Sally's, Pepe's, Abate's, Tony & Lucille's. And tucked among the pizza joints are Consiglio's and Tre Scalini, serving up delicious Italian fare, but with fancy linen tablecloths and candles on the tables.

At Sally's, you don't even get a plate. They serve the pizza on large cookie sheets, give you a few napkins and some cutlery, and there you have it. You might wait two hours to get your pizza, but it's so damn good it doesn't matter.

And then there's Libby's, in between Consiglio's and Abate's, where every kind of cannoli possible is sitting in the display. Libby's also makes amazing Italian cookies — the green acorns with jam are my favorite — and their Italian ice is perfect on a hot summer day.

But a hot cappuccino would be more appropriate today.

I parked in front of my building, deciding

to walk the rest of the way, and as I passed the snow-covered playground, a snowman watched my every move.

Frank and Mary's doesn't seem much bigger than my walk-in closet, but their subs can't be beat. I ordered a meatball and mootz (mozzarella, for anyone not from the neighborhood) and a Foxon Park white birch beer, a weakness of mine. Foxon Park sodas are made locally, in East Haven, and most of the Italian delis in the area carry them. You can't get them in Stop & Shop.

Since there are no tables at Frank and Mary's, I headed toward my apartment but was too hungry to keep myself from peeling back the paper and eating the sub as I walked, holding my birch beer under my armpit.

I came out onto Chapel Street, and Wooster Square spread out in front of me across the street. It was about a city block long and wide, circled by historic homes. The city's Italians had settled here from the Amalfi region near Naples; they'd been poor and exploited. In New Haven, they found what they thought was the American dream. The statue of Christopher Columbus stood tall among the bare branches; iron benches sat empty throughout the park. Off to my left, I could see the remnants of Prego, its blackened walls like shadows against the white snow.

I took another bite of my sub, but out of the corner of my eye, I saw movement. Looking back up, I squinted, not seeing anything and wondering if I'd imagined it.

I crumpled the sub paper into a ball and shoved it into my pocket, leaving the soda bottle on one of my building's steps. It wouldn't hurt to go over there. It might be Tom or even Jeff Parker.

I crossed the street and moved down the sidewalk a little precariously, since some of the snow had turned to slush and then frozen over. When I got to the restaurant, I didn't see anyone. Strips of yellow police tape were wrapped here and there, allegedly to keep people out, but I wouldn't be contaminating the scene since all the forensics guys had been here and gone for at least twelve hours. I made my way around to the back door that led to the kitchen, and I peered in through the holes where the glass used to be. Everything was sooty, and the smell moved quickly into my nose and down into my lungs. I'd be coughing up black shit for days after all this if I wasn't careful. But not breathing wasn't exactly an option.

'Are you looking for the chickens?' The voice startled me, and I turned to face that crazy old guy I'd seen here yesterday.

'Who are you?' I asked.

He smiled, a toothless vision, but somehow it made him seem less crazy. 'Mario.'

'Do you have a last name?'

He shook his head. 'You're with the newspaper,' he said flatly.

I nodded. 'And what about chickens?'

Mario's face fell. 'They must be dead.'

'But why would they be here in the first place?' I asked.

'I shouldn't say. When people talk, look what happens.' He waved his arm toward Prego's remains.

'You can tell me,' I tried in my best conspiratorial voice.

But Mario just started mumbling under his breath. Fortunately, I've had to deal with a lot of weirdos in my job and could hold my own with the best of them.

'Nothing will happen if you tell me about them,' I promised.

He cocked his head, his eyes searching my face, and I saw a glimmer of clarity. 'Don't bet against the chickens. You'll lose. Ask your father.' And with that, he scurried off around the building and out of sight.

By the time I rounded the corner, he'd vanished. I had no clue what he'd been trying to tell me. And what did he know about my father? Did he even know who my father was?

I made my way back to my building, where I picked up the soda bottle I'd left on the steps. When I opened my apartment door, a flash of white on the floor caught my eye, and I picked it up.

It was another vegan recipe, courtesy of Amber. I'd been finding recipe clippings under my door for about a month now. I didn't say anything, though, because I thought if I ignored it, maybe she'd stop. So far, no such luck.

I crumpled the clipping and tossed it in the trash along with my sub wrapper, Mario's words swirling around in my head. Ask my father. Since I had no other options at the moment, I would have to do just that.

But when I dialed and waited for him to answer, I realized I couldn't do this on the phone. He wouldn't answer me, and I couldn't see his reaction.

'Hello?' I heard noises in the background, but I couldn't identify them.

'Hey, Dad, what're you up to?'

'Hold on a minute, okay?' I heard him tell someone he was going on the porch, and then, 'That's better.'

'Where are you?'

'An old friend's. We're catching up, haven't seen each other in a while.' His voice was light. 'Are you still at work?'

'I came home for lunch, but I have to go back.' I paused. 'I'm heading to Mom's for dinner. Do you want to come?'

'That sounds great. What time?'

The sad thing is that despite Suzette, my father still loved my mother. My mother is the one who ended their relationship, choosing to move on to law school and a very lucrative career. She insisted that she'd fallen out of love with him, but I wasn't convinced. My father had a roving eye, and I think it was more a matter of pride for her to get out while she believed he was still faithful. I never wanted to delve too deeply into their personal shit, so I don't know whether he ever cheated on her or ever would have.

I told my dad what time to be there, and I knew I'd have to call my mother so she'd be prepared. At least with another table setting.

'I'm bringing someone tonight,' I told her when I got her on the phone.

'Oh, Annie, really?' Her voice sounded strange.

'What's up, Mother?'

'Nothing.' She paused. 'It isn't that policeman, is it?'

'No, Mom, it's not a date.' I debated whether to tell her. If I did, she might try to find a way out of it. If I didn't tell her, she could see him and then tell everyone that I tricked her, it wasn't her idea. That would be the best way.

'Who?'

'Just someone, okay? You might want to set another place.'

'Well, Annie, since we spoke last, our dinner has gotten a little larger.'

Oh, Christ, another dinner party. Now I would have to get dressed up. 'Bill Bennett isn't going to make it after all, is he?' I asked. That's all I would need, my father and Bill Bennett in the same room. My father would chew him up and spit him out. Then again, that might not be a bad idea.

'No, Bill can't make it. But I've invited a few other people.'

While I didn't like the idea of a dinner party, having a bunch of other people around meant I wouldn't have to deal too closely with my mother. I tried to look on the bright side of this situation.

My cell phone started to chirp inside my purse. 'Fine, sure, I'll see you later,' I mumbled as I hung up and rummaged through my bag until I found my phone.

'Annie' — it was Marty — 'I just got a call from a friend who works over at the medical examiner's office.'

'Did they finish up with LeeAnn's autopsy?'

'You won't believe this.' He paused.

'What?'

'She didn't die from the fire, Annie. She was shot. A single gunshot to the chest.'

10

Marty got it from his source that LeeAnn's wound couldn't possibly have been self-inflicted because of the angle of the trajectory. Which meant someone else had pulled the trigger.

I tried calling Tom for an official comment, but either he wasn't answering his cell phone because he had it turned off or he knew it was me and opted to ignore it. Probably the latter. So I had to change my strategy.

I needed to get in touch with Mickey Hayward, get a comment from him. But where the hell would he be? He didn't have a job anymore since his place of business had burned down. I called his house after finding his number in the book, but he wasn't home and didn't have an answering machine.

Maybe Mac would know where he was. I should talk to her again about Sal anyway, and I could even get a couple of quotes from her about LeeAnn. I went back out into the cold and crossed the park to her house.

Just my luck, Mrs. DeLucia answered the door. Her glare accused me of being the hussy she thought I was, the hussy her son hoped I would be. I straightened my posture. I was a grown woman, and I couldn't let myself be intimidated. For Christ's sake, I'd seen dead bodies. This should be nothing.

'Hello, Mrs. DeLucia. I'd like to talk to Mac for a few minutes, if she doesn't mind.' I didn't wait for an answer — I knew I didn't have a lot of time — so I moved through the foyer and into the living room.

Mac was on the couch in a green flowered housecoat, her eyes puffy, her gray curls a little flat in the back where her head had been on the pillow.

'Hi, Mac. I hope you're doing okay.' I plopped down in the chair across from her. 'I have some news,' I started, and both Mac's and Mrs. DeLucia's eyes rested on my face. It was a little disconcerting, but I reminded myself about the dead bodies and forced myself to continue. 'We heard about the autopsy. LeeAnn Hayward was shot. That's how she died. Not from the fire. Gunshot to the chest.'

Mac frowned. 'What?'

I repeated my news. Mac snorted. 'I knew that Mickey Hayward would kill her one of these days.'

'So you think Mickey killed her?'

'They fought like cats and dogs all the time, it was just a matter of time.'

Mrs. DeLucia was nodding in agreement. I hated to admit it, but the more I thought about it, the more I also wondered whether he killed her. It wouldn't be out of character with their relationship.

'I heard LeeAnn was Dominic Gaudio's niece,' I asked.

They exchanged a look, then Mac smiled tightly at me. 'That's right. Dominic asked Sal if he could give her a job. She was a hard worker, at least when she and Mickey weren't fighting.' She toyed with a curl near her ear. 'She was a big help to Sal with the books. She put everything on computer for him. Of course, Sal had trouble working that thing, so she would put all his numbers in the computer after he did them by hand. She could've done something with that, her computer skill, but she wanted to stay at the restaurant.' She paused. 'She was a smart girl, but stupid when it came to Mickey.'

'Why did Sal keep him on?' I asked. 'If he caused so many problems with LeeAnn?'

Mac smiled. 'The man was a genius in the kitchen, Annie. We'd had chefs before who were trouble, but they couldn't cook like Mickey. His pasta fagioli was like nothing I'd ever tasted, and he's not even Italian. When he was in the kitchen, he was a different man. Too bad he couldn't stay in the kitchen all the time.'

'So LeeAnn was pretty involved with restaurant business?' I was treading on thin ice, but while I was here, I might as well get what I could. 'Did she know what the FBI was looking into?'

Again they exchanged a look, and Mac frowned. 'She wasn't killed over that.' She said it as though she knew it for a fact. And by saying it, she was telling me that she knew exactly what Jeff Parker was nosing around for.

'Is it the chickens?' I asked. 'Did LeeAnn know about the chickens?'

Mac started chuckling. 'Annie, everyone knows about those stupid chickens.'

Everyone but me.

'Mario said the restaurant burned down because someone knew about the chickens.'

Mac's eyes flashed. 'Mario? That man can't keep his mouth shut, even now.'

'What happened to the chickens, Mac? Did they die in the fire?'

'Sal wouldn't let anything happen to them,' Mac said, obviously believing that I was privy to whatever was going on. 'I'm sure if he could have, he would've gotten them out.'

'So where is Sal, Mac? Where is he hiding?'

Mac sat up straighter. 'I have no idea where

my husband is. I've hired Vinny DeLucia to find him.'

Mrs. DeLucia was strangely quiet during this rant, and I watched her.

'What else did Mario tell you?' she asked quietly.

I shrugged. 'Not much.'

I was just about to get my ass out of there when Mac stood up and pointed her finger at me. 'You better not tell that policeman about any of this. That's all I need right now, more questions from the police about those damn birds when I'm worried sick about my husband.' She clutched her chest.

'You wouldn't by chance know where I could find Mickey now, would you?' I looked from Mac to Mrs. DeLucia and back to Mac again.

'Try Café Nine,' Mrs. DeLucia said. 'He and Pete said they were going over there an hour ago.' As she spoke, her hand was under my arm, herding me out. Once on the doorstep, she stopped, her eyes boring into mine.

'Don't listen to Mario. He lost his wife and his house, and he's not right in the head.'

'But he was concerned about the chickens,' I said.

She chuckled, which surprised me. 'Those chickens have been here a long time. No one paid any mind to them before, but one person loses and all hell breaks loose.' She eyeballed me again. 'Vinny was pretty good. He beat them once.'

Jesus, what the hell was going on? Beat them at what?

'You shouldn't see Vinny,' Mrs. DeLucia warned me.

'It's just business,' I insisted, but she shook her head and gave me a sad smile, like I had a big 'L' for 'Loser' on my forehead.

The rock salt on the steps and sidewalk was hard under my boots as I left.

★ ★ ★

I found Mickey Hayward at Café Nine on State Street. He was drowning himself in shots and beers, telling anyone and everyone how much he loved his wife and how much he missed her. I moved closer and saw Pete Amato on the bar stool next to Mickey. Pete looked as if he'd had more than his share, too.

At night, a bar comes to life when the band is cranking out tunes, people have to squeeze between and around one another, and everyone and everything is hot. But now, in the middle of the day, my stomach turned with the smell of stale beer, cigarettes, and body odor. The light coming in from the window bounced off Mickey's face, giving him the haggard look of someone who's just got to have a beer at two o'clock in the afternoon in order to get through the rest of the day.

'Hey, Annie.' He spotted me before I was ready, but I collected myself and made my way over to the bar. 'Can I get you anything?'

I shook my head. 'A little early in the day for me, Mick,' I said, trying to keep my voice light. From his reaction to seeing me, it was clear he hadn't heard yet about LeeAnn being shot. I'd been the bearer of bad news before, and it was never easy. But I knew from experience that the first quote was always a good one, even though killing the messenger was always a possibility.

I was glad Pete was here. Even drunk he could be a good buffer.

'Hi, Annie.' Pete raised his glass to me.

Pete Amato was a carbon copy of his father: medium height, a little on the heavy side, black hair, eyes that could be brown or green depending on the light, a nose that was a little too long for his face. He was a couple of years behind me in school, one of those football players who was too busy being an asshole to get good grades or have a steady girlfriend. He'd gone to college for a couple of years but dropped out and went to work for his father — but not in the kitchen. Sal taught him the business side of the restaurant, and Pete helped him run it. He'd done well there. He had a flair for marketing; he was the one responsible for the classy exterior and sign, and it was his idea to update the interior, taking down the dated 1970s wood paneling and Thomas Kinkade paintings and replacing them with a soft eggshell paint and copies of old photographs depicting New Haven and Wooster Square in bygone years, giving Prego a place in history and the community. Unfortunately for his personal life, he still hadn't moved out of his parents' house, and since he was thirty-six, that would send warning signals to any single woman.

I nodded back. 'Hi, Pete. You okay, you know, after the accident and all?'

He grinned, his teeth a perfect example of teenage orthodontia. 'The guy's going to be okay.' He paused. 'Well, he's come through surgery okay, and the doctors say he's going to make it.'

I bit my tongue. I'd seen that car and what Pete's truck had done to it. It was a miracle the guy wasn't dead.

'Wasn't his time yet,' Mickey was saying. Oh, Christ, he was getting philosophical on

110

me. I had to do what I'd come here for.

'Hey, Mick, autopsy report's back. Has anyone told you?'

All eyes were on me; even the guys at the booth in the corner near the door seemed to be waiting to hear what I had to say.

Mickey shook his head, but he didn't say anything. I took a deep breath.

'She was shot, Mick. She didn't die in the fire.'

Mickey's eyes widened. 'What the fuck are you trying to tell me, Annie?'

'She was murdered, Mick. Do you have any idea who would do that?'

'Why the hell would anyone kill LeeAnn?' With each word his voice got a little louder. I took a step backward.

'I suppose you think I did it.' He was shouting as he slammed his glass onto the bar, shattering it. Bits of glass sprayed across the room, and I instinctively closed my eyes before feeling some hit my forehead.

'Hey, Mickey, get ahold of yourself,' I heard Pete say.

I turned back around to see the bartender wiping up the glass, Pete's hand on Mickey's arm, holding him down in his seat. I glanced at myself to make sure I was okay. I felt my forehead and gently brushed off a piece of glass that stuck there but hadn't done any damage. And damn but if there wasn't a fucking shard sticking out of my puffy coat. I picked it out carefully and put it on the bar.

'I didn't say you did it, Mick, I just asked if you knew who might have done it,' I said calmly, although my heart was beating way too fast and I wanted out of there. He was drunker than I'd thought.

He was shaking his head violently. 'No — I mean, maybe.' He paused. 'No, I don't know of anyone.'

'Annie, you might want to try to talk to him later,' Pete said, taking my arm and steering me toward the door and out onto the sidewalk.

'What the hell is the matter with you?' he demanded as the cold air hit me in the face and the door slammed shut behind us.

'I needed some sort of comment, Pete. You know, it's my job.'

Pete Amato sighed. 'Yeah, Annie, I know, but he just lost his wife, whether she's murdered or not. You also seem to forget that I lost a friend and my father's missing. I don't really want to field questions, either, right now. You may think that you know us because you live in the neighborhood, but you don't. Now go do your reporting somewhere else and let us be.'

He left me on the icy sidewalk. Something

caught my eye, and when I stared it down, I saw it was a feather, a small white feather. It came from the small hole in my coat, from which several other little white feathers were trying to escape.

Jesus. Now I needed a new coat.

★ ★ ★

The feathers reminded me that I still needed to find out about those damn chickens. Since Vinny's mother had spilled the beans about Vinny 'beating' them, I was going to try my best to get it out of him.

Vinny's SUV was in front of his office building on Trumbull Street. Cobb Doyle, attorney-at-law, was coming in at the same time.

His big, saucerlike eyes would've looked surprised if they didn't look that way all the time. 'Oh, hello, it's you.'

Cobb Doyle and I had met under some rather stressful circumstances a couple of months ago.

'Hey, Cobb, what's up?'

He opened the door for me, proving that chivalry isn't completely dead yet, just comatose most of the time.

'Are you and Vinny working on something together again?'

I nodded, although 'working together' was a stretch, and he nodded solemnly in response as he moved down the hall, past Vinny's office and to his own.

A familiar odor brought me back to my college days.

'Who's got the incense?' I asked, walking into Vinny's office without knocking.

'Madame Shara's upstairs with a client.'

Madame Shara will read anyone's palm for a price. I hadn't had the pleasure of meeting her yet.

Vinny closed the door behind me and motioned for me to sit in a chair in front of his desk. As he rounded the corner of his desk and sat down, I glanced at the door.

'You know, frosted windows are clichéd. Who do you think you are, Sam Spade?'

'Maybe. And maybe you're the femme fatale.'

'Your mother seems to think so, but I think she'd like to see Rosie take me out.'

Vinny smiled. 'My mother doesn't know what's good for me.'

'Do you?'

His eyes moved across my face, into my hair, and I swear I could feel them through the front of the goddamn puffy coat. My nipples grew hard despite myself.

'Why don't you take your coat off?' He was

114

teasing me. I pulled my coat closer.

'No thanks. I'm fine.' But it was fucking hot in here. Oh, yeah, that was the idea.

'What's up?' he asked. 'I'm in the middle of something.'

His immaculate desk didn't indicate that.

'Your mother said you beat the chickens once.'

'You talked to my mother?'

'I ran into her at Mac's. So what about the chickens?'

Vinny hung his head back and sighed. 'Okay, I beat them. But it was a fluke. They really do know what they're doing.'

'Is this really why the feds are after Sal? The chickens?'

Vinny nodded. 'Yeah. Can't have something like that go on for a long time before the feds find out about it.'

'So how does it work, the chickens, I mean?' I had no idea what I was talking about.

'Christ, Annie, you've played it. Every kid has. But it would be more fair if the chicken didn't go first.'

My brain was trying to compute this. What sort of game does a kid play that he should go first? My thoughts were jumbled all over the place, running through every game I could think of.

I didn't really take notice when Vinny got up and moved around toward me. He perched on the edge of the desk in front of me, his arms folded, a little smile playing at the corners of his mouth. 'You have no idea, do you,' he said quietly.

I cocked an eyebrow at him. 'Sure I do.' Checkers? Chess? That was stupid. A chicken couldn't do those things.

Vinny was staring at me, and I could see he was waiting for me to figure it out.

Poker? A chicken couldn't play cards; they don't have hands. Forget card games. Bingo? No, that wasn't a two-man game, it was for the little blue-haired old ladies at the casino. Casino . . .

I felt something on my leg, and I looked down to see Vinny's fingers on my knee. I went back to my thoughts and tried to keep my mind off Vinny's hand. But the hand was winning. It was unzipping my coat. And I was letting it.

'Give me some hugs and kisses,' he said softly.

My coat was unzipped all the way now, and he was leaning over me, his face closer and closer . . .

Hugs and kisses?

'I got it!' I jumped up, throwing Vinny to one side. I remembered a story I'd seen about

116

chickens in Atlantic City. They were making a mint for one of the casinos. And the symbols for hugs and kisses were X's and O's.

'It's tic-tac-toe, isn't it?' I shouted. 'Sal trained those chickens to play tic-tac-toe!'

11

It took a minute for both of us to recover, but then the lightbulb went on over my head again. If I didn't watch out, I'd have a fucking strobe light sending signals from my eyeballs.

'Jesus, Vinny, why couldn't you have just told me from the start?'

'Don't want to be giving neighborhood secrets out to the press.' Vinny smiled. It was that smile that always got to me, and I had to look away.

'Mac and your mother said everyone knew about the chickens. But that's obviously not true.'

He grinned. 'Well, when they say 'everyone,' it's everyone who counts.'

I made a face at him. 'So Sal was running a little gambling thing with the chickens? How long?'

'How long what?'

'How long had he been doing this? And how did the FBI suddenly become so interested?'

'First of all, this is more than just a 'little' gambling operation. Tens of thousands of dollars have been made and lost on a daily basis. And the feds have been trying to get into it for years.'

'You're shitting me.' But it seemed he wasn't. 'Tens of thousands in a day? How can that happen?'

Vinny smiled. 'Degenerate gamblers can and will bet on anything anytime. Did you know there was a craps game going on in New Haven for twenty years? On some nights, thirty-five thousand dollars went across the table.'

Jesus. No wonder the FBI was poking around.

'So how does it work?'

'What?'

'How do the chickens play the game?' I wanted to know how chickens could be such a huge moneymaker, my curiosity thoroughly piqued.

'They use a computer. At least now they do. Sal had it all set up in the basement at the restaurant. The chicken is in a box with one screen, you're on the other side of the box with your own screen. The chicken always goes first. It'll peck the screen where it wants to place its letter. And then it's your turn.'

'And there's no one in there with the chicken, helping him along?' I was rather dubious of this arrangement. Chickens have brains the size of a pea.

'Sal built the box. It was on a sort of pedestal in the corner, with three wooden walls and a curtain on one side over a wire door so the chicken couldn't get out.'

If I was that chicken, I'd probably want to fly to freedom as fast as possible.

'So the curtain keeps everyone from seeing what the chicken is doing?' This was really bizarre.

'Yeah. Sal's always got someone watching, to make sure no one peeks in at the bird.' Vinny was saying all this with a straight face. A chicken bodyguard. Go figure.

'How many people?'

'What do you mean?'

'How many people each night?'

Vinny cocked his head, looked up at the ceiling for a second, then back to me. 'Fifty. Sometimes more, sometimes less.'

'How the hell could all this go on without anyone in the restaurant knowing?' I asked.

Vinny smiled. 'That was the beauty of it. Sal had the basement soundproofed. They started coming in around eleven, when the restaurant closed, but even if people were lingering, because of the work he'd done, no one could really hear anything. It was fucking genius.'

'What about employees?'

Vinny laughed. 'Hell, they knew what was

up. Mickey was down there every night.'

Figured. I had another wrench to throw, though. 'What about cars? I never noticed any extra cars anywhere.'

'Back lot. Prego's got a pretty good parking lot back there.'

I thought about that a second. He was right. And it was always full. I never noticed the hour, though. And I never thought anything of it. Vinny was right. It was fucking genius.

'How many chickens are there?'

'At least three or four.'

I had another thought. 'Where were the chickens that weren't playing?'

'He had a portion of the basement set up for them, a room no one was allowed in.' Vinny rubbed the back of his neck.

'So where do you think the chickens are now?' I asked.

Vinny shook his head. 'I don't know. They might have been in the basement and died in the fire.' He narrowed his eyes at me. 'Did Tom say anything about finding anything unusual in there?'

'No.' I doubted he'd tell me if he had.

This was pretty weird shit, though. And my next question was: Who the hell would be stupid enough to let themselves lose to a fucking chicken?

'There's a guy up in Middlefield who trains them,' Vinny was saying. 'Pavlov's dogs and all that shit. Some sort of behaviorist who teaches at Central. He's into this big-time.'

Oh, Christ, I was going to have to find that guy and interview him. When Marty caught wind of this, I'd have a week's worth of stories about where they get the chickens, how much time to train them, where else might the chickens play their game. I wasn't sure I wanted to get into the chickens right now. The bigger story was still who killed LeeAnn Hayward and where Sal was. If the FBI said anything about the chickens, I guess I could get into it then.

Maybe I really *was* burned out, since I was making so many excuses why not to write a story. This was good shit. Tic-tac-toe playing chickens that had generated possibly millions of dollars over the years. Don't see those stories every day.

The phone interrupted my thoughts. Vinny moved back around his desk and picked it up.

'Private investigations.'

He was quiet a minute as he listened, then: 'Sure, half an hour?' A pause. 'I'll be there.'

He hung up. 'I hate to break up this little party,' he said, 'but I've got some stuff I need to do.'

'Who was that?'

'No one you need to know about.'

I got up and started out but paused at the door. 'Oh, by the way. LeeAnn Hayward was shot before the fire. That's how she died.'

Vinny jumped up, getting to the door so fast that I barely had time to open it. 'What?'

'You heard me.'

'You spent all that time on chickens when you have real news?'

So I got a little distracted. It happens. I shrugged. 'I have to go write the real news now.'

'Have the police got a suspect?'

'I haven't talked to the cops yet.' That reminded me I had to find Tom, even if he didn't want to talk to me. Time was running out; I had a deadline to meet and dinner at my mother's. If I was lucky, I'd have to work late and wouldn't have to go to my mother's. But I remembered my father, who was going to show up there with or without me. He needed me as backup.

Vinny had a funny look on his face. 'Well, I guess I'll see you later.'

Something wasn't right, but I couldn't put my finger on it. I started the car and sat for a few minutes, letting it heat up and running everything over in my head. As I was about to pull away from the curb, I spotted Vinny pulling out of the back parking lot and turning toward the highway.

The old Honda can move when I want it to. I didn't know why I was following Vinny, but it seemed like a good idea. He was about three cars ahead of me — thank God for those big SUVs, it's not easy to lose them — and heading toward the Q-Bridge that connects downtown New Haven with the East Shore. People who lived there were technically in New Haven, but they had East Haven zip codes and got the earlier edition of the *Herald* that covered the shoreline more than the city. The East Shore was split up into the Annex and Morris Cove; Townsend Avenue led you down through both to Lighthouse Point Park, a city beach with a huge old carousel and a lighthouse, of course.

Next to Wooster Street, this neighborhood was considered one of the safest, and for the same reasons.

Vinny's Explorer was moving at a pretty good clip down Townsend, until he slowed for the hairpin turn along the water, which spread out like glass under the gray winter sky. Sometimes, on a clear day, you could see Long Island from here. Today, I couldn't even see West Haven.

The SUV turned suddenly, and I slowed, turning down the same street. But he was already gone by the time I reached the next intersection. The blocks were short here, so maybe I could just drive around a little and I'd find him again. I took a right, then another right; going in circles seemed appropriate somehow, and my instincts were rewarded. I pulled over to the curb at the top of the street and watched Vinny emerge from his SUV in front of a small yellow Cape about halfway down the street. He climbed the steps, and I inched a little closer to see who was greeting him.

My father stepped out onto the landing.

12

Whose house was this?

And in a second, my question was answered when Dominic Gaudio joined my father, shaking Vinny's hand before they disappeared inside.

I leaned back in my seat and pondered the situation. There might not be anything fishy about this at all. It wasn't surprising that my father would know Dominic Gaudio, considering that he grew up in New Haven and they traveled in similar circles. And Vinny, well, he was a private investigator and was looking for Sal. Why not ask Dominic Gaudio and my father if they knew anything? That's what I would do in his shoes.

But they had called him.

A black Cadillac with New York plates moved slowly past me and almost came to a stop in front of the yellow house before speeding up and moving on. I watched it turn the corner, out of sight. I felt my chest constrict. That wasn't someone I was inclined to follow, and I began to worry about what my father was into.

Now I wasn't a kid, and I knew my father

wasn't squeaky clean, but it did seem his position in Vegas was on the up-and-up. I wanted to believe that whatever he'd been involved with earlier in his life, he'd gotten out of it.

I glanced at my watch and back up at the house. I didn't have a lot of time. I needed to get back and write up the story about LeeAnn getting shot, with Mac's and Mickey's comments, before going to my mother's for dinner.

I'd see my dad there anyway. I could ask him about this then.

★　★　★

Once back at the paper, I tried to call Tom for an official comment about LeeAnn's murder but got his voice mail. I did reach the cops' public relations officer, who told me they were 'following several leads.' Which meant they didn't know shit. But at least I had something on the record to make Marty happy.

And he smiled. Really smiled after he read my story. I'd even slipped in a sentence about how Vinny was investigating Sal's disappearance. He liked that.

I left out the stuff about the chickens. I didn't have time to get into it, and I needed something from the FBI first, to confirm what Vinny told me.

I had to admit that the newsroom was strangely quiet without Dick, and I kept expecting him to come in. It was still damn cold, though. I hoped they'd get the heat cranking by tomorrow at least.

'I hate to file and run, but I have to get to my mother's for dinner,' I told Marty. 'If you need me for anything else, you can call me on my cell.'

I had to go home and change. I couldn't show up at my mother's in a torn puffy coat and dirty jeans. There were rules to follow, and even though I thought they were stupid, I followed them rather than face the wrath. Anyway, if I was dressed properly, maybe she wouldn't mind that I was showing up with my father.

Because of the snow, I was faced with a fashion dilemma. I couldn't wear normal shoes, I had to go the boot route. But would it be snow boots with regular shoes in a bag — my preference, but the bag would be considered gauche because undoubtedly it would be a plastic supermarket bag — or my incredibly uncomfortable but fashionable plastic boots that would be serviceable both in the snow and on dry land? I went with the plastic boots, even though I'd bought them in a hurry in New York City last winter because it had started snowing unexpectedly and I'd needed footwear. I cringed as I forced my feet into them. I have no idea what sort of fashion devil had possessed me that day. Except that my friend Priscilla had tickets to *The Producers* and we couldn't be late.

My old standby black A-line skirt and a striped turtleneck completed the ensemble. I dabbed on a little makeup, thought better of trying to do something with my hair, and put on my dress coat and leather gloves. Respectable and uncomfortable. Everything my mother wanted me to be.

Fortunately, my father pulled up in front of my mother's at the same time I did. It was better that he didn't go to the door alone.

He snickered a little when he saw me. 'Still trying to please her?'

His own dress shirt and tie did not go unnoticed. 'Can't teach an old dog new tricks?'

'She still bugging you about getting your hair straightened?'

'Yeah.'

'Don't do it. Vinny thinks it's hot.'

I didn't have time to respond, because my mother had thrown open the door and we could see the holiday party taking place inside. A small gathering, she'd said. Yeah, right. A small gathering for my mother is fifty people at a sitdown dinner. How she'd pulled this off in one day would be one of those unsolved mysteries of time.

True to form, she was gracious to my father even if she didn't feel like being gracious.

'Joe, I'd heard you were in town,' she said as she pulled us inside and shut the door, trapping us like the sitting ducks we were.

'Oh, Annie, what lovely boots!' she exclaimed, herding us into the study.

In moments we each had a bourbon in our hands, without really knowing how she did it. We stared at each other numbly.

'And you had a problem with this lifestyle?' I asked my father while my mother went off to tend to a guest who needed another martini.

He was shaking his head, but I could see the smile playing near the corners of his mouth. 'I don't know how she does this. Suzette has a panic attack if we're having one couple over for drinks.'

'Are you ever going to marry her?' It was a loaded question, one I asked him on a regular basis. He never had a good answer for me. Tonight wasn't going to be an exception.

'It's better if we're both free to come and go as we please.' I saw his eyes following my mother around the room, taking in the elegant red crepe dress that hung just right over her slender frame. I had to admit that my mother was a damn good-looking woman, and I guess I didn't blame Bill Bennett for succumbing to her charms, but I wish she'd picked on someone else rather than my boss. I also harbored secret thoughts that maybe she'd realize what an idiot she was about my father and they'd end up together again.

I'm almost forty, and that's a kid's dream, for my parents to get back together. But we all have our little secrets.

'I'm glad you got rid of that awful down coat.'

I turned to see Vinny DeLucia smiling at me. What was worse was that my father was looking at him approvingly. It was weird having my father like the guy I had a crush on. It seemed wrong somehow.

'You could've mentioned you were invited.' I tried not to look at my father, whose eyes were twinkling.

'We could have breakfast again tomorrow,' my father was saying.

'And I could become anorexic and never eat again.' I downed my drink. Actually, it wasn't bad that they were both here; I could kill two birds with one stone, so to speak.

But before I could ask them anything about

this afternoon, my mother returned to our little corner.

'Where's Bill Bennett tonight?' I asked.

She hesitated, and for a second I thought perhaps it was over, that I could get on with my life and not have to cringe every time I saw him in the cafeteria, on the way to the bathroom, or in the executive editor's office.

'He may be by later. His daughter is visiting from Wisconsin, and he wanted some time with her. I met her at lunch. She's a lovely girl.'

Might as well plunge a wooden stake through my heart and get it over with.

'Is this serious, Alex?' My father tried to keep his voice light, but I could see his hand twirling his glass, making the bourbon swish a little too hard.

She smiled at him condescendingly. 'Oh, Joe, you never know.' But she knew. And we knew. This was serious, more serious than I'd ever imagined it could be. Oh, Christ, my life was going to be really fucked up.

My only hope was that the corporate suits would decide they needed new blood and fire Bill Bennett. It had happened before. Someone looks at someone cross-eyed and they're gone, leaving no sign they'd ever even existed. We'd watched four publishers come and go in the past six years. One managed to hang on for two years, but profits went down and he was gone along with the advertising and circulation directors. Bill Bennett had been around for about eight months. Word was he was in tight with the CEO, who was based somewhere in Texas. Since I never had any plans to visit Texas, I didn't think it mattered whether I knew exactly where he was or not. It was a big state. And far away from Connecticut.

We were being led into the dining room. I counted heads once we were seated. Twenty-five. My mother was the odd person out. I wondered if she was saving a plate for Bill Bennett in the kitchen. She used to do that for my father.

Vinny was across the table from me. I was sandwiched between my mother's best friend, Freda, and an old man with Bozo hair. I introduced myself, since it would undoubtedly be a long, painful meal during which I'd have to make small talk. I might as well know who the guy was.

'Mitchell Cartwright,' he said in a low, rather Sean Connery-like voice. I took another look at him. If he'd trimmed his hair, he would actually be a good-looking older man, with a long nose and high forehead. I wondered if my mother had made a mistake and Freda should be sitting next to Mitchell

Cartwright. Freda's husband had died the year before of prostate cancer, and she was on the make. Really. I could tell. She'd obviously had her hair and makeup done, and her blouse was low and clingy. And it even looked as if she'd visited Victoria's Secret and invested in one of those bras that push your breasts up and out over your clothes in an attempt to look appealing.

It was working. Mitchell Cartwright didn't seem to give a shit about me, even though I am thirty years younger than Freda.

Vinny caught my eye, and I could see he was trying not to laugh. I just wanted to go throw up and tell my mother I was too ill to stay.

My father was across the table, about five people down. No breasts in his soup. He was stuck between my mother's law partners.

Halfway through the fruit cup, I traded seats with Freda. My mother frowned at me from the head of the table, and I frowned back.

'You know, you could've been more social,' she whispered to me after we'd gotten through the marathon dinner and finally were knocking back brandies in the study.

'I've been working almost straight through since yesterday morning,' I said, maybe a little too loudly, because I noticed Mitchell

Cartwright glance up at me from Freda's chest. I jerked my head in their direction. 'Freda's getting laid tonight.'

My mother shook her head. 'Don't be crude, Anne.'

One of the hired help for the night appeared mysteriously at my mother's side with the cordless phone. My mother took it, got a funny look on her face, and wandered into the hall. At first I thought it was Bill Bennett, but the look on her face told me no, it was someone else. And since her ex-husband, daughter, and law partners were here, I couldn't help but be curious.

I followed her as she scurried into the kitchen and put the phone back in its cradle. I startled her when she turned around and I was in her face.

'Oh, Anne,' she said, her voice breathless. 'I have to go.'

'Go?'

'I have something important to attend to.'

Something important during one of her soirees? I studied her face. This was fucking big; there was no way she would be able to get me off her case until she told me what was up. And she knew it.

She sighed. 'You're going to have to take over, take care of everyone until they leave.'

'When are you coming back?'

She shook her head. 'Probably not for a while. They'll all filter out soon, anyway.' She pulled a jacket out of a closet near the back door. I blocked the door.

'You have to tell me. Otherwise I'm leaving. Now. And your guests will have to fend for themselves.'

Leaving a party host-less was something I knew she couldn't do. It was against her nature. She was struggling with herself, trying to decide whether it was worth it to tell me.

Finally, I could see her relenting. 'All right, but you have to promise me that you won't do anything about this.'

It was a story. A story I would still be able to get into the paper because it was early enough for tomorrow's edition. And she was making me promise I wouldn't. I crossed my fingers behind my back. 'Okay,' I said.

'I have to get to the police station. They've arrested Mickey Hayward in LeeAnn's murder.'

13

While I wasn't completely surprised that Mickey was arrested, considering his and LeeAnn's volatile relationship and his reaction earlier in the day, I was surprised about one thing.

'He called you to represent him?' I didn't think he could afford my mother, even though she did pro bono work from time to time. But Mickey Hayward didn't seem the type of guy she'd take on. He was a little too smarmy for her.

'Oh, no, dear. That was Mac. Mac Amato. He called her and she called me. I told her I'd help out.' And with that she was out the door, leaving me with a decision to make.

Actually, it wasn't too hard. I picked up the phone and called the paper. Marty was still there, like I knew he would be.

'Gotta top my story off,' I said.

'Better be good. Deadline's in fifteen minutes.'

I told him about Mickey's arrest. I could hear his fingers moving on his keyboard. 'Can you call the cops and get it confirmed?' he asked.

'I'll call you right back.' I hung up and dialed Tom's cell phone number. This was no time to respect our breakup. This was news, and I was going to get it before deadline.

'You heard.' He didn't even say hello.

'My mother's on her way over. When did you pick him up?' I had to ask him the questions quickly, before he realized what he was doing.

'Half an hour ago. Your mother?' Fortunately that was news to him, and it distracted him.

'Yeah. Left a dinner party.'

'Holy shit.' My mother was a good lawyer. She got criminals off. The cops didn't like her. Of course, she also got innocent people off, too. But the cops think everyone's guilty, so that didn't matter to them.

'What's the evidence?' I asked.

'No comment.' He hung up, and I quickly dialed Marty and fed him the news.

'We don't have a picture of him, do we?' he asked.

'I don't think so.'

'Too bad. And it's too late to try to find one now. Gotta get one tomorrow.' I agreed to try to get my hands on one.

It wasn't until I hung up that I realized I had to go out there and tell my mother's guests that she wasn't there anymore. My father was lurking just outside the kitchen.

'Where'd she go?'

I told him what was going on, and he rubbed his chin thoughtfully but didn't say anything.

'Mac said she thought Mickey had killed her, but when I saw him, he seemed really surprised she was murdered,' I told him.

'Hmmm.' His mind was definitely elsewhere.

Might as well get it over with.

'Why were you at Dominic Gaudio's today?' I asked.

He looked me straight in the eye. 'He's an old friend, Annie. Why wouldn't I go see him? I think I told you I was visiting friends today.'

He was calm, but I was flustered and frustrated. This wasn't the whole story, I would bank on that. 'Why did you call Vinny and tell him to meet you there?'

His expression didn't change, but I could see his shoulders tense slightly. 'How do you know Vinny was there?'

'Because she followed me.' Vinny stepped around the corner.

I glared at him. 'How do you know that?'

'You'd make a lousy private eye.'

So sue me. 'Why were you there?'

'We were talking about Sal,' Vinny said. 'I still have to find him.'

I remembered the Cadillac. 'You know, someone was watching you besides me.' And I told them how the car had slowed down in front of the house.

My father smiled. 'There's nothing to worry about.'

But Vinny looked a little distressed at this news. I was going to have to get him alone. My father was too smooth, too used to evading questions.

'What's going on here?' Vinny asked. 'Where's your mother?'

I told him how Mickey had been arrested. He frowned and bit his lip. 'Shit.'

'I have to go be the host,' I said with a grimace, indicating the people we could hear murmuring down the hall.

My father grinned. 'Are you up to it?'

'No.'

When everyone found out my mother had left, they quickly donned their coats and said their own good-byes. My father, Vinny, and I settled into the leather chairs in the den with more drinks as the hired help scurried around like mice, cleaning up. We'd wait until they were done and gone before we left.

I tried to talk to them again about Sal and their meeting this afternoon, but my father refilled my glass and changed the subject to golf, something he and Vinny seemed to have an affinity for. It was easy to drift off into my own thoughts as they chatted. They talked in that way guys do when they're alone together, even though I was sitting there with them.

'Hey, Annie, wake up.'

My dad was leaning over me the way he used to when I was little and having a nightmare. I smiled at him. 'I fell asleep?'

'You've been snoring.'

I sat up straight, looking around for Vinny.

'He left.' My father paused. 'Before the snoring.'

'How long have I been asleep?'

'About an hour.'

'Really?'

'You've been working hard the last two days, and I know you don't sleep well when you're wired about something.'

The lights were dim, and I had a throw blanket on top of me. I pulled it up to my chin, savoring the smell of the chair leather and my dad's cologne.

'Are you sure you can't come back?' I asked softly.

My dad settled back into his own leather chair and sighed. 'I really can't. Especially now that your mother . . . ' His voice trailed off.

'If she wasn't involved with someone, would you come back?'

He smiled, but I saw a twinge of sadness in his face. 'I've got a life in Vegas, she's got one here, whether she's seeing someone or not. She made it clear I wasn't going to be a part of that life. And you, well, you're doing fine on your own. You've built a nice career for yourself, you've got some good friends.' He winked. 'And Vinny is good people.'

I saw what he was implying. 'But he's engaged.'

'For the wrong reasons. I have confidence — '

But before he could finish his thought, we heard the front door open and shut.

'Back so soon?' I asked when my mother walked by. It startled her, and she peered into the den.

'You're both still here?'

'Annie fell asleep,' my father said.

'How's Mickey?' I asked.

'He's there until Monday morning's arraignment. I couldn't get him out.' That was a surprise. She could always get them out.

She took off her jacket and poured herself a brandy. 'They've charged him with the fire, too.'

I sat up straighter. 'Arson murder?' Pretty damn serious charge. 'No one would say whether it was arson.'

'It was. In the dining room. They found accelerant. Gasoline.' I knew she was telling me this because I'd find out anyway.

'But he was in Boston,' I said.

She shook her head. 'He can't prove it. Hotels have that express checkout now, you don't even have to turn in a key or check at the desk when you leave. The maid found the computer printout on the floor in the room, but Mickey says he just forgot it when he left because he was worried about LeeAnn. He could've left anytime.'

This didn't bode well.

'Do they have the gun?' I asked.

'Yes. They found it in the trunk of his car. He says he didn't know it was there.' She looked me straight in the eye. 'I believe him.'

So did I. Why the hell would someone murder someone and then not get rid of the weapon? Nobody would be that stupid. We all watch TV.

'The gun was wiped clean,' my mother added.

'No fingerprints?'

'No. But in their minds, possession is nine-tenths of the law.'

It seemed a little weak to me, but I could see her trying to keep her eyes open. Now wasn't the time to get into it. My father stood up and got our coats.

'It was good seeing you, Alex,' he said when

she walked us to the door. He kissed her cheek, and for a second I thought I saw her lean in toward him. But then she pulled back. 'I hope we can talk before I leave,' he added.

'When will that be?' She was tired, but she was back in the game for a minute.

Dad shrugged. 'I'll let you know.'

My mother gave me a hug. 'Thank you, Annie, for helping out.' I didn't have the heart to tell her I hadn't done a damn thing.

We stepped out into the frosty air, and if I'd been sleepy before, I was wide awake now.

'How long are you staying?' I asked my father on the sidewalk.

'As long as I have to.' He walked me to my car and made sure I got in safely. He kissed my cheek. 'I'll see you tomorrow.'

I followed him as far as downtown, when I turned off toward Wooster Square. I pulled up in front of my brownstone and parked. The streetlights played against the snow, casting weird shadows. I didn't look toward Prego as I got out of the car and started up toward the steps.

Someone grabbed me from behind, and an arm stretched across my chest, keeping me from turning around, my arms pinned behind me.

'What?' I started to say, but a hand clasped over my mouth.

'Listen,' a voice hissed in my ear, 'you better stop messing around in things that don't concern you.'

The arm wrenched my body backward, and it felt as though I were going to snap in two. I tried to catch my breath, but the hand over my mouth was tight and sweaty.

'Hey!' The shout came somewhere from my left, and in a second the grip loosened and I fell to the ground, the slush seeping into my skirt. I heard footsteps off to my right, and with a stab of pain in my side, I looked toward them. A large shadow disappeared around the corner.

14

I managed to get up, but it felt as if my back were still twisted, and I hobbled toward the stairs. Once inside, I made sure the front door was locked, and I climbed the stairs to my apartment. My door swung open, and I reached in and turned on all the lights before locking myself in.

What had happened really didn't sink in until I pulled off my coat and fell onto the couch with another stab of pain. Maybe it was the brandies I'd had, but until that moment, I had experienced some sort of weird calm. Now I started to hyperventilate, and my whole body shook.

The buzzer screeched, sending me into a new panic.

My heart beating madly, I walked over to the switch and turned off the overhead light. I made my way through the dark to the window and peered down at the stoop. Vinny was standing underneath the light post outside, looking up at my window, his arms outstretched, sort of like Marlon Brando in *A Streetcar Named Desire*.

I buzzed him in.

His hair was mussed up, his shirt open to reveal a small tuft of dark hair, his bare hands red from the cold.

'Are you okay? I saw what happened. I shouted, but I was across the park, I couldn't get there in time. He was gone by the time I got here.' He took me into his arms, and I drank in his spicy, sexy smell, my panic attack subsiding.

'You okay?' he asked again; I could feel his lips on my hair.

I pulled away and took a deep breath. 'Yeah, I'm okay, I guess.' I told him what the guy had said to me.

'This is what happens when you follow people around, when you pretend to know more than you do.'

'Give me a break, Vinny. I didn't ask for it, if that's what you're implying.' My voice was harsh, but I could feel myself on the verge of tears again, and I bit my lip to keep them at bay.

He sat down. 'I didn't mean that, but maybe you need to be a little more discreet.'

I tried to smile. 'Not my strong suit.' I sat next to him.

'No kidding.' He leaned toward me, and for a second I thought he was going to kiss me, but he merely reached up and moved a curl off my forehead. His fingertips were cold against my skin, and I shifted a little.

'Tell me what's going on at Dominic Gaudio's,' I said.

He moved away from me a little. 'Don't you think you've learned enough?'

'No. What's up with that Cadillac? And why is my father meeting with strange men in diners?'

'Why don't you ask him?'

I snorted. 'Yeah, right. Like he'd tell me.'

'So you want me to tell you?' Vinny's eyebrows arched, and he smiled. 'They may have to kill me.'

'I'll make that sacrifice,' I said, my eyes meeting his.

Suddenly the smile disappeared and his expression grew serious. 'What I tell you can't leave this apartment. You can't put anything in the paper. This is only for your personal information, okay?'

I frowned. 'What's with the secrecy?'

Vinny shook his head. 'I'm serious, Annie. I shouldn't tell you anything.'

'But everyone seems to know everything, and I don't know shit.'

'Because you're not part of us.'

I knew what he was saying. My mother is Jewish, my father isn't my biological father. So I wasn't even Italian. I wasn't second generation like Vinny or the kids I'd gone to school with. I wasn't part of the inside circle, and even my father had left me out all these years. 'Okay, fine,' I grumbled. 'But this better be good. You just made me feel like crap.'

He chuckled. 'You might change your mind when I tell you.' He paused. 'The guys in the Cadillac, well, they might be the FBI, or they might be . . . ' His voice trailed off.

'The Mob?' Even as I said it, I wasn't sure I believed it. It seemed so clichéd.

'Sal's game wasn't his own. He paid protection.' He paused. 'Okay, in a nutshell, the Mob still has gambling interests here, even though it's not as big as it used to be. The feds took down most of the New England organization back in the late eighties after a major player was murdered, but it's still active. And New Haven is stuck between New York and Boston, which means both organizations own a little piece here. They know about each other, they work together sometimes. Sal's was one of those operations that was shared.'

'Did the Mob burn down the restaurant?' I asked. 'My mother says Mickey Hayward was charged with arson, so the cops think he did it.'

I could see Vinny was struggling with how much more to tell me, even though a history of the Mafia in New Haven certainly wasn't going to tell me too much about Sal Amato and his game-playing chickens.

'They wouldn't destroy something that was making money, but they would try to recoup some cash if they thought it was owed to them,' he finally said.

I got up and took a couple of beers out of the fridge, handed one to Vinny.

My head was swirling, and I thought of something else. 'LeeAnn Hayward was Dominic Gaudio's niece. Do you think that has anything to do with what happened to her?'

'I don't know.' Vinny got up and started pacing. 'You know, Mickey hired me six months ago.'

'For what?'

'LeeAnn. He was convinced she was having an affair.'

I stared at him. 'So what did you find out?'

He sat down, shifted in his seat, and took a drink before answering. 'She wasn't having an affair, at least not from what I saw. But there was something odd. Every week she would go to the farmers' market on DePalma with a cloth bag full of something, and it would be empty when she left. I tried my damnedest to see what she left and where, but it was always too busy, and she was fast, moving around those stalls. Hardest fucking job I've ever had, and it should've been the simplest.'

He paused, and I waited. 'I didn't tell Mickey about that, it didn't seem relevant to what he'd hired me for, but even when I stopped working for him, I continued to follow her to the market. When the market closed for the season, I didn't see her anymore. I did a little surveillance on my own, but she never did anything like that again.'

'The Mob deals in cash, doesn't it?' I asked quietly. I wasn't completely ignorant; I'd heard things through the years — rumors, innuendos — and I read wire stories about the crime families in New York and Boston. I'd known there was a history here, too, but not that it was still as active as it seemed to be if Vinny was right.

Vinny's eyes bored into mine. 'Yeah,' he said, and I knew we were on the same page with this one. Sal was paying protection, and LeeAnn Hayward was a courier.

'Why did you follow her, knowing what she was probably doing?' I asked.

He chuckled. 'Curiosity. I've heard about this all my life, but besides the chickens, I'd never seen it in action. And it was sort of a challenge to myself. I wanted to see how good I was.' He paused. 'Guess I'm not that good.'

'Jesus, Vinny, you're dealing with the Mob. They've been doing this a helluva lot longer than you have.'

We drank our beers without saying anything else for a few minutes. But I had a nagging thought.

'The guy who jumped me, was he going to kill me?' As I said it, I began to get a little panicky again.

Vinny smiled. 'Of course not.'

'How can you be so sure?'

'The Mob doesn't kill honest journalists or honest cops.' He said it so matter-of-factly.

'So that's some sort of rule?'

His smile turned into a grin. 'Yeah.'

That was about all I wanted to know tonight. I took Vinny's empty bottle and put both in the sink.

'Do you want me to stay?' Vinny was right behind me, close enough so I could feel his breath on the back of my neck.

I shook my head without turning around. 'No.'

'Are we ever going to talk about this?' I felt his hand snake around my waist.

I turned and pushed him an arm's length away. 'There's nothing to talk about.'

He studied my face for a few seconds, then said, 'Okay.' He walked to the door; I was right behind him.

'Thanks for telling me all that,' I said as we stood in the open doorway.

He nodded, and before I could stop him, he leaned over and kissed me, sending tingles down into my toes. When he pulled away, he smiled. 'See ya,' he said casually, and went down the stairs.

★ ★ ★

I woke up the next morning with more resolve. Resolve to find out what my father and Dominic Gaudio were up to, resolve to find out where Sal was, resolve to keep my head around Vinny. That kiss had made it very hard to fall asleep, and it also proved that maybe there *was* something to talk about after all.

I pulled myself out of bed, and the pain in my arm and back made me catch my breath, reminding me that being a pain in the ass wasn't all it was cracked up to be. I gritted my teeth, made my way into the kitchen, and put on some coffee. As I poured the water into the machine, I thought about LeeAnn Hayward and her visits to the farmers' market. It was time to call Paula again, try to get something official from the FBI.

But all I got was her answering machine. It was 9:00 A.M. Saturday morning. She was

153

never up early. I tried her cell phone.

'Annie, I'm working. I can't talk.'

'I know about Prego and the gambling operation, Paula.' Well, not everything, but she didn't have to know that. 'And someone threatened me, jumped me outside my apartment last night. So maybe I need to know more of what's going on. It might save my ass.'

'Or it might not.' I hate it when people play devil's advocate.

'Okay, but don't you think I'll find out anyway?'

'Not from me.' But she still hadn't hung up, which made me start wondering why.

'Are you working on it?'

'Yes.'

'Does it involve only Sal or other people, too?'

'Other people.'

So playing twenty questions might actually get me somewhere, as long as I asked the right ones.

'Besides his gambling operation, is there anything else?'

'I can't tell you.'

I reminded myself that this was her job, like mine was to annoy her enough to get her to talk to me just so I'd leave her alone.

'You know,' she said when I took too long

trying to think of my next question, 'you might want to talk to your father.'

'I already tried that. He won't tell me a damn thing. You're not after him, too, are you?'

'We're watching him, I'll give you that. But as of right now, no, we're not after him.'

He wouldn't have come back if the FBI was after him. He would've gone off somewhere, like Sal, maybe with Sal.

'You know Mac hired Vinny to find Sal.'

I heard her chuckle. 'If he finds Sal before we do, we're going to be really embarrassed.'

'Can you tell me anything else?'

'No. Not now. I'll talk to you later.' The phone went dead in my hand, and I hung it up.

I pulled on my coat, stuffed an extra notebook in my purse, and went downstairs. I could smell snow in the air, like we needed more of it, and I glanced reflexively toward Prego. Someone was moving around over there. Maybe Mario had come back. I still had some questions for that guy.

Once across the square, I went around the remains of the restaurant and into the back where I'd seen Mario the last time. But there was no one there.

There were two doors in the back of the restaurant, and I recognized the one that led

155

to the kitchen. But I'd never really noticed the other one before, because it seemed to blend in with the rest of the building and was off a bit to the side. I turned the knob and gave the door a little push. It creaked inward, and I stared down a set of stairs into darkness.

The basement was down there, where the chickens played and the gamblers made their wagers. The soundproof room that Sal kept hidden from regular customers. A dim glow emanated below.

Before I could talk myself out of it, I was moving down the stairs. The stench of smoke invaded my lungs, and I coughed. There was another door at the end of the stairs, and I opened it.

The room was about the size of a tennis court, with a large roped-off section underneath what would be the front of the restaurant. That was probably where the chickens played their game. Most of the ceiling was burned away, and I could see the gray clouds overhead. Debris surrounded me on the floor, drowning in a few inches of water, probably from the firemen's hoses. The fire smoke smell was mixed with something else — cigars and cigarettes. But what caught my attention more than anything else were the feathers floating on the water's surface. My eyes moved quickly around the room, and the body made me freeze.

A chicken lay about four feet from where I was standing. Two more were in the far corner, opposite the roped-off section.

Their heads were nowhere to be seen.

Someone had killed the chickens down here. But before or after the fire? Maybe someone *was* a sore loser.

I stiffened as the sound of voices reached me. There was ceiling just above me, but to my right, I could see straight through to a corner of the kitchen. There was an argument going on up there, but the voices were too muffled for me to hear what they were saying or to recognize any voices.

A loud crack echoed down through the hole. Even if I hadn't ever heard a gunshot before, I would've recognized the sound. As if my body had a mind of its own, I found myself racing up the stairs and out the door into the back parking lot.

I almost jumped out of my boots when a figure came crashing out the kitchen door, nearly knocking me over. Whoever it was was wearing a coat puffier than mine, and a hood hid its face. It was sexless and quick. I stepped back as the figure ran past me and out of sight.

It happened so fast, I didn't realize until it

was gone that it was holding a gun.

My body tensed. I peered around the open door and into the kitchen. The hole in the floor was far enough away, so I stepped inside and around the stainless-steel island in the middle of the room. The walls were charred, and debris and water were everywhere, like in the basement. A gaping hole was where the ceiling should be, and a few snowflakes had begun settling among the ruins around me. I didn't want to go any farther, realizing now that the building could be very unsafe. I was an idiot to have gone downstairs.

'What the hell are you doing in here?' came a voice from behind me.

I spun around so quickly, I slipped and fell forward onto Vinny. He steadied me, but he was distracted; his eyes were taking in everything.

'Jesus Christ, Vinny, you scared the shit out of me,' I scolded.

'I heard something over here. Sounded like a gunshot. What's going on?'

'You might want to ask the guy with the gun who just left.'

Vinny stared at me. 'What?'

'I saw someone over here, and I figured I'd check it out. I was downstairs looking at the dead chickens when I heard the argument and then the shot and came up here. I saw someone dressed in a huge jacket, so I couldn't see who it was, and he ran out with a gun.'

'You're okay?' Vinny asked.

'He just ran past me, didn't stop.' I hated to admit it, but seeing Vinny slowed my heartbeat, even though it was still pounding so hard that I was sure he could hear it.

'Dead chickens?' Vinny's brain seemed to be catching up with what I'd said.

'Downstairs. Three of them. No heads.'

'You heard an argument?' Vinny's eyes narrowed as he took in this information.

'I don't know who it was or how many people there were. But then I heard the shot.'

'Have you looked around farther than this?'

I shook my head. 'No. It doesn't seem like there's much more to look at, and I don't think it's safe.'

The skies had opened up again, and snow was falling about ten feet away from us into the rubble. Vinny grabbed something, a blackened table leg, I think, and started poking around.

'What are you looking for?' I asked.

'I don't know. You heard voices, but you said only one person came out. There was a gunshot. Something doesn't feel right.'

'Oh, yeah, you're the great private investigator.'

He shot me a look that made me sorry I'd said it. But I didn't apologize. I just started looking around a little more, too.

I stepped tentatively a little farther to the right, past where the doors to the dining room would've been.

I saw blood on the ashes. I took another step. The scream caught in my throat.

Sal Amato lay among the rubble, his eyes staring lifelessly at nothing, a neat hole in the middle of his forehead.

15

Vinny grabbed me from behind and pulled me back. He then stepped around me and took a closer look before leading me outside. I was hyperventilating again.

Vinny stroked my hair and whispered, 'You'll be okay,' over and over until I could feel myself breathing almost normally again. I nestled my face against his shoulder, breathed in his scent, and it calmed me.

'I guess you found Sal,' I said quietly. But after a second: 'Well, I guess I found Sal.'

'You're in shock,' Vinny said matter-of-factly as he pulled his cell phone out of his pocket, but I could see his hand shaking as he punched in the numbers.

I couldn't stop thinking about what Sal looked like. It was just like in the movies, but this time it was Sal and not De Niro or Pacino. 'What was that Pacino movie where they cut up the body?' I asked Vinny, who was calling 911.

'Which one?' he asked as he stuck the phone back in his coat.

The snow was falling gently as Vinny steered me back around to the front sidewalk.

I could hear sirens approaching. That was fast. But the gunshot was so loud, someone in the neighborhood had probably called 911 before Vinny.

I didn't even notice Vinny had made another call until he was finished talking.

'That was my father, wasn't it,' I said in a moment of lucidity.

He nodded. 'You don't look too good.'

I didn't feel too good. I didn't give a shit about the snow or the slush or my jeans, and I sat down, putting my head between my legs. Vinny's fingers massaged the back of my neck. It felt pretty damn good.

The sirens were closer now, and when I looked up, the cruisers were pulling up in front of us. Tom stepped out of a Crown Vic and looked down at me.

'I should've known you'd be around here somewhere,' he said accusingly.

'I saw something over here. I didn't think it would be anything like this,' I said.

'She saw someone leaving with a gun,' Vinny added.

Tom stared at me. 'You saw whoever did this?'

I shook my head. 'Not really. I couldn't see a face, or even a body, really. He was wearing a big puffy coat and a hood that came up over his face.' I thought a minute. 'I don't know who killed the chickens.'

Tom's face scrunched up with confusion. 'Chickens?'

'There are three dead chickens in the basement,' I said.

Tom shook his head. 'Dead chickens?' he said incredulously.

'I think they were the tic-tac-toe chickens,' I said after a minute.

Tom snorted. 'I can't believe this,' he said, and moved past us into the restaurant, where the crime scene guys were already at work.

'He thinks we're crazy,' I told Vinny.

Vinny grinned. 'No, he thinks you're crazy.'

That wasn't news.

Speaking of news, I wondered where Dick Whitfield was. I hadn't seen him in two days, and usually I was tripping all over him. A thought dawned on me, one that would verify Tom's suspicions about my mental health. Maybe it was Dick Whitfield. Maybe he was like a Jack the Ripper or a Boston Strangler. Maybe it was Dick in that puffy coat — the Michelin Man with a penchant for chicken blood.

I had to get ahold of myself.

'Do you think that guy killed the chickens, too?' I asked Vinny.

Vinny shrugged. 'Maybe.'

I had another thought, one that made me

shiver again. 'Why didn't he kill me when I saw him run out? He could've, he had that gun.' I thought about what Vinny had said about the Mob not killing honest journalists, but Vinny suggested something else.

'Maybe he knew you wouldn't be able to identify him with a big hood over his head.' He paused. 'How tall was he?'

'I dunno. Little taller than me, maybe six feet, six two.'

'You're not that tall.'

'I can be, in heels,' I argued.

'But you're not wearing heels now.'

We stared at my big snow boots.

'I like a girl in boots,' Vinny whispered. He was smiling that sexy smile again.

'Keep your eyes off my boots or I'll slap a sexual harassment complaint against you.' Sparring with Vinny was keeping me from thinking about Sal, who should've been basking in the sun on some Caribbean island, hiding from the feds. 'What was Sal doing here, anyway?'

'He was waiting for something. Had to be. Or he would've been gone by now,' Vinny said.

I saw a silver Town Car out of the corner of my eye. I thought about Dominic Gaudio, but his car was white. This one pulled up to the curb and parked behind one of the cruisers. My father stepped out into the street, spotted me and Vinny in the driveway, waved, and came over, ignoring all the cops and activity around us.

'Are you okay, Annie?' His voice was soft, and he bent down close to me.

I nodded.

'What happened here?' He asked this of Vinny, who straightened up and shoved his hands in his pockets, probably to keep anyone else from noticing they were still shaking. I wasn't the only one affected by this.

Vinny told him about me finding Sal.

'Shit,' Dad said quietly.

I stood up. It would be futile to try to brush off the slush. I looked back at the restaurant but didn't see Tom. I was going to have to change my clothes or I'd freeze to death out here.

'I'll go find Tom and tell him you'll be right back,' Vinny offered, and I watched him until he disappeared around the building.

My father took my arm and led me across the square.

'I don't get why Sal was still here,' I said, stopping and looking at my father. His eyes were tired, and his mouth hung slack. 'Why didn't you help him?'

His eyes grew a little harder. 'How could I do that?'

'You must have known where he was.'

He didn't say anything. I knew I couldn't push it much further. If he didn't want to tell me anything, he wasn't going to. There was nothing I could say or do that would change his mind.

'Did Mac know that Sal was here? Was he at the house?'

'Why don't you let it go for now?' There was something in his voice that told me to stop.

At the bottom of my steps, I turned to him. 'You can go back over there, talk to Vinny or something,' I said. 'I'll be right back.'

'I could send Vinny over,' he suggested, trying to make things lighter between us.

'No. I'll be right back,' I said, and went up the stairs and through the heavy door.

Amber's door cracked open as I came up the stairs.

'What's going on over there?' she asked. I could see only half her face.

I shook my head, not wanting to get into it.

'Did you get the recipe?' I heard her ask as I started up the stairs.

I turned back and stared at her. 'Listen, Amber, I like meat. I hate tofu. Sorry, but you're wasting your time.'

The door creaked open a little farther, and I saw a bit more of her face, a lot of hair.

'You should stop the suffering,' she started, but I just snorted and turned my back on her, going up the stairs and into my apartment.

The phone rang just as I pulled off my pants. I was considering a quick hot shower when I picked up the receiver.

'If you keep poking around, you'll be next.' The voice was muffled, as if he were talking through a pillow.

'Who is this?' I asked, my own voice trembling.

The dial tone echoed through my ear, and my hand started to shake. Whoever had been in that restaurant knew who I was.

Of course he knew me. Jesus, everyone in the neighborhood knew who I was. And this had to be someone from the neighborhood. Someone who knew about the chickens and their Mob connection.

I sat on the bed, wrapping the comforter around my middle to warm myself up. I still wore my wool sweater and turtleneck, and my hair was wet with melted snow. I don't know how long I sat there, my head swimming, until I heard the door buzzer. I pulled the comforter off the bed, clutching it around me as I went to the window. Vinny was laying on the buzzer like there was no fucking tomorrow. I buzzed him in, and I could hear his heavy boots pounding against the wooden stairs in the hall.

He stared at the comforter around my waist, my bare feet on the floor.

The smile told me he'd guessed correctly that I was wearing nothing but my birthday suit under there.

'I was going to take a shower,' I tried lamely.

'You shouldn't do that to a man, Annie. You're making me crazy.'

But he didn't come any closer. I might have let him. I might have let him do a lot of things right then and there, but be didn't move.

Damn.

I went back into the bedroom, found a dry pair of underpants and an old pair of khakis in the drawer, and locked myself in the bathroom to put them on. When I came back out, he was pouring a snifter of brandy.

'Drink this. It'll relax you,' he said, handing me the glass. 'Tom said he'd come by here in about ten minutes.'

I took the glass and drank. I felt the warm liquid down to my toes. He was right. I started to relax, and I knew it would brace me for facing Tom again with Vinny by my side.

I took another swallow, then handed the glass back to Vinny. 'I shouldn't have more, that was enough. Thanks.' I sat on the couch, staring at my Japanese print of Mount Fuji across the room.

Vinny put the snifter on the counter, then plopped down on the couch next to me. Our legs were touching, and neither of us pulled away. 'Why didn't my father get Sal out of town?'

'Maybe he really didn't know he was still here.'

'Maybe.'

But we didn't believe that. We couldn't prove it, but we didn't believe it.

'I got a threatening call.' I paused.

Vinny sat straight up and stared at me. 'From who?'

I shrugged.

'What'd he say?'

'Told me to stop poking around or I'd end up dead like Sal.' As I said it, it sank in and the trembling started again.

Vinny pulled me close, and I rested my head on his chest. I could hear his heartbeat underneath his chamois shirt. I felt his hand stroking my hair, just as he'd done outside, and it had the same effect.

'What happens now?' I asked.

'You have to talk to Tom. Try to remember everything. I told him everything I saw. We have to find out who did this.'

169

'So he doesn't come after me,' I said quietly.

'Want to hire me to protect you?' Vinny teased.

'Are you cheap?'

'No, just easy.' And he lifted my face with his hand and guided my lips to his. I forgot about Sal and the Mob and the chickens and the phone call. For about two seconds, until the buzzer interrupted us.

'That'll be Tom,' I said, pulling away reluctantly. I wanted to forget everything that had happened this morning, and here it was again, knocking on my door like an annoying Jehovah's Witness.

Tom didn't like it that Vinny was there. But he pulled out his notebook and didn't say anything, just started writing down everything I told him about going over there and finding the chickens and then the figure rushing past me with a gun.

He closed his notebook when I was done and started for the door.

'That's it?' I asked.

He stopped and looked at me, his blue eyes almost violet in the light from the window. 'That's it.' And he walked out.

'Boy, that was cold,' Vinny said quietly.

I didn't want to think about it. I had to keep my mind occupied with something else.

I needed to call Marty. I picked up the phone, ignoring Vinny's raised eyebrows.

'Hey, Marty,' I said when he answered.

'What's going on over there? I tried to call your cell phone, but all I got was your voice mail.'

My cell was in my purse, turned off.

Marty was still talking. 'Dick Whitfield called. He's over at Prego. Says Sal Amato was found dead. And you found the body.'

'Yeah, that's about right.'

'You'll need to talk to him.'

'Who?'

'Dick. For the story. Eyewitness and all.'

'You want Dick to interview me?'

Marty sighed. 'Listen, Annie, obviously you can't write this yourself. You're part of the story.'

'Jesus, Marty. He'll get the quotes wrong, and then who do I complain to?'

'You can read the story before we print it, okay? Will that ease your mind?'

'Yeah, I guess that would be okay.' It was a lost cause. I'd lost my story because I was stupid enough to go into that shell of a building.

I looked out the window at the crime scene. The cops all looked like ants, and there was Dick Whitfield — I could pick out his skinny fucking frame anywhere.

'I'll go talk to him now,' I volunteered. I hung up. 'Maybe I should have some more brandy. Getting interviewed drunk by Dick Whitfield might be the best way.'

Vinny smiled. 'I could take advantage of you instead.'

I could see the merits in that. I wouldn't have to be interviewed and misquoted by a moron, the killer wouldn't be able to get to me right away, and it would satisfy the itch that I'd had for Vinny for two months now.

I wondered what Vinny would do if I said yes. Would he shout 'Yippee!' and carry me into the bedroom, or would he get that 'deer in the headlights' look a guy gets when a girl tells him she loves him and he's just not quite ready for it?

'I didn't think you'd have to think about it so long,' Vinny teased, although I could see some relief in his face that I wasn't completely enthusiastic.

'It's not really a good time,' I said. 'Finding a dead body and getting threatened isn't good foreplay.'

'I know. I just thought I'd get your mind off those things for a few minutes.'

I tried a smile. 'Thanks. I gotta get back out there.'

He nodded and picked up my coat. I frowned. 'What're you doing?' I asked as he came around behind me.

'Haven't you ever had a man help you on with your coat before?' he asked as he did just that.

As I slid my arm into my coat, another thought crept into my brain.

'Vinny, the guy called me on my phone.'

He shrugged. 'Yeah?'

'My number's unlisted.'

16

Vinny grilled me about who might have my home phone number. I always gave out my cell phone number.

'My parents and Tom have my home number. So do you, as a matter of fact.' I thought a second. 'Oh, and Marty, but he doesn't give it out to anyone, he knows better than that. Priscilla in New York has it, too, and Paula.' I paused for a minute, thinking about Paula. But the FBI wouldn't have cause to threaten me. They might want to question me, but certainly not threaten me.

'So you're fairly sure no one but those few people would have your number?'

I shook my head. 'I don't think anyone would give my number out.' But then I wasn't so sure. My number was in the phone list at work, and even though it was flagged as being unlisted, that didn't really mean much if an editor or reporter was on deadline and someone was bugging them to get in touch with me.

'Well, if no one spilled the beans, and that's a big 'if,' you just named your closest family and friends as suspects. Me included,' Vinny said.

'But you were here.'

'No, I wasn't.' Vinny paused. 'You remember our conversation last night?'

I nodded.

'Normally the Mob doesn't physically threaten people like you. But threatening phone calls are another matter.'

'So what are you trying to tell me?' I asked. 'The guy last night might not be a mobster, but the phone call was?'

He shrugged. 'Possibility.'

Way too much shit going on right now. And the worst was yet to come. 'We'd better get going. I have to talk to Dick.' I cringed as I said it, but something had to go in the paper, and I wanted everything to be right.

The sky had a pinkish hue. I felt the flakes melting on my face, the cold biting into my cheeks.

'How are you doing?' My father approached us as we crossed the street and stepped onto the sidewalk. He put his arm around me.

I nodded. 'I'm fine.'

I pulled away, and for a second thought I was going to slip, but I steadied myself. 'I have to go talk to Dick,' I said, and I left my father with Vinny and made my way over to Dick, who was unfortunately talking to Tom.

'Did you forget something?' Tom asked, his eyes darting over to Vinny and back to me.

I sighed. 'I have to talk to Dick.' I felt like a goddamn broken record. But I'm dating myself. Did CDs repeat themselves when they wore out? I think they just skipped. My thoughts were swirling around, making no sense, sort of how Dick's story would end up.

Tom turned and walked away without another word. I was like fucking Typhoid Mary, bringing death and destruction to all I met.

Except Dick, whose eyes were bright with the fact that I was actually seeking him out. I should've stayed home, I shouldn't lead him on like this. Marty needed to know better than to give Dick the illusion that I actually thought he was competent, because that's what was going on in his head. I could see it, as clear as a goddamn bell.

I heard a clicking behind me. Wesley Bell's face was covered by a camera aimed at me.

'Don't you fucking dare,' I hissed.

The camera fell to his chest, and Wesley's eyes were wide. 'We won't use it,' he promised, but I knew better. Maybe it wouldn't get in the paper on purpose, but some asshole with a lame sense of humor might decide it was the only picture that illustrated the crime scene.

I shook my head. 'You know better than that,' I said condescendingly, and waved him off. I watched as he shrugged and disappeared behind the back of the building. I had to talk to Dick quickly and get the hell out of there. I turned to him.

'Marty says I have to give you some quotes and tell you what happened,' I said flatly. In an equally monotone voice, I told Dick everything I'd told Tom. I threw in some more details about the dead chickens; Marty would like that. 'Marty says I can read it when you're done,' I added.

Dick frowned. Like he had a right to object. But before he could say anything, I was standing face-to-face with Immaculata Amato, now most certainly a widow.

'They tell me you and Vincent found him.' Her eyes were red and puffy from crying, but her voice was harsh, and I sensed something in her tone that seemed to accuse me of causing Sal's untimely demise. 'You just can't leave well enough alone, can you.'

I saw that in her grief she was lashing out at me — I was the obvious choice — and braced myself for more, but Vinny stepped in between us.

'It's a good thing she found him, Mac,' he said. 'Otherwise he would've been chewed up by the bulldozer that's coming to level the place.' Not a pretty image, but it was accurate.

I wanted to know where the animosity was coming from. It wasn't my damn fault that Prego burned down, that Sal went missing and now was found dead.

Movement caught my eye, and Pete Amato came up next to his mother. He ran a hand through his thick hair, then stared at me. 'Why are you always around?'

'I'm just doing my job,' I said. 'You know, I cared about Sal, too.'

'You have a funny way of showing it,' Pete growled.

'You really don't have any reason to talk to her like that,' Vinny said.

A shadow moved across the snow, and my father stood silently by my side. Pete's scowl wavered a little.

I wanted to get out of there. But before I did, I wanted to ask some questions. I mean, they hated me anyway — it couldn't get much worse.

'So did either of you know that Sal was in the neighborhood? I can't imagine that someone didn't see him over here.'

'Did you see him?' Pete asked. 'You live across the square. If one of us could see him, then you could, too, right?'

'He wouldn't exactly seek me out, but he

might go home,' I said, feeling my face grow hot.

Pete leaned over and whispered something to his mother, who held tightly to his arm but didn't look at me. 'I can't have you disturbing my mother,' he said, and paused. 'First LeeAnn and now my father. Maybe you should be questioning Mickey Hayward.'

'He's in jail. He couldn't possibly have killed Sal,' I pointed out, ignoring his remark about disturbing Mac. She'd disturbed me, but who the hell was keeping score?

'How do I know you didn't kill him?' Pete glared at me.

My father stepped forward, his expression calm. 'Now, Pete, don't overreact.' His voice was soft, smooth.

Vinny was nodding. 'And if you keep talking to Annie like that, I'll have to do something about it.'

'What do you think you can do?' Pete's voice was ugly, but he glanced nervously at my father before looking back at Vinny.

'Remember Malone's?' Vinny asked.

Pete stiffened. 'You're all talk,' he said, but I was surprised to hear a tinge of fear in his voice. I stared at Vinny with a little more respect. Malone's used to be a bar on State Street, and I would have to ask Vinny what happened there so that Pete, who was a few inches taller and more than a few pounds heavier than Vinny, would be concerned about his well-being.

My father smiled at Pete. 'Why don't you and I help your mother back to the house? I think she needs you now.' In one move, he put his hand on Pete's back, the other under Mac's elbow, and steered them toward their house. They had no time to refuse.

'He's good,' Vinny said softly.

I nodded. My father always knew the right thing to say and do. I'd always thought he should get into politics. He and my mother would've given Bill and Hillary a run for their money.

'I have to get going. I need to get to work.' I glanced around for Dick, but he'd vanished.

'I'll drive you,' Vinny said.

'I'm okay.'

Vinny smiled sadly. 'No, you're not.'

Vinny took my arm and led me catty-corner on the square to his Ford Explorer.

'So what happened at Malone's?' I asked as soon as we were both strapped in. I looked around the SUV. It was just as neat as his apartment, which I'd had the opportunity to survey a couple of months ago. Not a scrap of paper, not a soda can in sight.

'Nothing.' Vinny turned the key and the engine started to purr, reminding me that my own Honda Accord had some sort of knocking noise that might need some attention from a mechanic in the near future.

'Hey, come on. You can tell me.'

He cocked his head and winked at me. 'And you won't tell anyone, right?'

He had me there. My job was to tell things to the world. But it didn't mean I couldn't keep a secret. I told him as much.

'Okay, okay.' He let the engine run while we sat there, waiting for the SUV to warm up. 'It was a few years ago. I was in Malone's playing pool with Mickey Hayward.'

I raised my eyebrows, and he grinned. 'I have friends, and Mick's one of them. He's not a bad guy.'

I nodded. 'Go on.'

'LeeAnn was there, at the bar. She was flirting with the bartender, which Mickey wasn't too happy about, but he didn't say much about it. We kept playing pool.' Vinny's voice got quieter, and he stared out the windshield at nothing in particular as he remembered. 'Pete Amato came in, he was drunker than hell, and he went over to LeeAnn. She started flirting with him, too. You know the way she was.'

He didn't need me to say anything. We all knew LeeAnn.

'Anyway, Pete started getting a little too

physical with her. He kissed her, right there in the bar, right in front of Mickey, who couldn't get there fast enough to beat the shit out of him. I was closer, and Pete thought he was swinging at Mickey, but he managed to get me in the eye.' Vinny rubbed his right eye absently. 'Hurt like a son of a bitch, and since I'd had a few beers, I swung back.' He paused and turned to look at me. 'I'm not a violent guy, not really, but Pete came at me with a beer bottle. I don't know where it came from, but it was there, and I had to do something about it. I took some boxing lessons in college and learned how to fight, so I did. But that beer bottle kept coming at me from all angles.'

He stopped suddenly, and I took a deep breath, holding it until he started again.

'I pulled out my gun. I had it under my jacket, I'd just come off a situation at work where I'd thought I would need it, and I pulled it out and pointed it at Pete and told him to fucking drop the bottle.' I could see Vinny reliving it as he spoke, and I didn't move.

Vinny dropped his eyes. 'Scared the shit out of Pete, and he dropped the bottle. I guess he never thought I would do something like that.' He looked at me. 'When he dropped it, I put the gun away, but he knew if he'd pushed me, I would've used it. I would've gone as far as I had to.'

We sat for a minute without speaking. 'So I guess he knows that if he keeps at me, you'll really do something about it,' I finally said.

He shrugged and looked at me sheepishly. 'Stupid, huh?'

'What the hell was wrong with him, anyway? Wouldn't he know Mickey would've probably killed him for that? He got off lucky with it being you. Especially since Mickey carries around that bag full of knives with him everywhere.' Everyone knew about Mickey's bag of chef's knives. He loved his knives, and he loved carving up shit with them. He wouldn't have stopped himself from carving up Pete Amato for kissing his wife. 'And what's with kissing LeeAnn?'

Vinny laughed. 'Pete's a bad drunk.' But I could see he was still thinking about his own actions.

'I don't blame you for doing what you did,' I said. 'You thought your life was in danger. You protected yourself.' I didn't want to tell him that I was a little shocked with the story. He used to be a marine biologist and studied whales for a while until the program's funding was cut. He went to work for a friend of his father's who was a private detective and managed to get his own license. But even though I knew what he did for a living, I'd certainly never seen him violent with anyone.

'What did LeeAnn do?' I asked after the SUV started moving.

'When?'

'After the fight.'

He smiled, more to himself than to me. 'Oh, she got on my case for being an asshole and scaring the shit out of everyone in the bar.' He paused. 'And then she and Mickey went home.'

'What did you do?'

'I went in the men's room and threw up.'

'You did not.'

'I did too. I was drunker than I thought.'

We were quiet the rest of the way to the paper. I mulled over this latest information about Vinny, a story I never would've believed if someone else had told it. But it reeked of truth, especially the vomiting part. He wouldn't have ever told me that if it hadn't really happened.

We pulled into the visitors' parking lot, and when the Explorer stopped, I opened my door.

He opened his at the same time.

'Where are you going?' I asked.

'I'm going to come in and wait until you're done. Then I'll drive you back home.'

'You are not my bodyguard.'

'I am today. You're stuck with me.' He followed me up the steps.

I swiped my card key through the thing by the door, and Vinny opened the door when we heard the buzz. I wasn't going to get rid of him, and this was going to be incredibly embarrassing.

The newsroom was hardly busy, since we only had skeleton crews on Saturdays, and this one was a holiday weekend to boot. Kevin Prisley was on the phone, and Renee Chittenden was pondering which Munchkin to eat from the box on top of the file cabinet near the wall. That's where we put all the communal food. There would be more later, when the copy editors came in with their chips and salsas and brownies and cookies. Occasionally raw vegetables would make an appearance, but only if someone was on a diet.

Even though he normally didn't work weekends, Marty was there. It was because of Sal and LeeAnn — he didn't trust the other editors on these stories, wanted to see them first, get them into shape before the copy editors got their hands on them later in the afternoon.

Dick was there, too, back from the crime scene and writing up the story.

I peeled off my coat, because now the

newsroom was hotter than Hades. 'Guess they fixed the heat,' I said.

Marty and Dick looked up at the same time; Marty's shirtsleeves were rolled up, and sweat beaded his forehead.

'I don't know what's going on,' Marty said. 'Maintenance guys aren't around this weekend.' He glanced questioningly at Vinny.

'This is Vinny DeLucia,' I said. 'He's just going to hang out while I check Dick's story.'

Just my luck, Henry Owens was filling in for the regular weekend metro editor, who was basking on some beach in the Caribbean. I didn't bother introducing him to Vinny. I didn't want everyone getting too friendly.

I pulled a chair over from Renee Chittenden's desk — she was nibbling on a Munchkin while talking to Kevin, who was off the phone now — and put it on the other side of my computer terminal, indicating Vinny should sit there. This was way too weird for me. While it was okay to have Vinny in my apartment and run into him at crime scenes and on the streets, it didn't feel okay to have him in my work space. And considering what a neat freak he was, I was more than aware of the stack of newspapers under my desk and the pile of old press releases that spilled across the top of the desk. Not to mention the clutter on my computer terminal: Old comic strips were taped to the sides, along with a postcard-size magazine photo of Frank Sinatra that seemed even larger as Vinny checked it out, his lips curling into a small smile. Stripped across the top of the terminal were two headline clips: IT COULD HAPPEN ANYWHERE and FIRE SUSPECTED AS ARSON GUTS BUILDING. It was too bad the new flat screens hadn't been installed yet; there was just too much room on these behemoths to fill up with shit.

And I had forgotten about my screen saver. Someone had sat here weeks ago and as a joke decided that I had to have a full-screen mug shot of Karl Rove. The joke was that I couldn't figure out how to get rid of it, so every day I got to stare at all the pores in his face as I booted up the computer.

'Where's the story?' I asked Dick, who was still typing across the desk from me, although he kept checking out Vinny beside me. 'Just ignore him, pretend he's not here,' I advised.

'Hey, Vinny.' Dick's smile spread from ear to ear.

'Hi, Dick. Good story, huh?' Okay, now Vinny was getting downright chummy.

Dick's eyes went from Vinny to me. 'I'm almost done. It's in my queue.'

I didn't wait for him to finish, I just pulled up the story on a read-only and scanned his words. As usual, I couldn't make heads or tails out of the lead, which was about fifty words too long. My fingers itched to get into the copy, to give it my own tweak.

'It's Dick's story, Annie.' Marty had come up behind me and was reading over my shoulder. But he gave me a wink that told me he'd take care of it. It would be readable by the time it got into the paper.

I got down to my quotes, which were fairly simple: 'I stepped into the rubble and Sal Amato was in front of me.' Then some stuff from the cops. 'There were three dead chickens.' And then some more stuff from the cops.

'Why the hell were there dead chickens there?' Marty muttered as he read.

I sighed. 'Seems Sal was running a gambling operation using chickens that play tic-tac-toe.'

Marty snorted. 'Gimme a break, Annie. Really, what's the story?'

'Apparently it was going on for years in the basement at Prego. Lots of money, lots of high rollers, lots of degenerate gamblers. I've got it on a good source.'

Marty stole a glance at Vinny.

Dick stirred. 'But how can chickens play tic-tac-toe?'

'Guess they're in Atlantic City and Vegas

and have been in Chinatown for a long time. Not to mention the Pennsylvania fair circuit.' I'd done a little research on the Internet while waiting for callbacks. I'd seen the stories about the chickens that got kidnapped from a fair a few years back. They were never recovered. Probably ended up on someone's barbecue plate.

'We need this on the record,' Marty said. 'This is a helluva story.'

'I don't know if anyone will talk about it,' I said. 'I found out some stuff about Sal's operation.' I paused. 'The Mob is involved.'

Marty just stared at me.

'New York, New England, guess Sal was paying protection,' I said to break up the silence.

'How long have you known about this?' Marty asked, drawing his words out slowly.

'Not long. Really.'

Marty looked at Vinny again, and he knew that Vinny was my source. But from the look on Vinny's face, he guessed right that Vinny wasn't going to go on the record with shit. He bit his lip. 'The FBI was there, at the fire. They know what's going on. You're going to have to get Jeff Parker to tell you on the record.'

I couldn't stifle a snort. 'Come on, Marty, that's a big order.'

'Maybe you should call your source, then.'

Paula. It would add to the story if we could include the gambling operation. But she didn't answer her cell. I left a message but wasn't optimistic about getting a callback, considering her reactions when I'd talked to her before.

Marty was disappointed but told me I had to keep trying. 'We've still got time. When you know anything, you have to let me know.'

I nodded and finished reading the story. 'It's okay,' I said with a sense of loss. Dick was hopping up and down like a rabbit.

'Really? You really think so?'

It was pathetic. He was pathetic. It was bad enough that I lost my story, but having to pump up Dick's ego was more than I could handle.

But before I could say anything, Dick's eyes strayed past me, his lips curling in an odd way. I turned to see what was distracting him and looked right into Cindy Purcell's breasts. She was wearing four-inch heels, 'fuck me' shoes, if I remembered the phrase right, and I must have, because Dick was drooling.

'Oh, hello,' she said to me, but looking at Dick in the same gross way he was looking at her.

My God, I had to get the hell out of here or I'd throw up all over my own desk. I looked over at Vinny, who was watching the whole show. In fact, everyone in the vicinity was watching it — and me, to see my reaction.

'This is the most disgusting thing I've ever experienced firsthand,' I whispered to Vinny.

'I think they're cute,' he said, his lips twitching.

'You do not.'

'You're just pissed because he didn't pick you.'

Now I really was going to be sick, and I punched him on the shoulder. 'Shut up.'

He was going to bust a gut if he didn't let himself laugh.

Renee Chittenden sauntered over and sat on the edge of my desk. 'What's wrong with her?' she whispered.

I raised my eyebrows at Vinny. 'See? It's not just me.'

Their bodies were too close together, their faces inches apart. Dick's was bright red, and Cindy was laughing.

Marty finally stopped the show. 'Dick,' he called over from his desk, 'I've got some questions for you.'

Dick's face was still flushed as Cindy sashayed her way back across the newsroom to her little corner, where her cameraman was waiting, looking pretty pissed.

I grabbed my coat and stood up, Vinny on my heels, chuckling. I didn't say anything as we walked out of the newsroom. For the first time ever, I was completely speechless.

17

As I climbed back into Vinny's Explorer, my cell phone chirped. I dug it out of my purse as Vinny started the engine. I felt a blast of cold air but knew it would warm up soon. I turned my attention to the phone.

'Hey, Annie, how are you doing?' I could hear the worry in Dad's voice.

'I'm okay. I'm at the paper, well, just leaving.' I had to wipe the vision of Dick Whitfield and his main squeeze out of my head or it would be swirling around there all day. But then again, it kept me from thinking about Sal. 'How are you doing?'

A pause. 'I'm all right. Can you meet me?'

I glanced at Vinny. 'I'm with Vinny.'

'Not right now. Dinner? Seven o'clock?'

I looked at my watch. It was just 1:00 P.M. 'Sure. Where?'

'Consiglio's?'

A restaurant similar to Prego, with mouthwatering fried calamari and marinara sauce. Since it was after lunchtime and I hadn't eaten since breakfast, my stomach growled. 'Sounds great,' I said, ending the call.

'What's up?'

'Dad wants to have dinner at Consiglio's later.' I thought a minute. 'I should probably give my mom a call and tell her what's going on.'

He nodded absently; I could tell his mind was elsewhere.

'What's up?' I asked.

Vinny sighed, and his eyes found mine. 'You'll probably find out anyway, so I might as well tell you. Sal hired your mother three weeks ago because the feds were coming down on him.'

Oh, Christ. I should've known. My mother's law firm — Hoffman, Giametti and Cohen — had a reputation for representing our city's residents who happened to have a vowel at the end of their names and happened to be involved in questionable business practices. I knew it was because they were all Jewish. For some reason, the Italians in the neighborhood trusted that — and trusted my mother because of my father.

So even my mother was on the inside. Everyone knew everything, and I was the last one to know. Great fucking reporter I was. 'Why didn't you tell me this before?'

'Sorry. Your mother hired me to look into some things pertaining to the case, and I couldn't say anything. But now that Sal's dead, well, I guess it won't matter if you know that.' He paused a second, biting his lip.

'What sort of things were you looking into?' I prompted.

Vinny shook his head. 'That I can't tell you.'

'So what exactly do you do for my mother's firm?' I asked.

'I check out alibis, backgrounds, witnesses.' He paused. 'I was working for your mother when I had the gun on me that time at Malone's. She was representing someone who had trouble telling her the truth about things.'

I realized that I'd been too self-centered two months ago when we met to really find out what his day-to-day life was like. 'So what else do you do, besides working for my mother's law firm? I mean, I know about that, and finding missing people, but is there anything else?'

'Why, Annie, I never knew you cared,' Vinny teased.

I waited.

'Okay, if you really want to know, I do a lot of divorce cases. You'd be surprised how many people are cheating on their spouses out there. I take pictures, take notes, follow people around, like I did with LeeAnn for Mickey.'

'You like it, don't you. Even though you

didn't start out doing that.'

Vinny sighed. 'Yeah, well, when I was at Cornell — '

'You went to Cornell?' I interrupted, frowning. Now this was a tidbit of information I hadn't known.

He shrugged. 'Yeah. It's no big deal.'

But it was a big deal to me. I hadn't strayed too far from home, studying journalism at Southern Connecticut State University right here in New Haven, although I had lived on campus. My grades weren't always the most important thing. I spent a lot of time working on the school newspaper. 'I didn't know you were that smart.'

Vinny's mouth twitched, but I couldn't tell if it was with annoyance or that he wanted to smile. 'I got my undergrad in biology and my graduate degree in marine science at Northeastern. I was working toward my PhD at Woods Hole Oceanographic Institution on the Cape just before I came home.' He stared at me for a long minute.

I was still reeling from 'Cornell,' 'Northeastern,' and 'PhD.' Christ, Vinny was fucking smart.

'You know, Annie, it's not a huge stretch between my research and this. Lots of analyzing data, looking at the minutiae. Trying to see what's really going on.' He pulled out of the lot. 'So where to?'

A phone call to my mother wouldn't be enough now. I had to see her and ask her about Sal directly. But I didn't want Vinny tagging along. 'Can you bring me home? I'm beat. I just want to take a nap.'

He looked at me out of the corner of his eye, and I'm not sure he believed me, so I faked a yawn. 'I'm sure you've got stuff you need to do,' I added.

'Okay,' he said simply, and it was too easy. But I couldn't call him on it.

Vinny brought me back to my brownstone and walked me up to the apartment, making sure I locked the door when I got inside. I watched him from the window — he looked up and waved — and saw the SUV go down the block and out of sight. I was suspicious that he knew I wasn't going to stay home but figured I'd take my chances. If he followed me, at least he wouldn't be with me when I talked to my mother, the way he would if I'd invited him along. But if someone else tried to assault me, he would be close by.

I didn't think that was a bad plan.

I ran down the steps and got into my car, slipping in the Rolling Stones tape and turning up the volume as I pressed on the gas.

My stomach growled as I drove up Chapel

Street. I glanced in the rearview mirror, didn't see the Explorer, and thought that a late lunch might be a good idea. I could also postpone the most likely unpleasant encounter with my mother. Miraculously, a car was pulling out of a spot on Chapel as I went through the light at Temple. I eased the car against the curb and found myself standing in line and reading the blackboard menu at Claire's. It was a vegetarian place, and while I definitely like meat and wasn't into a big salad or alfalfa sprouts, the cheese-and-bean enchiladas were always good. I took my lemonade to a table, staring out the window, until a tall, skinny girl wearing a white apron called my name and I waved her over. The plate of food smelled fantastic and tasted even better with sour cream slathered all over it.

One of the best things about not dating anyone was eating anything I wanted, with no regard for calories. Fortunately, while I certainly wasn't skinny like the girl who gave me my food, my metabolism hadn't slowed enough yet so I would have to do something drastic, like buying into the latest diet fad. I couldn't see myself resigned to a life of constipation, eating only bacon and cheese.

I suppose I could've been considered callous, enjoying my meal after finding Sal dead, but I don't argue with my stomach, and dealing with my mother would be much easier if I didn't feel like I was going to pass out from hunger.

★　★　★

My mother opened the back door for me when I pulled into the driveway. 'Your father called me,' she said, holding me close. 'Are you okay?'

I nodded, and although I'd had enough distractions what with Vinny and lunch that I didn't spend much time thinking about it, in just those few words my mother had brought the morning's events back full force in my head.

I tried to shake them aside, reminding myself what I was here for. Answers.

But what I didn't count on was her stonewalling me. As she sat across from me at the kitchen table, sipping ever so daintily from her coffee cup, her eyes were like steel.

'I can't comment on a client,' she said.

'Even though he's dead?'

She took a long drink and put the mug down in front of her, folding her hands behind it. 'It's now a murder investigation, Annie. I've already spoken to the police, and I expect I will again.'

I stretched my hands around my cup, warming them. It was chilly in this big, drafty, expensive kitchen. 'Listen, could you just tell me on the record what the federal charges were against Sal?' I heard the hard, cold reporter voice, and I knew that wouldn't get me anything. I switched gears, sighing, appearing as desperate as I was. 'I really need this, Mom.'

'Illegal gambling, tax fraud, and money laundering.' She paused. 'Some things may emerge from this that you won't like hearing about, Annie.'

'It's Dad, isn't it.'

She sighed. 'Your father is a good man, deep down. I always knew that. But I also knew that his, well, business interests were sometimes questionable.'

I sank back into the chair. 'They're not going to arrest Dad, are they?'

She laughed. Really laughed. 'Oh, goodness no, Annie. He's too damn smart, you know that. But there will be some who will try to get him in trouble, to keep the spotlight off them. Some of what they say will be lies. But some . . . ' Her voice trailed off.

I like stories that are cut-and-dried. Stories that involve strangers. Stories I can make gruesome sick jokes about with my colleagues because it's the only way we can tolerate the horrible things we hear and see. I didn't like this story, because I knew all the players and I was back in my childhood world again, when I hadn't become hardened by the world and my job. I never wanted to write a story in which I had to connect my father with a crime.

'Did Dad have anything to do with Sal's operation?' I asked.

'I don't know, Anne. I've never known too much and never wanted to know. But he showed up here unexpectedly, and I'm not sure he's the only one.'

I shook my head. 'Me neither. I know about the Mob connection to the chickens.'

Her eyebrows rose, and she opened her mouth, but I spoke before she could ask anything.

'Confidential source,' I said, not wanting to let anyone, not even my mother, know Vinny had told.

'How much do you know?'

I briefly told her what Vinny had said. She smiled. 'You have a good source.'

'So were you really going to defend Sal?' I asked. 'Even though you knew he was guilty?'

'Yes.'

'Why?'

'It's my job. And everyone deserves representation and a fair trial.' She picked up her mug and brought it to her lips, then put it down again. 'I believe in the judicial system.'

It sounded hokey, but I knew she meant it. And I was proud of her for that. Because I understood it. I felt as hokey about journalism as she did about the law, even though I was cynical and getting burned out. It didn't mean I didn't believe in it anymore.

I could see a few more wrinkles that hadn't been there a couple of months ago.

'You look tired,' I said.

She smiled wearily at me. 'I *am* tired.'

I glanced around at the white-tiled counters, the stainless-steel appliances, the spotless cherry cabinets. 'Where's Bill Bennett? He didn't show last night?'

'He's spending time with his daughter. I told you that.' Her voice grew tight, and I knew not to push.

'Do you think Mickey Hayward is innocent?'

She looked a little startled at the change of subject, but then she smiled again. 'Yes.'

'Really?'

She chuckled. 'Annie, there are some innocent people who are charged falsely.'

While I was tossing this around in my head, another question popped in. 'Why did Mac call you?'

'When?'

'To represent Mickey? Why did you leave the party for that?'

She got up, brought her mug to the sink, and started washing it out. 'It's my job, Annie. Mac knew I was trying to help Sal and thought I could help Mickey. And I left the party because the police were questioning him and he needed to be represented right away. That's the way it works.'

'Vinny said he was working for you on Sal's case,' I said.

She smiled. 'That's right.' The way she said it, I knew I wouldn't get a fucking thing out of her about what he was doing on it.

'Did he come up with anything that could've helped?' I couldn't give up.

'I've always been confident in his abilities. As you should be.' She narrowed her eyes at me. 'Are you?'

The smooth change of subject caused my face to grow hot. 'He's engaged.'

'I know. But I also see the way he looks at you.'

'What about Dad?' I asked, hoping to turn the tables on her this time.

She frowned. 'What about him?' She got up. 'Want more coffee?'

I nodded, and she brought over the coffeepot and poured me another cup.

'Are you ever sorry?'

'Sorry about what, dear?' She sat back down again.

'Sorry about the divorce.'

She smiled. 'Still hoping we'll get back together?'

I could tell by her tone that it wasn't going to happen. She didn't have to keep talking. But she did, and I nearly spat my coffee all over her fancy tablecloth.

'Bill and I are talking about moving in together.'

Bill? Bill Bennett? And my mother? Cohabitating? I must have heard it wrong. But like a moron, I said, 'Oh, really?' Like it wasn't a big deal. But it was a big fucking deal.

She knew that. She saw it in my face and the way my hands clutched the mug in front of me.

'But we're just talking about it right now.'

'So it's that serious?' I tried to keep my voice light, but it had an edge, kind of like stainless steel against your teeth, that I couldn't keep at bay.

'Yes.'

For some reason, all I could think of was how good it was that my mother was too old to have more kids, so I wouldn't be saddled with baby siblings that looked like Bill Bennett.

Too much stuff was going on right now. I might have to get some sort of antianxiety drug to keep myself going. And the more I entertained that idea, the more appealing it was.

I stared at my mother's smooth cheeks and deep green eyes. A thin streak of gray ran down near her ear, but the rest of her hair was still a bright chestnut. She looked happy despite her fatigue, and I vowed to try to be happy for her, even if I didn't approve of her choice of companion.

At least she hadn't divorced my father and sworn off men like a lot of women.

As I pulled it on, I saw that my puffy coat had dried nicely since the day before.

'Are you going to be okay?' my mother asked again at the door.

'Sure.' But my voice sounded a lot more confident than I felt.

'You should do something fun.' I don't know how many times I'd heard that from her. Our definitions of 'fun' were very different.

'Yeah, right,' I mumbled as I stepped out into the frigid air. It had gotten colder, and more clouds were moving in. Oh, shit. More snow. Just what I needed.

'You should wear a hat,' was the last thing I heard my mother say as I got into my car.

I should do a lot of things.

18

Just as I climbed into my car, a sleek black Cadillac crept past. I watched it as it braked at the stop sign farther up, then turned right, out of sight.

I thought about the car I'd seen at Dominic Gaudio's when I'd followed Vinny there. That one had New York plates. But I hadn't thought to look when this one went by.

No, it couldn't be the same one. It had to be paranoia after finding Sal dead and all those Mob stories Vinny told me.

Speaking of Vinny, I glanced around but didn't see him. Maybe he did think I'd meant to stay home after all. I thought of the fake yawn, and I yawned for real. Suddenly my whole body felt like a wet dishrag. Maybe a nap wouldn't be such a bad idea. It could rejuvenate me.

Unfortunately, with Tom now most definitely out of the picture and Rosie still in it, I had no one to be rejuvenated with.

I yawned again, heading my car across town toward my brownstone. I only hit every light on the way.

I was figuring just how much time I had before I had to meet my father for dinner when I spotted Dick Whitfield talking to Mac and Mrs. DeLucia in front of Mac's house. I couldn't hear what they were saying — they were too far away — but I could read Mac's body language, which was telling Dick to go fuck himself. It was plain as day. Uncle Louie was standing back a little on the porch, keeping an eye on Dick.

Around them, it was the same scene as two days ago. Women were bringing covered dishes across the square and into the house. This time there was most definitely a death in the family. I could almost smell the food from where I was. I found myself wondering if anyone had remembered LeeAnn this way. Did anyone put out a spread for Dominic Gaudio and his daughter?

Mac was trying to go back into the house, but Dick wouldn't let her. He stepped between her and the door. Not a good move. I saw Uncle Louie move forward and a lot of head shaking and finger pointing going on.

I wasn't on this story anymore, it was a weekend, and I was not inclined to help Dick out. But when a battered pickup pulled into the driveway and Pete got out, ran up the stairs, and grabbed Dick by the back of the collar, I figured I'd have to do something.

I jogged down the sidewalk, now close enough to hear Pete shouting, 'Get off our property!'

Dick, in response, was whimpering.

'What the hell are you doing here?' Pete yelled at me when I came into his line of sight.

'Come on, Pete. Let him go.'

To my surprise, he did, and Dick slumped onto the slushy sidewalk.

'He has no right to come here and ask all these questions,' Pete said, moving closer to me. I caught a whiff of booze. Shit. 'And you, too, you have to stop bothering us.'

'Perhaps you should get him out of here,' Uncle Louie told me softly, indicating Dick, and I nodded, noticing that Mac and Mrs. DeLucia had disappeared inside.

'All right, all right,' I told Pete. Dick was getting up, brushing himself off. 'Let's get out of here,' I hissed at Dick, grabbing his coat sleeve and pulling him up the sidewalk.

'What the fuck are you doing?' I asked when we were at the bottom of my steps.

Dick shrugged. 'I had some questions for them.'

'Questions that couldn't wait? Questions while they're having a spread for Sal? Jesus, Dick, the whole fucking neighborhood is there. This is not the time for questions.' I didn't like it that I had to explain this to him. He should know this shit by now.

Dick's expression was sheepish. 'But this can't wait.'

'What can't wait?'

'I got a tip.'

'A tip?'

'From a source.'

Dick had sources? 'What was the tip, Dick?' I asked.

He cocked his head at me, a look of confidence replacing the sheepish one. 'Sal set the fire.'

I frowned. 'What?'

'Sal set the fire at Prego.'

'But Mickey's been charged with arson murder. Obviously the cops think he did it.' But I was intrigued by this. He'd said this as though he knew it for fact.

'That may change.'

Jesus. I thought about how the 911 call had been made from inside the restaurant and how Sal had been hanging around at the scene. 'Who told you this, Dick?'

He shrugged. 'A source. I can't tell you.' But he blushed slightly, giving me an involuntary clue.

It could be Tom, and a pang of jealousy hit me in the gut. It was like finding out an ex-boyfriend was marrying someone else two months after our breakup. Christ, if Tom was talking to Dick and not to me, well, that was going to be a huge adjustment.

Before I could say anything, though, a black Cadillac sped past us and turned left onto Olive.

I stared after the car. Was it the same one? Had he followed me from my mother's? Or was my imagination just working overtime again?

'Annie?' Dick was asking.

'Yeah?'

'You okay?'

'Sure, why wouldn't I be?'

★ ★ ★

I followed Dick back to the paper. All thoughts of a nap were pushed aside as I speculated about Tom and how Dick could end up usurping me if I didn't watch out. In the newsroom, I decided to tell Marty about the federal charges against Sal; hopefully that would show him I could still be useful on this story, even though I couldn't write anything anymore.

'But you still didn't get anything about the gambling operation?' Marty asked.

'Christ, Marty, it's like pulling teeth getting anything out of anyone on this,' I whined.

'What about Vinny?'

I stared at him. 'What about him?'

'What can he give you on the record?'

I sighed. 'Nothing, Marty. Really. I can't ask him to go on the record with any of it. It would jeopardize his job if people found out he was telling me stuff.' Vinny was no Sammy the Bull.

'You're going to have to get something from someone.'

Which brought me back to Paula and Jeff Parker. The FBI might be easier to crack than my father or Dominic Gaudio.

'What can I do?' Dick came up behind us, practically salivating.

Marty shook his head. 'You need to stay on top of the charges against Mickey. Write up what you can from what you got from your source, and as soon as the charges are reduced, we're going to run with the story.' He paused. 'And I'd better not see it on Channel Nine first.'

Dick scowled and skulked back to his own desk.

'You need to get something on this,' Marty told me.

I nodded. 'I will.' I went back to my desk, picked up my bag, and grabbed my coat on the way out. I'd sounded a lot more confident than I felt.

I could've just called Paula from the newsroom, but I wanted to be home when I did that, and I didn't want to be within listening distance of anyone, especially Dick. My motives were moot, however, because all I got was voice mail, at her apartment and on her cell phone. This wasn't going to be easy.

I turned on the TV and channel surfed for a few minutes, landing on a showing of *Flashdance*, one of the best worst movies ever made and a guilty pleasure of mine. I remember seeing the part where Jennifer Beals is dancing with Michael Nouri on the railroad tracks before I fell asleep.

The buzzer woke me up. I glanced at the clock: 6:55. I'd been asleep for two hours.

Vinny came into my apartment and flopped onto the couch like he owned the place. I scowled at him, rubbing the sleep from my eyes. I saw him take in the blanket and the half-eaten bowl of microwaved popcorn.

'What's on?' He smiled, taking a handful of the popcorn.

I pulled the bowl away from him and brought it to the island that separated the galley kitchen from my living room. 'Nothing.' I could just hear it now if Vinny found

212

out I'd been indulging in *Flashdance*.

I looked at the clock again, and the alarm went off in my head. Shit. My father. I was supposed to meet him at seven at Consiglio's. I looked at the back of Vinny's head. I'd just have to tell him to get lost.

'I have to meet my dad,' I said. 'For dinner.'

He couldn't say much, his mouth was full of popcorn, but he nodded. 'I know,' he mumbled. 'He asked me to come along. That's why I'm here.'

I walked around the island and saw him taking in my yoga pants and sweatshirt.

'Are you wearing that?' he asked.

I grabbed a handful of popcorn from the bowl and threw it at him. It wasn't the brightest move, since now I'd have to clean it up. But it startled him, and the look on his face was worth it. 'I'll be ready in a minute,' I said, and went into the bedroom. I wondered why my dad had asked him to come, too. I'd thought it was just going to be the two of us, and I felt a familiar twinge of jealousy again. First Tom and Dick and now Dad and Vinny.

Get over it, I admonished myself. I was too old to be a daddy's girl.

I threw on a long skirt and a form-fitting blouse and pulled on a pair of ankle boots. I didn't give a damn about the weather anymore. I was tired of wearing snow boots, and we were just going around the corner. I dabbed on a little blush and some mascara, tossing my hair around a little so it would look as though I'd brushed it.

Vinny's face changed when I came back out, and if this was a date, I would've been sure I was going to get lucky later.

But it wasn't, and I wasn't, so I ignored him as I grabbed my wool coat from the small closet next to my front door. 'I'm ready,' I said, forcing myself to think about chicken with mootz and asparagus and a Caesar salad.

Vinny opened the door for me and followed me out closely.

We met Walter on the stairs. He looked from me to Vinny and back again, didn't say anything, and squeezed by us, clomping his way to his apartment.

'Gee, aren't we one happy family here?' Vinny whispered, teasing me.

I slugged him on the shoulder, and we went out into the frigid night without another word.

He wasn't in the restaurant, even though it was 7:15 now. My father was never late. I fumbled for my cell phone in my purse, but I had forgotten to charge it up and it was dead. Shit. My expression must have conveyed my worry, because Vinny immediately pulled out his phone and stepped outside while I waited.

He was closing the phone when he came back in. 'Voice mail.'

'Maybe he's on his way,' I said, but I wasn't convinced. We allowed the hostess to seat us and each ordered a bourbon. Ten minutes later, when he still hadn't arrived, I stood up.

'Something's wrong.'

Vinny helped me on with my coat and shrugged into his own leather jacket. 'Let's go back to your place and see if he tried to call there,' he suggested.

When we got to my apartment, I turned on the lights and moved the thermostat to a more comfortable zone. My message machine was blinking.

'Sorry, Annie,' my father's voice echoed through my living room. 'I left a message on your cell, and I thought I'd reach you at home, but I can't meet you for dinner. I need to straighten some things out.'

Just as I was about to say something to Vinny, a second voice emanated from the little box.

'Annie? It's Tom. Call me as soon as you can.' His voice was strange, but not as strange as the next one I heard:

'Annie, your father checked out of his hotel, and I'm trying to reach him. It's concerning Sal. It's important. If you hear from him, please have him call me immediately.' My mother was unfamiliar in her anxiety. Even during the divorce, she always managed to remain calm and keep any emotion out of her voice, something that's helped her immensely in her career.

Vinny was rummaging in my refrigerator, probably looking for something to eat. I ignored him as I dialed my mother's number. He wouldn't find much. I hadn't been to the supermarket in a week.

My mother picked up on the first ring. 'Hey, Mom, I don't know where Dad is, I thought he was still at the hotel. I was supposed to meet him for dinner and he never showed.'

She laughed, a high, twittery sound that scared me. 'He's going to have a lot of questions to answer.'

'What's up?'

'The police and the FBI seem to believe that your father is directly involved in Sal's disappearance and maybe even his murder.'

19

I sat down, dumbstruck. Vinny's head swung around quickly, and he frowned as he shut the refrigerator door.

'The police found out Sal had been staying in a house in Morris Cove,' my mother explained.

My body tensed. That was the neighborhood where Dominic Gaudio lived. 'And?' I prompted when she paused.

'A neighbor saw him there, recognized his picture from the paper, and called the police. They were waiting for him when they got the call that you'd found him at Prego.'

All this was fine and dandy, but it wasn't telling me about my father. 'And what's the link to Dad?' I asked.

'Your father's fingerprints are in the house.'

My heart caught in my throat, and it was a few seconds before I could speak. 'It wasn't Dominic Gaudio's house, was it?' I didn't want to know how they'd identified my father's fingerprints.

It was my mother's turn to hesitate. 'No, Annie, why would you ask that?'

'I saw Dad there, yesterday.'

Vinny was staring at me, and I could see his impatience, wanting to know what was going on. I shook my head at him and said, 'Mom, maybe there's a logical explanation for this.' But as I said it, I wasn't so sure.

'Maybe.' She wasn't sure, either. 'If you hear from him, tell him it would be better if he goes to the police himself, volunteers to answer their questions.'

Vinny was practically wetting his pants with curiosity. 'Hold on, Mom.' I put my hand over the receiver. 'Apparently my dad's fingerprints were found in the house where Sal was hiding.'

Vinny frowned.

I sighed and went back to my mother. 'Listen, Mom, I'll let you know if I hear from Dad. Did you call Suzette?'

'For God's sake, no, Annie. Why would I do that? I don't want to worry her. Please let me know if you hear from him.'

I promised to do that, and we hung up. I sat on the couch next to Vinny.

'What the hell is going on?' I asked. I tried to shake away my doubts. He was my father, for chrissakes. I had to get a grip. He did show up at the crime scene. He wouldn't have been that brazen if he'd really killed Sal. Would he? And so what if his fingerprints were found in the place Sal was hiding? Okay, so they might be able to get him on obstruction of justice, but it wasn't like the cops thought Sal had killed LeeAnn. Mickey was in jail for that.

But then I remembered how Dick had heard the cops were changing their tune about the fire.

Vinny's hand closed over mine. 'Where's my father, Vinny? If he's innocent in all this, where the hell is he?' A thought slipped into my head. At least I was off the story. I didn't have to write about this. As long as Dick didn't find out, my dad was safe from the Evil Media, at least for one more day.

I dialed another number, and Tom picked up on the first ring. 'We're looking for your father,' he said, but without any harshness in his voice.

'I know,' I said. 'I just talked to my mother. What's the story here?'

'You have to tell me where he is.' He didn't seem inclined to explain anything.

'But I don't know, Tom. Really. I was supposed to meet him for dinner, and he never showed.'

'It would be better for him if he just came in quietly.' The implication was that I did know where he was and wasn't telling.

'I really don't know where he is, Tom,' I repeated. 'Now I'm worried about him.'

Vinny rubbed my shoulders, and it helped a little.

'If you do hear from him, do you promise to let me know?' Let 'me' know, ha, that was a nice way of saying that I would be turning my dad over to the cops, but I could appease my conscience by saying I was just handing him over to my ex-boyfriend, who might treat him fairly. 'We just want to talk to him.'

'Yeah, right,' I said, hanging up. Vinny continued massaging my shoulders, and if I weren't concentrating on where my father would be, I might be concentrating on what his hands could do to the rest of me. But there was no time for that.

'Vinny, we have to find my father before anyone else does. There has to be some sort of explanation for this. So what if he was helping Sal hide, big deal. But I know he didn't kill him.'

Vinny's hands stopped moving, and he stared at me. 'You know, Annie, I don't believe he killed Sal, either. But I think my reason is different from yours.'

I waited for his reason, and I could see him struggling with what exactly to say. Finally, he opened his mouth again. 'He wouldn't have left his fingerprints anywhere, there wouldn't be any connection to him at all.'

'So you believe my father could actually kill

Sal but not leave behind any evidence?'

Vinny nodded. 'Yeah. And you know it, too, deep down.'

'Listen, my father is not Tony Soprano.'

'That's TV, Annie. It's a gross exaggeration.' He paused for a couple of seconds, and I could see him thinking. 'But your father has been part of a world that has courted people who could be Tony Soprano.'

I sat, dumbfounded. Somewhere inside my head I knew all that shit.

A memory flashed, and I stared at Vinny. 'You didn't know about this, did you? Where Sal was? What did you see my father and Dominic Gaudio about that day? Were you really working for Mac?'

My doubts about him hurt, I could see it in his face, but I wanted answers now. He studied my face, putting his palm to my cheek, and smiled.

'I was working for Mac. I asked them if they knew where Sal was. They said no, but I didn't believe them. Why Sal was still in the city is something I can't figure out. And why did he hide?'

I turned my head, and he dropped his hand. 'I'm sorry,' I said, 'I just needed to know.'

'Yeah, it's okay.'

'Do you think Sal set the restaurant on fire?

Maybe it was the Mob. And why was LeeAnn there?'

Vinny took a deep breath. 'LeeAnn was a courier, remember? She must have been involved in Sal's operation, she must have known everything.'

'So how did she end up dead? What went wrong? And why kill her and then burn down the restaurant?'

Vinny shrugged. 'There are more questions now than three days ago.' He cocked his head at me. 'Your father, though, he's kept his nose clean on the game. He's running an up-and-up operation out there in Vegas. He should never have come back, even for Sal.'

I heard Vinny's words, and they rattled around between my ears before settling down. I'd never wanted to know the truth, have it spelled out for me, like Vinny was doing right now. I go after other people in my investigations, real criminals, criminals who aren't related to me.

'Wouldn't he know that we'd help him?' I asked.

Vinny smiled. 'The cops and the FBI will be watching you and your mother like hawks. He knows what's up. He doesn't want to get either of you in trouble.'

'Do you think he's at Dominic Gaudio's house?' I asked.

'No. Dom's kept quiet the last few years, but the feds would still love to get him on something. They keep an eye on him, so if your dad showed up there, they'd know.'

'Can you find him?' Vinny was privy to the neighborhood secrets, so I was sure he had an inside line somewhere.

He smiled mysteriously. 'I'll see what I can find out.'

'I appreciate it.'

'Don't forget, you're going to be watched,' Vinny warned.

'Okay, but don't you think they're going to watch you, too?'

Vinny stood up. He walked over to the window and stood in full view, as if he were admiring the square, even though it was dark outside. With all the lights on, I knew everyone could see everything in my apartment. He turned back to me, his back to the window. 'They're probably out there now, they probably watched us come in.' He was quiet for a moment.

'They wouldn't have my phone tapped or anything?' I was getting paranoid.

Vinny tried to smile, but it didn't quite come off. 'No, I doubt it.'

I felt a heaviness in my chest, uncertain that I wanted him to leave but knowing he had to. He had to start trying to find my father as soon as possible. We were wasting time.

I took a deep breath and stepped toward him. He caught my arm with his hand, and he kept a foot or so between us. 'Do you really think you can find him?' I asked.

He nodded, and the smile finally creased his face. He looked pretty confident, his hand tight on my arm; the last few days' events bubbled up into my chest, and I bit back tears.

Vinny let go of me and went to the door. I turned, my back to the window.

'You'd better fucking fix this,' I said as he opened the door to leave.

I saw his mouth twitch; he wanted to smile again, but he just bit his lip. When the door was open and it hid half his face, I saw him wink. 'I'm expecting a pretty big thank-you. Up for it?'

20

As soon as Vinny left, I was on the phone to Abate's to order a small white-clam pizza. Abate's delivers, so all I had to do was give the guy a few dollars and bring my dinner upstairs, where I devoured it in about fifteen minutes. A beer chaser and I was sated, but not content. My head was swirling with what my mother had told me.

Just before I went to bed, I plugged my cell phone into its charger. I wasn't going to miss any more calls if my dad needed me.

⋆ ⋆ ⋆

The landline phone woke me up. The sun streaked into my bedroom, rushing across the walls. A glance at the clock told me it was 8:00 A.M. I reached out from under my comforter and pulled the receiver toward me. 'Hello?' I said, still under the covers.

'Hey, Annie, sorry it's so early.' Paula's voice was a little funny, a little too high, a little too nervous. They'd made her call me, the FBI. Her bosses. I should've expected this.

'It's okay. What's up?' I tried to sound nonchalant, but I knew I wouldn't be able to fool her, any more than she could fool me.

'I'm sorry I never really got back to you. Things have been pretty hectic.'

'Yeah, I know.' I wasn't quite sure what else to say.

I could almost see Paula's boss pantomiming that she should move the conversation along.

'Is your dad still in town?' Paula was trying to ask this casually, but it came out too fast.

'I don't know. Pulled a disappearing act on me last night. I was supposed to meet him for dinner at Consiglio's, and he never showed. My mother's looking for him, too.' I threw out the last bit of information to get them to leave my mother alone.

'So you have no idea where he is?'

I sat up, pulling my comforter tightly around me. How the hell had it gotten to this point? Three days ago I was covering a fire, and now the FBI was trying to get information out of me about my father through my friend.

'No. I don't,' I said. 'Listen, want to have some breakfast? I'll meet you at The Pantry on State.'

A second of silence, she was probably asking the boss, and finally: 'Okay. Half an hour?'

I leaned over and looked at myself in the mirror over the dresser. I looked like hell. 'Sounds fine.'

My stomach growled as I rummaged through my drawers and found a very old pair of jeans shoved in the back. Go figure, but the jeans actually fit. I should clean out my drawers more often.

I pulled on a turtleneck and glanced out the window. It was sunny outside, but I could see the layer of ice that had formed on top of the snow, and I knew it had to be really cold out there. I threw a sweatshirt over the turtleneck and put on a thick pair of socks. The snow boots were going out again. I couldn't wait until spring, and it wasn't even really winter yet.

When my hand was on the doorknob to go out, my thoughts strayed to my gun. Well, it wasn't really mine. It was Vinny's. He'd lent it to me after mine was used in a crime, and I'd never gotten around to giving it back. I yanked open the drawer on my bedside table and there it was. Granted, taking it along to meet the FBI might be stupid, but with all this Mob talk and Cadillacs all over the place, it might not be a bad idea to have it handy.

Paula was sitting at a booth when I finally walked into The Pantry. I ordered coffee and eggs before saying anything else. I kept my hand on my bag, like everyone was going to know there was a gun in there. But how the hell would they know?

'Why'd you bring the gun?' Paula whispered, leaning close to me across the table.

'Shit, Paula. And what's with the G-men hanging around?' I jerked my head toward the counter, where two guys tried to look as if they were interested in the menu, but I could see them sneaking peeks at us.

She sat back and sighed. 'I told them they shouldn't come in.'

'What's up?' I asked.

She shrugged. 'They think I'm going to fuck this up. Because we're friends.'

'Fuck what up?' I feigned stupidity.

The waitress came over with coffee for both of us and our eggs and toast. When she left, I smiled. 'Listen, Paula, I really don't know any more about where my father is than you people.'

' 'You people'?'

'You're using me. To get to him.'

'I'm sorry.' And she really looked it. I couldn't be pissed off at her. I'd do the same thing if I were in her shoes.

'Yeah, right.' I couldn't let her know I'd forgiven her that easily. I took a long drink from my cup and hailed the waitress back for more.

'Vinny doesn't know where your father is, does he?'

She was sneaky, but I had to give her that one. 'No, Paula. He doesn't know, either. And my mother's looking for him. He seems to have vanished.'

'I'm sorry, Annie, but it's my job.'

'They didn't even call you when the restaurant burned down and Sal was still alive.'

I could tell she didn't like being reminded of that. We ate our eggs in silence for a few minutes.

'How long are you guys going to watch me?'

Paula wiped her mouth with her napkin. 'Until he shows up again.'

'You know he won't contact me. He's not stupid.'

'Yeah, I know. But we have to try.'

One of the guys at the counter was getting up, doing something with his head that made me think he had Tourette's syndrome or something, except he wasn't cursing.

'Excuse me for a minute,' Paula said. She slid out of the booth and sidled up to him. They went outside, and I could see them on the sidewalk, the man gesturing wildly, his mouth moving faster than a fucking train, and Paula's eyes getting wider. She nodded, then came back inside and sat down.

'I have to get going,' she said, draining her coffee cup.

I was finished with my eggs and halfway through my toast. 'What's up?'

She grinned. 'Top-secret agent shit.' She swung her bag over her shoulder as she got back up. 'I'll be in touch.' The second guy at the counter followed her toward the door.

'Tell them to stop watching me,' I shouted after her, not caring who heard. And no one seemed to care, since no one even looked up to see what all the shouting was about.

I watched as Paula and the two agents walked around the side of the building to the parking lot. I threw down a $10 bill, put on my coat, and picked up my bag. If I hurried, maybe I could find out where they were going.

Paula had parked farther back in the lot, so when my car started, they were just turning onto State Street. I kept a car length behind them. If I was lucky, no one would notice.

I really had no idea why I was following the FBI. Maybe it was a sick sense of being more in control than I really was. I didn't know what that guy had told Paula, but if they were willing to have her stop grilling me, it must be important. I hoped they hadn't found my father before Vinny did. I was compelled to follow them to find out.

My cell phone rang as we passed the old Malone's, the place where Vinny and Pete Amato had gotten into their brawl.

I pulled the phone out of my bag and held it to my ear. I had to get one of those handless things. It would be a lot less awkward, and anyway, it was now against the law to talk on a cell phone without one while driving. With my luck, I'd get pulled over and thrown into jail for this. If they found my father, maybe we could share a cell.

'Hello?'

'Annie?' Jesus, it was my father.

'Can they trace this?' I asked. 'I'm following the FBI as we speak.'

I heard him chuckle. 'You're following them? And, no, I don't think they can trace this.'

'Are you sure?'

'You watch too much TV.'

I didn't see what TV had to do with it. I was pretty sure technology was advanced enough to trace a cell phone call. But before I could say that, he asked, 'Why are you following the FBI?'

'Oh, it's Paula and some guys she works with. They had her call me to find out where you are.' I paused, watching the car ahead of me. 'Where are you?'

'Don't worry. I'm sorry I didn't call you earlier.'

'Why did they find your fingerprints?'

'When I see you next time, I'll explain everything.'

He was a master of evasion. 'Mom said they think you're involved in Sal's murder.'

'They're wrong. Why would I kill one of my closest and oldest friends?'

Paula was turning left, onto Court Street. 'Hold on a minute, okay?' I put the phone on the seat next to me as I made the turn, then picked it back up. 'I need one of those handless things.'

'Christmas is coming.'

'Jesus, Dad, what the hell's going on?'

'That's what I'm trying to find out. I just wanted you to know I'm okay and I'll be in touch.' We were quiet a few seconds. 'Love you.'

'Love you, too,' I said, and the connection was broken. I put down the phone. Paula had pulled up in front of Vinny's brownstone. I kept going, parked in front of my building, and hopped out onto the sidewalk. I strained to see what was going on but couldn't, so I crossed the street and went into the park about halfway down, where I had a much better view.

I watched it like a silent movie. Paula

stayed on the sidewalk as her partner went up the steps and rang the bell. In a minute or so, the door opened, and Rosie stepped out in a bathrobe. And then Vinny came out; his hair was tousled, and he was also in a bathrobe. I watched him shake his head and say something, then the FBI guy indicated Paula should follow him, and they pushed Vinny and Rosie inside, and the door closed after all of them.

I must have held my breath the whole time they were in there, and when they came out, I let out a long sigh. Paula and her partner got back into their car. I saw Vinny looking out his window, watching them drive away. Oh, shit, he saw me, too, and there he was, waving like a goddamn flag.

I shot back across the park and to my car, which wouldn't start. I think I flooded it, laying on the accelerator as if there were no tomorrow, and it just whined at me. Vinny was knocking on my passenger-side window, now dressed appropriately in jeans and a leather jacket.

'Open the window, Annie,' he demanded.

I cracked it about a quarter of an inch. 'I'm on a secret mission, Vinny. I'm following the FBI.'

Just then my car started, and in the same second that Vinny opened the door and jumped in, the old Honda lurched forward, throwing him into the dashboard. The door blew back on his leg and he shouted, 'For God's sake, slow down!'

The car careened around the corner, and he managed to pull himself into a seated position and close the door. I turned to glare at him. 'What are you doing?'

'I'm going along for the ride. What do you think?' Vinny glared back. 'And I think you lost them.'

I craned my neck and spotted Paula's Toyota Camry turning back toward Chapel. I made a hard left turn, and Vinny nearly fell into my lap. 'What the fuck . . . ,' he muttered. 'How long have you been at this?'

I shook my head. 'I met Paula for break-fast, she asked about my father, she and the other guys left, I followed them to your place.'

I snuck a peek at him. His face had turned an odd shade of pink. 'Oh.'

I slammed on the brakes, and the car screeched to a halt in the middle of the street. 'I certainly don't have the right to be jealous, but I'm a little confused.'

He wouldn't look at me for a minute, and I could see him forcing himself to bring his eyes to my face. 'I've got some things to sort out.'

I snorted. 'No shit. So what did they want?'

'What?'

'What did Paula want?'

'Oh, they wanted to find out if I knew where your father was.' He was quiet a second. 'I went over to Dominic's last night after I left you, guess someone saw me there. But your father wasn't there.'

My brain tried to wrap itself around his words, but it was going in a hundred different directions.

'You lost them,' he finally said when I didn't say anything.

'They'll be back.'

'I'm sorry.'

At least he said that. But it didn't really help. 'I think I'm going to go to the paper. I'll drop you off.' The car started moving again, and I turned at the light.

'Drop me here,' he said.

'I can take you home.'

'I need to walk, to think.'

I pulled over on Wooster Street. He opened the door and was about to get out when he turned back to me. He tried a smile, but it didn't really work. 'I'll let you know when I find your father.'

'He called me.'

'What?'

'He called me on my cell phone when I was following Paula.'

'Where was he?'

'He didn't say. But he said he'd be in touch.'

Vinny frowned. 'I'll call you if I find out anything,' he said as he climbed out of the car. He slammed the door shut and tapped on the window a couple of times. I pulled out into the street. I looked back at him in the rearview mirror. Damn, he looked good. I was one sick puppy.

21

I turned the car around and started back up Chapel Street. I had to go to work. It was Sunday morning; it would be quiet, and I could go through my notes to try to make sense of everything that was going on, even though I wasn't officially on the story anymore.

But as I passed my brownstone, I had to stop. Amber and about six other people were stacking placards into a minivan. I caught a glimpse of one, which had big block letters announcing STOP THE SUFFERING. What the hell was this?

I got out of the car and scurried up the sidewalk, sidling up to Amber. 'What's going on?' I asked.

She seemed a little startled to see me, then: 'Oh, Annie, it must have been dreadful for you to see those poor defenseless chickens cut down before their time.'

Chickens? Sal's chickens? She must have seen the paper this morning. I choked back a laugh when I saw how serious she was. I could thank years of talking to crazy people about ridiculous story ideas for my ability to keep a straight face when I was looking at someone who was obviously deranged. 'It was pretty bad,' I admitted.

Someone jostled me, and I stumbled.

'Sorry.' Walter the Pit Bull didn't even stop as he carried two placards to the van.

'So what's up?' I asked Amber.

'We belong to a group called Vegans for Animals. We don't eat anything that has a mother.'

Christ, she was fucking serious about this. I could feel the laughter bubbling up inside me again, and I forced it back down. 'So you're protesting what?'

'The murder of those innocent creatures,' she said. 'We're heading for the Green, where we can talk to as many people as possible.' She waved her arm toward Wooster Square. 'Not enough people here. Want to come along?'

'No thanks. I really can't, you know, since I have to be objective and all.' I began backing up toward my car, then stopped. 'So what do you expect to gain from this?'

She shrugged. 'Community sympathy. We've planned a memorial service.'

'For who?' I asked, confused.

'The chickens, of course,' Amber said. 'It'll be tomorrow afternoon. Please come.' She paused. 'Do you think the newspaper would be interested in this?'

It was a publicity campaign. For her weirdo group. I shook my head. 'Don't think so,' I said as I climbed into my car.

'You really should be more aware,' she called as she went back to join her friends.

I watched them for a few minutes from the car as it warmed up, Amber's tall, slender figure weaving in and out of the group, obviously the leader. She really was nuts.

I was looking forward to going to the paper, where, after fifteen years, there were no surprises left. There would be one or two reporters reading the Sunday paper, waiting for their assignments to come up, and there wouldn't be any editors on yet. The room would smell like Chinese food or garlic, depending on what the Saturday night copy desk had ordered in for dinner.

They'd ordered pizza. A lone piece sat on the cardboard on the obituary desk. It looked tempting, especially since it was covered with pepperoni, and after talking to Amber, all I could think about was eating barbecued chicken or big slabs of meat. But I knew eating the pizza would be risky since it'd been there for more than twelve hours.

I pulled out the notebooks I'd kept since Thursday. I'd just started reading through them to see if I'd written down anything I'd forgotten when I heard them approach.

Bill Bennett and Dick Whitfield. Neither of them was smiling. In fact, Bill Bennett was looking downright disturbed about something.

'Hello, Annie.' Bill Bennett's voice grated on me like fingernails on a chalkboard. What the hell was he doing here on a Sunday morning, anyway? Maybe he was going to do something about the heat. But I doubted it. He didn't even seem to notice it was like a sauna in here — his tie was perfectly straight, his suit jacket neat and wrinkle-free.

I mumbled something that could have been construed as 'Hello' as I yanked off my sweatshirt, wishing I'd worn a sleeveless shirt rather than a turtleneck underneath it. I could feel a band of sweat forming on my neck. Maybe this was what it was like to have hot flashes. Something to look forward to.

'I'm glad you came in this morning,' Bill Bennett was saying. 'I was going to call you.'

I stared up at him without saying a word. It didn't seem to faze him.

'We have a bit of a situation.'

Dick was strangely quiet, his eyes on the ground. I waited.

'Alexandra Giametti received a phone call from Immaculata Amato. She wants to file a restraining order against you and Dick.'

'What?' I asked. 'Why?'

'She says you're harassing her in her time of grief.' He looked at Dick. 'She's very upset about your visit yesterday.' He turned back to me. 'And she says you threatened her son, you and that private investigator.'

'Hey, that wasn't me. That was all Vinny.'

He shook his head. 'It doesn't matter. All that matters is that the two reporters who are working this story have now been shut out by the victim's family because they overstepped their bounds.'

What the fuck was this all about? I wasn't even on the story anymore. And to be lumped in with Dick, that was the absolute worst thing.

'Your mother calmed her down, Annie, but you have to stay away from her and her son.' He turned to Dick. 'You're going to have to get this story without them.'

'What were you asking them about when I showed up there?' I asked Dick. 'Were you asking them about how the cops think Sal might have torched the restaurant?'

Dick nodded meekly.

'Was that all?'

He shook his head, like a kid who got caught coloring on the walls.

'So are you going to tell us?' I demanded.

He gulped. 'Well, Mrs. Amato told me to

go away when I asked about Sal's gambling operation. We still need to get that on the record. And then I said I wanted to see the garage, to see if the gasoline was there that started the fire. My source said the gasoline was found in the garage.' His voice was barely audible. Bill Bennett and I moved closer to him.

'First off, if the cops found gasoline in the garage, they probably took it for evidence, so it's probably not there anymore,' I said. 'Second, this is not exactly the way to get a story, Dick. You can't fuck with these people. They know people, if you get my drift.'

He snapped out of it. 'People like your mother and your father, right?'

'You can leave her mother out of this,' Bill Bennett said sternly. 'Where's your father, Annie? That's the other side of this.'

I shrugged. 'I really don't know where he is, Bill. He's disappeared, like Sal did, and I sure as hell hope he doesn't end up dead like Sal.' I hadn't voiced that fear before, and it sent shivers down my back.

Bill Bennett scratched his chin. 'So where does all this leave us? Do I need to get another reporter on this story?'

An ugly thought had started swirling around in my head. If Mac wanted to file a restraining order against us to keep us from asking any more questions, maybe Dick was right, maybe his source was right. Maybe Sal had torched the place.

'We can't let Mac and Pete keep us from doing our jobs,' I told Bill Bennett. 'We can get to the bottom of this without them. They know something, and maybe they think this will stop us. Mickey Hayward's arraignment is tomorrow. Dick can cover that and he wouldn't even have to see Mac or Pete. That's pretty simple. If you want, I can nose around about the gasoline thing.'

'But you're a part of the story, you found Sal Amato. You shouldn't even be covering this anymore.'

I had to find out what was going on, and I was going to do it whether I covered it or not. The look on my face must have told Bill Bennett everything I was thinking, because finally he said, 'All right. Can you try to get this gasoline thing confirmed? Just stay away from the Amatos. If you can do this without bothering them and getting the paper in trouble, do what you need to.' He got up, and I thought that was it, but then he stared me straight in the eye. 'If your father contacts you, I want to hear about it. I don't want you to protect him. He needs to turn himself in. If he's innocent, it will be proven.'

He didn't need to know that Dad had

already called me. Because I still didn't know where the hell he was, so what difference would it make?

Dick and I watched him walk through the newsroom and disappear around the corner, going back upstairs to his cushy office.

'We're still on it,' Dick said quietly.

'Only because there's no one else to put on this right now. He didn't have a choice. And it's the biggest thing since that Yalie got murdered in September.' I paused. 'So tell me more what your source' — and I emphasized the word *source* — 'told you about this gasoline.'

'Accelerant was found in Sal's garage,' he said.

'And the accelerant that started the fire was gasoline?'

He nodded.

That's what my mother had said, too, so this wasn't off the mark. 'So maybe he had some left over from the lawn mower. A lot of people have gasoline in their garages.'

'Annie, he doesn't have a yard. What would he need a lawn mower for?'

He had a point. Mac had turned what little property they had into flower gardens a long time ago.

'What about a snow blower?' I suggested. 'Or a generator?' I was grabbing at straws; I

244

had no clue about what sorts of machinery found in a person's house would need gasoline.

That stumped Dick. He shrugged. 'Don't know.'

'We have to tread lightly on this. We can't find ourselves in a middle of a libel suit if we're wrong.'

'I'm not wrong,' Dick insisted. 'I've got a reliable source.'

If it was Tom, he certainly was reliable.

'Did your source say anything else?' I asked.

Dick stared at the ground a second, then looked back up at me, his eyes bright. 'Sal's finances weren't what they should be.'

'What was wrong with them?'

He shrugged. 'I don't know. That's all he said.'

We had precious little to go on.

I got up, put on my puffy coat, and picked up my bag. 'Dick, keep your head down.' I left him there, and I could still feel his eyes on me as I walked away. It was a creepy feeling.

22

I had no choice but to go to the police department to find Tom. I didn't have any ideas about how to find my father, so following up on this gasoline thing was the next best thing. Dick had certainly fucked up his end of it. He should never have confronted Mac and Pete with that, unless he had absolute proof. And then he should have called them only for a comment, not parked himself on their doorstep and demanded answers.

He was a little too eager, a little too 'in your face.' I guess I could've tried to explain the rules to him, but I had to be honest with myself. I couldn't give him my secrets without giving him my job. Dick was cheap labor, unlike me, who had been hired when money was still used as a lure. And if he could do my job as well as I could, then I'd be out as fast as Bill Bennett could say 'layoffs.'

So in a way, it was good that he'd gotten us in trouble, although I wish Mac and Pete had kept me out of it. I hadn't pushed them like Dick, but I guess they were just lashing out at the paper. But as I'd told Bill Bennett, I didn't really need them right now, so it wasn't a huge problem.

I could've called Tom, but I wanted to see him face-to-face when I asked about the gasoline and Sal's mysterious financial situation. Even if Dick had gotten this from someone else, Tom would know about it, since he was the primary detective on the case. And if he didn't, it would be either because someone hadn't told him and it would piss him off or because it wasn't true. I was pretty sure I would be able to tell just by watching his eyes.

As luck would have it, he was coming out of police headquarters as I was going in, and we stood in front of the doors awkwardly, neither of us sure how to greet the other.

Finally, I said, 'Hey, there. Just the guy I wanted to see.'

He smirked and ran a hand through his hair. 'Just my luck.' But he didn't run away, he didn't even start walking. We continued to stand there like idiots, staring at each other for another few seconds.

'Got something to ask,' I said.

'Figured that.'

'Will you answer?'

'Depends.'

We weren't getting anywhere with this shit.

I motioned him to follow me down the steps and onto the sidewalk, where we'd be in less danger of being overheard.

'Heard some gasoline was found in Sal's garage and it might have been the gasoline that was used to torch the restaurant.'

His eyes flickered for a second, and he couldn't hide it. 'Where'd you hear that?'

'Around.'

'Around where?'

'I can't say. Is it true?' I asked.

'Maybe. Maybe not.'

'Oh, cut the shit, Tom,' I said a little too loudly. A couple of uniforms turned around to look at us as they went up the steps a few feet away. 'I know you already talked to Dick, so what harm would it do if you talked to me, too?'

Tom grabbed my arm and pulled me along the sidewalk, farther away. 'There may be some question as to who set the fire,' he said, his voice low. While I was happy he actually told me something, it was only because he'd confirmed he was Dick's source without saying so. Which wasn't good. But I might as well try to get more out of him while I could.

'So the arson charge might be dropped against Mickey?'

'Could be. We're still gathering evidence.'

'What about the murder?'

'Hell, we've got him there. Gun in the car. It had been shot recently, and forensics matched it to the bullet found in LeeAnn.'

Seemed pretty clear-cut to me, too. 'So it's the fire that's in question.'

'Possible Sal didn't know she was in there. She was on the floor in the front corner, the fire was set near the restrooms in the middle of the building. He may not have even gone in any farther.' He rubbed the back of his neck, and there were bags under his eyes.

'You okay?' I asked softly.

His eyes hardened, and he snickered. 'Yeah, like you care.'

I did care. I cared a lot. But how much? Who the hell knew. I certainly didn't.

'Is there any other proof?' I asked, not wanting to remind him that he'd shut me out. For some reason he was talking, and I wasn't about to stop him.

'Of what?'

'That Sal was the one who set the fire, not Mickey.'

'Other than it was his place, and he'd just taken a huge loan out for renovations?'

This could be the financial problem Dick mentioned. 'Really?'

Tom nodded. 'Yeah, he'd just taken a loan out. Talking about fifty grand to do some renovations.' He paused, then smiled as my mouth opened to ask the next question. But I didn't have to ask. 'The money was deposited Wednesday afternoon, then the place burns to the ground before morning.'

'So the money's in the bank?'

His smile got larger; he was loving this one. 'There was a cash withdrawal about an hour after the deposit.'

'Oh, Christ. Cash?'

'Yeah.'

'How much?'

'More than half of it.'

'So where's the money?'

Tom shook his head. 'Beats the hell out of me.'

Shit. Money disappears, the restaurant goes up in flames, Sal vanishes. But then again, he didn't, did he. He was still here, all that time. And that's what I couldn't figure out. And what Tom couldn't figure out, either, because I could see the same look in his eyes as I probably had in mine.

'So something got screwed up,' I said.

'Yeah. Maybe it was LeeAnn, maybe not. But for some reason, Sal didn't get out of town like it seems he was planning to.'

'Why do you think my father is involved?' I had to ask.

Tom narrowed his eyes at me, as if he thought I knew more about my father than I did. I started to protest, and he put a finger to my lips. 'His fingerprints were found at the house where Sal had been staying. We got a tip Sal was there. He was gone by the time we got there, but we dusted and found his fingerprints, and your father's and Dominic Gaudio's.' He paused. 'You should tell me where he is.'

That's why he was talking to me. He thought if he told me stuff, I'd give up my dad. One hand washes the other and all that shit.

'Have you been to Dominic Gaudio's?'

Tom snorted. 'Yeah, sure. We had a search warrant. Clean as a goddamn whistle. The old man just sat in his fucking Barcalounger and pretended he didn't know who we were. His daughter followed us around so close we kept tripping over her.'

'If my father's not there and he's checked out of the Omni, then I don't have a clue where he is, Tom,' I said. 'I haven't seen him.' I didn't mention the phone call this morning. 'You know, this sounds a little too familiar. The gun that killed LeeAnn was found in Mickey's car, my father's fingerprints show up in Sal's hideaway, what's up with that? Seems both of them would be smarter than that.' At least my dad would be. Mickey, well, it was a crapshoot.

Tom nodded. 'You're right. It does seem a little too pat. But fingerprints don't lie.'

'But they might obscure the truth.'

'Your father showed up almost immediately after the fire.'

'Because he's an old friend of Sal's.'

'Or maybe because he was going to help Sal get out of here.'

It was exactly what I'd thought, but I couldn't admit it. I had to give him something else, someone else to concentrate on other than my father.

'I've heard my dad's not the only one who's blown into town, if you know what I mean,' I said quietly, thinking about that Cadillac with the New York plates.

Tom nodded. 'Yeah, we know about that.'

They did? 'But you still think my father is involved?'

'Your father probably knows everything that's going on.'

I was quiet for a second. He probably did. Which didn't bode well for him.

'Does your boyfriend have any ideas about this?' Tom emphasized the word *boyfriend* as if he were saying the word *diarrhea*.

I shook my head. 'No, Vinny's in the dark, too.' It wasn't until after I said it that I realized I hadn't disputed Tom's use of the word *boyfriend* to describe Vinny, even though it certainly wasn't accurate.

'Are you sure about that?' Something in his voice made me look more closely at his face.

I wasn't sure, but I didn't want to say so. 'Why?'

'Feds think he's up to something.'

'Paula and her partner went to see him this morning, I know that.'

His eyebrows shot up.

'Oh, shit, Tom, I know about it, but not because I was there. I was following Paula. They went there. That's all I know. But I don't know what Vinny knows or what the feds think he knows. Are the feds saying anything to you?'

Tom snickered. 'They're taking everything we're finding out and not telling us a damn thing in return.'

'So what's your next move?'

'What's yours?'

I shrugged. 'No clue.'

'If you hear from your father and you don't tell me and I find out about it, I'm going to be pretty pissed at you. I could bring you in on obstruction of justice.' His blue eyes were dark, and I knew he meant business.

'Yeah, sure, I know.'

'Your boyfriend, too.' It was the way he said it that made me think if he could've, he would've shot me right there and put us both out of our misery.

Which reminded me I still had that stupid gun in my bag. I got in the car and headed toward my apartment so I could put the gun back in its drawer. I'd been out all day; no one had threatened me, no one had jumped me, I was in one piece. The FBI was probably following me. So there was no need for a firearm. I sighed with relief. I hated the thing.

But when I turned off State Street onto Water, Vinny's SUV came up on my ass. I pulled into the parking lot at what used to be Big Tony's bar but is now something else, I always forget the name.

'Did you get anything out of Tom?' Vinny asked, climbing out of the Explorer.

'No.' I'd rolled down my window and could see my breath practically reach Vinny, who was a good three feet away but getting closer. How the hell did he know I'd talked to Tom? Jesus, I wasn't being followed by the FBI. It was Vinny. 'I'm on my way home,' I said curtly.

He shook his head. 'Get out of the car and come with me. I have something to show you.'

I must have looked annoyed, because a slow, sexy smile crawled across his face. 'Aw, come on, Annie. It could be fun.'

I hesitated, thinking about this morning. He opened the door. 'Get out, okay? It's important.'

My feet moved without telling me, and I was in the SUV before you could say 'home wrecker.'

He started up the engine, but before he pulled out, he turned and looked at me, right in the eyes, for what seemed like an eternity but was probably only about three seconds. 'I know I shouldn't expect you to believe anything I say because I certainly haven't shown you in the right way how much I care about you, but when this is all over, I promise you, things will be different.'

The tires screeched as the Explorer skidded on some ice and found dry pavement, and Vinny was watching the road instead of me.

I didn't think he was expecting any sort of response, so I asked, 'Have you found my father?'

His mouth twitched as though he were going to smile, but he didn't. 'Just relax, okay?'

I clutched my bag in my lap, and I could feel the outline of the gun inside. It preoccupied me long enough so that when I finally focused again on where we were, we were pulling up in front of Vinny's office on Trumbull Street.

Just our luck, Madame Share was coming in from the opposite side of the sidewalk. I knew it was her, because who else would be swathed in brightly colored scarves wrapped from her head to her knees?

'Ah, Vincent!' she exclaimed as she came up the steps beside us. 'And who is the lovely young lady?'

I tried to ignore her as we stepped inside, but Vinny stopped at his box to collect his mail, which encouraged her.

'Is this the fianceé?' Madame Shara asked, her eyes peering into my face. 'Ah, no, I'm wrong.'

No shit, Sherlock.

'You are very troubled,' she continued. I remembered the gun in my bag, and that I didn't want to use it.

I shook my head and pushed my way through the next set of doors behind Vinny, hoping she'd go into her own little space and leave me alone. But it was my lucky day. She followed us into Vinny's office and started peeling off the scarves. Vinny still hadn't said anything, like, go away, which I was hoping he'd do. He just had a faintly amused look on his face as he dropped the mail on his desk.

'I can help you, my dear.'

I pulled my coat tight around me. 'We're pretty busy,' I said, looking at Vinny and

256

pleading for help. But he had gone behind his desk and was booting up his computer.

Madame Shara took my hand and started leading me out the door. 'We'll be back in a minute,' she said over her shoulder to Vinny, who merely nodded. I couldn't break away from her grasp.

Madame Shara led me up the stairs and into her 'office.' She actually had a crystal ball. A crystal ball on a red table in the middle of the room, which smelled like incense and honey. The walls were covered with red and purple sheer fabric with yellow and green beads that shimmered when she turned on a muted lamp.

'Take off your coat,' she said, and it was not a suggestion.

I figured I was in for the long haul; Vinny hadn't come to get me, and what the hell else did I have to do today but talk to some nut? It wasn't like I had a job to do or anything.

She made me sit across from her at the red table, the crystal ball between us.

'Does that thing work?' I asked, and in a second it lit up like the fucking Fourth of July.

Madame Shara had a small smile on her lips. 'You're a skeptic.'

I snorted. 'Okay, so tell me my future. Tell me what you think I want to know.'

'What you want to know is different from what will happen,' she said in a deep voice.

What the hell did that mean?

'You are very troubled,' she said again.

And who wasn't?

'There are three men,' she said.

Three?

'One of them you have known a long time,' she said, her voice barely a whisper. 'And one only a very short time. The third has been your lover.'

Vinny had been talking out of school. He'd been telling this woman stuff about me. He was obviously the man I'd known for a short time; Tom was the lover. But who was the third man?

'Ah, you're curious,' she said.

'You're kidding, right?'

'Curiosity has always been your strength.'

Okay, so Vinny must have told her I was a reporter.

'But it will not help you this time. It is there, in black and white for you. But you must figure out the puzzle before you can see the whole picture.'

This lady was a fucking whack job. I hoped she wasn't going to charge me for this little session. Maybe I'd let Vinny pay for it, since he hadn't done anything to get me out of this.

'He cares about you, more than even he

knows. He will come to you. But you must be ready.' Maybe Vinny took his mind-reading lessons from Madame Shara. 'Once you find him, it will be over. But you will have been betrayed, and forgiveness is difficult.'

Madame Shara leaned forward, her pointy nose practically touching the crystal ball.

'Don't let your feelings for him cloud the truth. He is guilty, and the sooner you see that, the sooner you can begin to love him again.' She leaned even farther, and a spark from the crystal ball shot up and bounced off her nose. She jumped up, her eyes wild with pain, but didn't break her stare.

'Go home and lock the door. They're after you,' she whispered.

23

I don't even remember leaving the room, but I was holding my coat as I slammed Vinny's office door shut behind me.

He looked up, laughing. 'What the hell happened up there?'

He looked so damn normal; I couldn't admit the woman had spooked me. 'She's insane,' was all I said as I plopped down on the couch next to the desk.

'Are you afraid it's catching?'

'Can you tell me why we're here? If you can't, then take me home.' I hugged my coat and noticed that the hole had gotten larger and I'd left a trail of feathers across the floor.

'This was just a pit stop. We have to go,' Vinny said, standing and putting on his leather jacket.

I was trying to close up the hole, but to no avail. Vinny suddenly was beside me, a roll of tape in his hand. 'Use this.' I pulled off a piece and stuck it over the hole. I moved the fabric around a little. Seemed to work. I put on the coat and didn't notice any feathers escaping. 'Thanks,' I said, following him back out. I left a wide berth in the hallway, just in case Madame Shara wanted to come back out and reel me in again. But there was no sound from upstairs.

The SUV heated up fairly quickly, and Vinny still hadn't said a word.

'What did she say to you?' he finally asked, chuckling. 'She got to you, didn't she. She can do that. Once she told me that I'd end up working for the FBI because I'd go broke working for myself.'

'She wasn't that specific with me.' I looked out the window.

'So, what did she say? Don't keep me in suspense.'

I took a deep breath. 'She just told me that someone would betray me and I'd have to forgive him.' I paused. 'Did you ever tell her about me?'

He laughed. 'Why the hell would I do that? She's one of those people you can't encourage with any sort of contact whatsoever, otherwise she'd be in your face all the time. When I see her, I just lock my office door and tell her I'm busy.'

'So you don't know if . . . ' I had to stop myself. It sounded too crazy even to ask.

'Don't know if what?' He wasn't really paying attention to me; his eyes were darting back and forth from his rearview mirror to the road in front of him.

'Nothing.'

'Come on, Annie, you don't really believe her mumbo jumbo, do you?'

'She seemed to know a little bit about me, and I certainly didn't say anything.'

Vinny thought a minute. 'You know, Cobb Doyle is pretty friendly with her, which makes sense in a weird sort of way. They're both odd ducks. Anyway, Cobb knows about you, maybe he said something.'

I didn't say anything.

'What else did she say?' He turned down a side street and then came back around, doing a perfect U-turn.

'She said someone's after me and I should go home and lock the door.'

He laughed out loud.

'Fuck you,' I said loudly. 'Where are we going, anyway?'

We were back in front of his office on Trumbull Street, but instead of stopping, we headed toward Interstate 91. Within minutes we were on the highway and going over the Q-Bridge, which stretched over the Quinnipiac River. Its official name was the Pearl Harbor Memorial Bridge, but no one ever called it that. If we put that in a story, most people scratched their heads and said, 'What bridge?' It had always been the Q-Bridge, and it would be that forever.

'I don't think anyone is following us,' Vinny said quietly, more to himself than to me. So that was what all that street maneuvering had been all about.

We got off on Woodward Avenue in the Annex. I was having serious déjà vu. This was where I'd followed Vinny the other day.

Vinny turned down a side street to our left and then turned again. He pulled up in front of the familiar small Cape, its yellow paint faded by too much sunshine and rain. He opened his door. 'We're here,' he announced.

'The cops have already been here,' I said as I scrambled out, following him up the front steps. 'My father's not here. So why are we?'

At that moment, Dominic Gaudio came out on the landing, his red plaid flannel shirt and khakis making him appear just like someone's grandfather and not a well-known mobster. When he looked up at me, he grinned, his teeth flapping against his gums.

'So nice to see you again, dear,' he said.

Vinny and I stepped into the house, into a wall of hot air that slapped me in the face.

'I've got coffee on,' Dominic Gaudio said, and disappeared into another room.

'This is a wild goose chase,' I whispered to Vinny.

Before he could respond, Dominic Gaudio came back into the room with a tray full of steaming cups. I took one and sipped. This was no Maxwell House, that was for sure. The liquid warmed my mouth and throat, its milky taste touched by a hint of cinnamon.

'This is delicious, Mr. Gaudio,' I said.

'Please call me Dom. There's no need to be formal here.' His eyes twinkled, and I could see the young man inside the old one. He turned to Vinny. 'I know why you're here, but I'm not sure I can help you.'

Vinny grinned. 'Sure you can. It's whether you want to or not.'

Dom laughed. 'You're just like your old man. But the kitchen was too hot for you, you needed more action? Private detective, what do you want to do that for? Your father has a wonderful restaurant and no son to take over when he retires.'

'I don't have to tell you about wanting more action,' Vinny said.

Dom opened a box that sat on the table and pulled out two cigars. I wrinkled my nose, and he caught me and smiled. 'My dear Anne, these are Cubans. Their aroma is nothing like you have ever experienced.' He handed one to Vinny, and they both lit up.

He was right. I didn't even give a damn about the secondhand smoke. But how the hell did he get Cuban cigars?

Oh, yeah, right. Dominic Gaudio could get

anything, anytime. The man was a fucking magician.

And I was sitting on his couch, drinking his coffee and listening to him bullshit with Vinny about the Red Sox.

Why were we here? I glanced around the room, taking in the sepia pictures on the mantel, the lace draped over the armrests on the sofa and chairs, the collection of Hummels in the glass cabinet in the corner.

My eye caught something outside, and I craned my neck to look out at the street. A dark car was crawling along, the driver invisible.

'Vinny,' I said quietly, cocking my head toward the window.

Vinny didn't even turn around.

'They come by every now and then to make sure the old man's still alive,' Dom said. 'They still have hope.' He laughed, his cheeks dimpled.

Shit, I liked the guy. I remembered all the stories about him, and I still liked him. What sort of journalist was I?

Oh, yeah, one who was dodging the FBI. Just like Dom. Well, not exactly.

'I know where he is,' Dom was saying, 'but I'm uncomfortable telling you.'

'It's for his own good,' Vinny argued. 'The longer he hides, the more guilty he looks. And

Annie and I know he didn't do anything.'

So Dom knew where my father was. No surprise there.

'I know that, too, but if you leave here, that car out there is going to follow you, because everyone who leaves here gets followed. And they're after you, too, right now.'

'Listen, Vinny, let's just leave. We can come back later.' I stood up, Madame Shara's warning echoing in my head.

A loud crash rang through my ears, and I felt my body jerk back as Vinny dove underneath me, bringing me to the floor. 'What the fuck,' I whispered.

Dom was next to us, and we huddled on the rug, glass from the broken window covering us and everything else.

'Have they ever done that before?' Vinny asked Dom, who shook his head.

'First time.'

'What happened?' I asked, although I didn't really need an answer. I'd heard gunshots before, and that window hadn't broken on its own. 'Who the hell did that?'

Neither Dom nor Vinny said anything. I started moving my leg. 'Can we get up now?' I asked.

Vinny shook his head. 'Whoever it is didn't leave yet,' he said, and I noticed for the first time that there was a gun in his hand.

There was one in Dom's hand, too. Where the hell did those come from? I saw my purse sitting on the couch. If it had been within reach, we could all be armed. But I was better off this way, since I'd never actually fired a gun outside the shooting range.

I heard footsteps coming up the front steps, heavy, boot-clad feet. I wished Dom hadn't put out as much rock salt as he had; if he hadn't, maybe the guy would've slipped and fallen on the concrete.

'Annie, on the count of three, we're getting up and running down the hall toward the bedrooms.' Vinny's voice was low, hurried. 'You up for this?'

Did I have a choice? The footsteps were almost to the top of the steps.

'One, two, three!'

Vinny, Dom, and I scrambled to our feet, glass crunching under our boots, and we shot through the dining room and toward the back of the house. Another bullet crashed through the dining room window as we ran, and I ducked into the first room I saw, which was the bathroom. Vinny and Dom bounded in after me. Vinny looked around quickly, then said quietly, 'Get in the tub.'

Seemed like a good idea to me, too. So I stepped in, hoping the tiles would protect me if someone decided to shoot through the wall.

I don't think I took a breath the entire time.

I brought my hand up to my face and started to brush my hair back, but Vinny's hand stopped me.

'Don't touch it,' he said. 'You're covered in glass.'

I saw then that he, too, and Dom were shimmering because of the slivers of glass on them. The two of them were perched by the door, their guns pointed out into the hall. The footsteps had stopped somewhere in the living room.

Vinny peered around the door, and I heard another shot, then another. I sank into the tub, my arms around my chest.

That's when I heard the sirens. They were faint at first, I could barely hear them, but they got louder and louder. The footsteps started again, but they were getting quieter and quieter.

'Jesus, he's going to get away,' Vinny muttered, and he ran into the hall, his gun leading the way. Dirty Harry didn't have anything on him. His footsteps got quieter, too, as he ran through the house.

The sirens were now screaming through my ears. I looked up at Dom, who had a bored look on his face.

'This sort of shit happen here all the time?' I asked.

'Had to be the guy next door who called the cops,' Dom said. 'He never knows when to mind his own business.' He held out his hand to me and helped me out of the tub. I left little glass shavings behind.

'Don't worry about that. I've got a cleaning woman,' Dom said as we went back out into the hall. I saw he'd brushed off his own head and shoulders.

Vinny was standing on the front porch, talking to two uniformed cops. His hair still shone with glass, but his gun was gone, stashed somewhere on his person, I was sure.

'Mustang,' I heard Vinny said. That's right, that was the kind of car it was. I wasn't very good about identifying cars. They all looked alike to me.

I recognized one of the cops. It was Ronald Berger, the cop who'd responded to Pete Amato's accident. He saw me, his eyes wide with surprise. 'What the hell are you doing here?' he asked through the hole in the window.

I shrugged. 'I always like a good party.'

Dom started chuckling.

'Don't encourage her,' Berger said. 'She's in a shitload of trouble.'

I frowned. 'I am?'

'Don't tell me you don't know the FBI's been asking questions about you, your father's wanted for questioning, and now this.'

So it'd been a bad day. I had a lot of those.

Berger turned back to Vinny. 'You don't have a license plate number, there isn't even any proof anyone else was here. The old man's got a gun. Sure he didn't shoot the window out himself?'

'If you got some crime scene guys here, you'd find out that the window was shot from the outside in, not the inside out. And it's too cold for anyone to go outside to shoot in the window when it could be done easily and comfortably from that chair over there.' Vinny pointed to the Barcalounger across from us. When he moved, some of the glass shavings flittered to the ground like snow.

'I don't like your attitude,' Berger said.

Oh, Christ, we were all going to end up in jail.

'Are you going to charge anyone with anything?' I asked.

Berger and his partner took a long look around, at the broken window, at the scattered glass shavings on Vinny and Dom and me, at the gun in Dom's hand. They looked at each other and sighed. 'We could charge you with breach of peace,' Berger said, 'but this is too crazy to try to explain.' He paused. 'But we have to file a report.'

It took about half an hour, with each of us telling the story of the unknown assailant who escaped. Berger was very matter-of-fact about it and told me when I asked that I could pick up a copy of the report in the morning. He shook Dom's hand, scowled at Vinny, and went back outside, stepping over the debris from the window.

I saw the neighbor across the street run to the cops as they climbed back into their patrol car. He argued for a few minutes, but then the cops drove away. The neighbor glared up at the house.

'I gotta call someone to come over and get this patched up quick,' Dom said. 'Think it's going to snow again.' He went into the kitchen to make his call.

Vinny started picking glass out of my hair again. 'You're covered in this.'

'So are you.'

'You know, this is all your fault.'

'Mine?'

'You should've gone home and locked the doors like Madame Shara said to.'

I frowned at Vinny. 'You're lucky I'm still talking to you after that . . . '

My voice trailed off as I heard something else, something muffled, coming from behind a door just a few feet down the hall. Vinny put his hand to his lips and pulled his gun out from under his jacket. He took two steps toward the door, which had started to open.

I stepped backward, away from the door, and Vinny pointed his gun at it. His finger tickled the trigger but stopped when we saw who it was.

'And I thought I only had the cops to worry about,' my father said as he stepped into the hall.

24

You were here the whole time?' I wanted to kill him myself.

He smiled sheepishly. 'When I heard the shooting, I figured I should stay put. I knew Vinny could take care of it.'

I snorted. He'd taken care of it all right. Before I could say anything I might regret, Dom came out of the kitchen with a tray of glasses and a bottle of wine. A man after my own heart. 'I thought we could use a drink,' he said, understatement of the year.

He poured, and I took a sip of the red liquid. It wasn't what I was used to. It was sweeter and had an unusual but not unpleasant flavor. 'What's this?' I asked.

Dom smiled. 'My own wine. I make it in the basement.' When he caught my confused look, the smile grew into a grin. 'My dear, all us old-timers make our own wine. That's how we beat Prohibition.'

Vinny chuckled, and Dom looked at him. 'What's so funny?'

'New Haven never honored Prohibition. My grandmother told me that on any day after the Winchester factory let out, there were five or six bars running openly downtown. Wasn't Connecticut one state that didn't ratify the amendment?'

Dom was nodding. 'You know your history. Your grandmother taught you well.'

We drank quietly for a few minutes.

'So who was the shooter?' my father finally asked.

Vinny shook his head. 'I don't know. We didn't see him. My question is, though, who was he after?' He looked from Dom to me to my father. 'Dom, well, we know people are after him. And someone threatened Annie anonymously. And you' — his gaze lingered on my father for a long minute — 'you are a wanted man. But do you know something that we don't?'

My father smiled and took a long drink from his glass before answering. 'I want to clear my name, and Sal's name, and then I want to go back to the desert.'

'Do you know what happened to Sal's money?' I asked. 'The money for the renovations that disappeared?'

My father gave me a look, one that said, *How the hell did you find out about the money?*

'I know about it, okay, so where did it go?'

'I don't know.' My father took another long drink from his glass, but I saw him glance at

Dom for a second. They both knew something, that was for sure.

'What about the people Sal was paying protection to?'

My father's eyes slid from me to Vinny, but I stayed mum. Dom shifted in his seat a little, and he and my father exchanged another glance. This time I noticed Vinny caught it, too.

It was a few seconds before Dad spoke again. 'Sal was having some financial problems.'

That was pretty goddamn vague. Vinny was watching Dom, who was running his thumb around the rim of his glass over and over, his eyes following it. Vinny placed his empty glass on the coffee table and looked at my father. 'Did Sal explain to you what his financial problem was? Did he mention the missing money?'

Another look between my father and Dom. When Dad looked back at Vinny, his expression was apologetic. 'The loan money wasn't the only money that had gone missing lately.'

We were as quiet as a fucking graveyard as we pondered that for a few seconds, until I had another thought, one that complicated things even more.

'Was it the Mob's?' I asked softly.

No one said anything, but I saw my father and Dom exchange a look that indicated I could be right. Maybe LeeAnn took the money Sal owed them for protection, and that's why she was killed. But if the fire was set to cover up her murder, why would the Mob want to burn down a property they were making money off of?

'LeeAnn was some sort of courier,' I said matter-of-factly.

'Where did you hear that?' my father demanded, his eyes flashing. I could see I'd surprised him.

I wouldn't look at Vinny. I didn't want to give him up. 'Heard it around,' I said as calmly as I could, even though I was certain everyone could hear my heart beating, sort of like in that Edgar Allan Poe story where the guy goes insane after he hides the body under the floorboards. Yeah, that was me. Crazy as a fucking fox.

Dom cleared his throat, took a sip of wine, then leaned toward me. It was all I could do not to pull away. 'My dear, you can't believe everything you hear.'

'Got it on a good source,' I said, not taking my eyes off Dom's.

He smiled. But he underestimated me. I always won staring contests. He could ask my dad.

'Did she get killed because of it?' I asked when he didn't say anything.

He shook his head and finally looked at my father. 'I don't know.'

And in that, he confirmed my worst fears: that LeeAnn might have been killed because of her connection to Sal's operation and that same person may have been the one who had just blown out Dom's window.

'Why would someone come here and try to kill us?' I asked no one in particular.

Vinny glanced at the shattered window, and no one said anything.

We heard a bad muffler pull up in front of the house, and three guys in grungy jackets, jeans, and work boots clumped up the stairs.

Dom got up. 'Hi, guys. This is the window.'

'No shit,' said one of them, eyeing the damage. 'What the fuck happened here?' He saw me then and quickly said, 'Sorry.'

He had no way of knowing he was apologizing to the wrong fucking person.

'That's okay,' I said, not surprised at the speed of service afforded Dom. He commanded a lot of respect, and getting his shot-out window fixed certainly was a favor being returned. If it were me, I'd still be waiting two weeks from now.

They surveyed the window frame and pulled out the glass pieces still stuck inside.

Dom picked up the tray. 'Let's go into the dining room,' he said, and we followed.

'I might be able to find the money,' Vinny said when we were out of earshot.

'How the hell are you going to do that?' Dom asked.

Vinny smiled. 'I have my ways.'

I rolled my eyes at him. 'Show-off.' I grinned at Dom. 'He thinks he's some sort of computer genius.'

Dom frowned. 'Really? You can find this out on the computer? I'd like to see how you do that.'

'I can show you sometime,' Vinny said.

My father laughed. 'Don't encourage him. That's all we need, Dom using a computer to break into bank accounts.'

Vinny smiled, turning to me.

'Annie, I'll bring you back to your car,' Vinny said, then he turned to my father. 'I guess you'll stay here.'

My father nodded. 'Let me know what you find out.'

He gave me a kiss, and Vinny and I went out to the Explorer. Neither of us said anything as we rode back over the bridge. But my stomach interrupted our silence. Vinny grinned. 'I'm hungry, too,' he said. 'Where should we stop?'

'I don't care. Anywhere.'

'Indian?'

It was perfect weather for Indian food, and Vinny steered the SUV off the Route 34 connector and down Church Street before turning left on Chapel Street toward Tandoor. Snow was falling again, lightly, dusting the windshield.

'Do you really think you can find the money?' I asked. 'You weren't just bullshitting back there, were you?'

Vinny eased into a parking spot right in front of the restaurant, which used to be a diner, with its stereotypical silver siding. He stared straight ahead for a few minutes, and I could see his eyelashes in the light from the streetlamp. Finally he turned to me and smiled. 'Yeah, Annie, I think I can find this out. It's my job to do this sort of stuff.'

'Okay, I was just checking,' I said lightly, although I hoped it didn't take him too long or we'd all end up dead. I thought a second, then added, 'I think LeeAnn was ripping off the Mob. I think she may have taken some of that money she was supposed to deliver. I think that's why she got killed.'

'It's a pretty good theory.' Vinny cocked his head at me. 'Thanks for not telling them how you found out about LeeAnn.'

'I told you I could keep a secret.'

Vinny grinned as he opened the door and

climbed out of the Explorer. 'You know,' he said as we crossed the street, 'when we were talking about New Haven's Prohibition history?'

I nodded.

'What I didn't say was that the Mob first moved into New Haven by taking control of the sugar and grapes.' He paused. 'The two things those people needed to make their wine.'

We ordered a couple of Kingfishers and way too much food, losing ourselves in rogan josh, tandoori chicken, and a shrimp birayni, swishing our naan around in the remnants on our plates. We were too hungry to talk, and when we were done, it hit us both at the same time that under different circumstances, this could've been a date.

'Is Rosie going to mind you being out this long?' I asked him.

Vinny shrugged and took another swig of his beer. 'My job's not conventional, she knows that.'

'But she doesn't like it, does she?'

Vinny smiled sadly. 'She hates my job. She wants me to teach. She's got some sort of weird idea that I should get a job as a professor at Yale.'

I couldn't see it. Yeah, maybe when he was the dorky kid in high school, but not now. He wasn't college professor material; he'd have to trade in that incredibly sexy leather jacket and gun for a cardigan and a piece of chalk.

'What about going back to your research?' I could definitely see him out on a boat — it was so George Clooney and *The Perfect Storm*.

Vinny smiled then, a wide grin that took over his face and spread into his eyes. 'If I wasn't doing this, I would be doing that.' He reached across the table and took my hand, which was resting next to my glass.

The heat from his hand moved up my arm and through my body. Even Tom had never had this effect on me. I pulled my hand away. 'We'd better go,' I said curtly, standing.

We didn't talk on the way back to Big Tony's to pick up my car, but I could feel his eyes on me every now and then.

'Thanks for dinner and the ride,' I said as I climbed out of the SUV. I'd argued that I should pay half the check, but he wouldn't take it.

I started getting into my car when I heard, 'Annie, wait.'

I paused as Vinny came up to me; he brushed his hand along my cheek, moving my hair back. My whole body felt like it was on fire, even though it was about twenty degrees outside. 'I'll call you tomorrow,' he said right before I closed the door and sped out of the lot.

★ ★ ★

The phone started to ring the moment I put the key in the lock. I swung the door open, bounded across the living room, and picked it up.

'Yeah?' Phone etiquette isn't always my thing.

'What the hell is going on with you, Annie?' Tom's voice was angry, angrier than I'd heard it for a long time. 'Where have you been? I've been trying to reach you for two hours.'

'What do you mean?' I took off my coat, kicked the door shut, and plopped down on the couch. 'I was out having dinner.'

'Involved in a shooting, at Dominic Gaudio's house? Jesus Christ, what the hell is going on with you?'

'I didn't know we were going to get shot at. It's not like I put an ad in the fucking paper or anything.' I needed another beer. I took the phone over to the refrigerator and pulled out a Heineken. Even though I was shivering a little, the cold liquid moved down my throat and warmed me.

'You're like a goddamn train wreck, you know that? Why the hell I ever got involved with you is beyond me.'

'You were taken in by my natural charm.'

'I was temporarily insane.'

'For a year?'

He was quiet for a minute. 'Did you find your father?' he asked softly, but I could still hear the steel in his voice.

'No,' I said, not wanting to hesitate and give him any more ammunition.

'You'd better be telling me the truth.'

'I am, I am,' I insisted.

How could I explain to him that my father, while possibly dangerous, was one of the most gentle people I'd ever known? That I missed him so much when he was gone that even though all this shit was happening, he at least was here and I could see him. I couldn't tell him that. It was way too corny. And he knew I certainly wasn't corny.

Horny, well, now, that was another story. But the way things were going, it was going to be like that for a while and I'd have to get used to it.

I hated it when things didn't go my way.

'I heard none of you even saw the guy,' Tom said, and I heard the words he didn't say: so we can't catch him. He was still out there somewhere, and I was sitting on my couch, drinking a beer as if I didn't have a fucking care in the world.

It was Sunday night and *The Sopranos* were due. I hung up with Tom after promising to keep him informed if anything else happened, and I turned on the TV. Cable TV is my luxury item; even if I was broke, I'd still find a way to get it. The show wasn't on yet, so I went into the bedroom, put on my flannel pajamas, washed my face, and settled in front of the TV.

Maybe I did watch too much TV, but what the hell else was I supposed to do? I had books I kept meaning to read, but after a long day chasing after cop cars and fire trucks and seeing way too much death and destruction, I needed to veg out, to let someone else do the thinking for me.

And I was doing just that when the buzzer startled me.

Dick Whitfield stood on my stoop.

I could pretend I wasn't home. But he must have seen my lights and me moving around. This wasn't good.

I buzzed him in, and I held open the door as he came up the stairs.

'Hey,' he said as he walked into my living room. I didn't like having him here.

'Make it quick,' I said. *The Sopranos* was starting, and I didn't want to miss anything. I hadn't set up the VCR, so I needed to catch it now. Who knew if I'd be around when they replayed it during the week.

His eye caught the TV. '*The Sopranos?*' It looked like he was going to get comfortable, and I moved between him and the TV, still standing so he wouldn't get any idiotic ideas, like that he was welcome and could sit down.

'What's up?' I asked.

'I was just over across the square,' he started.

'Are you crazy? Mac'll file a restraining order against you. Do you really want that?'

He shook his head. 'No, no, she wasn't home.'

'Then what's the problem?'

He sniffed and bit his lip, looking down at the floor.

'Dick,' I said, 'what the hell's going on?' I realized I was standing there in my flannel pajamas that had little blue clouds and stars on them. It really wasn't a good thing that Dick Whitfield saw me in my jammies.

He sighed and looked back up at me. 'I don't know how to say this.'

'Just tell me,' I said sternly, knocking him out of his trance.

He blinked a couple of times before speaking. 'I saw something over there.' He paused.

'Spit it out.'

'You know they're looking for your father, right?'

I nodded, wishing he'd just get to the point.

'Well, I just saw him over there, and he had a gun in his hand.'

'How do you know it was my father? I don't remember you two meeting,' I said skeptically.

Dick rolled his eyes at me. 'He was at the restaurant, you know, after you found Sal. I saw him there with you. The detective pointed him out to me.'

Okay, so he probably had seen my father. I just knew that no formal introductions had been made.

'So where was this person with the gun, exactly?'

Dick leaned a little to look out my window. 'Over near the Amatos' house, along the side.'

'What the hell were you doing over there?'

'Nothing.' But his blush gave him away. I had to give him credit for not backing down, but it was still stupid of him to be over there.

'Why would my father sneak around with a gun out?' I asked, more of myself than of Dick.

'There wasn't anyone home,' Dick repeated.

I left Dick standing in my living room as I went into the bedroom and pulled off my pajama bottoms and put on my jeans. Tony Soprano was going to have to wait.

'You're still wearing your pajamas,' Dick said as I came back out, threw a scarf around my neck, and put on my boots. The puffy coat was going back outside, a little less puffy, but it would still keep me warm.

'Just the top,' I growled. 'You better be wrong about this.'

25

It was still snowing, harder now than when I'd gotten home, and I could feel my hair getting wet. Next it would start freezing, and I'd have icicles hanging from my head.

I really hoped he was wrong. I hoped whoever it was just maybe looked like my father in a certain light but certainly was not my father. It wasn't too long ago I'd left him at Dom's, and it hadn't seemed like he was planning to go out anywhere.

We crossed the street and hopped over the small fence at the square. I looked up at the statue of Christopher Columbus. I never really paid much attention to it, it was just there, like a piece of furniture that you always walk around but sometimes you bump into and notice every now and then.

I just walked around it; Dick was trying to keep up.

'So how's Cindy?' I asked, trying to act as though I didn't care what we were doing.

'She's great,' Dick panted from behind. 'We're going skiing in Vermont next weekend.'

Skiing? Dick didn't strike me as the athletic

type, but then I never thought he'd have a girlfriend, either.

We were getting close to the house. I started walking a little slower, and Dick caught up. The shadows were playing games with my eyes, and the snow wasn't helping much. We were next to the house, which was dark.

'Where was he?' I whispered.

Dick pointed to the other side of the house, and I tried to look all around me as I circled the front porch. There was no one I could see anywhere.

'You must have imagined it,' I said out loud, my voice startling both me and Dick, who jumped.

'I know I saw him,' he insisted.

I shook my head. 'No, Dick, there's no one here, and if he'd been here, we would've seen him leave as we crossed the park.'

I turned, and from somewhere behind the house a loud noise echoed through the trees and made me freeze. Dick grabbed my arm. 'What was that?' he whispered.

It was most definitely a gunshot, although it sounded like a much bigger gun than the one this afternoon. I could have been wrong, though. I'm not an expert on guns. Obviously, Dick wasn't, either.

Another shot rang out, and I pulled on

Dick's sleeve until we were both in the neighbor's driveway behind an old Dodge pickup. 'Can you tell where that's coming from?' I whispered.

Dick's head shook back and forth until I realized it wasn't going to stop. I put my hand on the top of his head to steady it.

'You're going to have to stay with me here, Dick,' I said.

He frowned. 'Why would someone be shooting at us?'

He really seemed to be curious about that, as though spying on someone and trespassing wouldn't cause that same person to feel slightly threatened and try something a little over the top. While I didn't like the position I was in, at least I could understand it.

Lights had gone on in the house next to us, and I could see two faces at the window. The shooting had stopped. I forced myself to stop thinking and listen. Silence. Except, maybe, someone slushing through the snow in back of Mac's house. Whoever it was was getting away, and I could hear sirens coming closer. I thought quickly about what was behind Mac and Sal's house. Another house on the street parallel to this one. I straightened up.

'I'm going through the back,' I whispered to Dick, who was crouched behind the truck bed. He might have been weeping.

'You're not leaving me alone here,' he said.

'The cops are coming. Tell them where I went and where I think the guy with the gun went.'

Dick pawed at my sleeve, and I tossed off his hand. 'He's gone, Dick, so get the fuck to the cops and tell them where he is.'

'You're crazy, you know that?' I heard him say as I went around the front of the truck and into the backyard behind the garage.

I might have been crazy to go after someone with a gun, but if it was my father, I had to help him. He could just disappear into the night, and I could tell the cops I never saw anyone. It was simple.

Like anything in my life is fucking simple.

I saw the figure a few feet ahead of me as I came around the garage in the yard behind the one I'd just left.

'Dad,' I whispered loudly. 'Dad!'

The figure stopped, not close enough to the streetlight for me to see his face, but the long coat swung around his body, and I could see the glint of metal in his hand.

'Dad!' I said again, louder this time.

I felt more than heard the next shot. Fortunately, he was not a good shot, and I fell to the ground as he turned again and ran down the street.

I hadn't gotten a good look at him, but I

didn't think my father would actually shoot at me.

'What the hell are you doing?' Tom's voice crashed into my head, and I looked up from the snowy mess I was lying in.

I pointed to the street as I got up. 'He went that way.' I felt like I was in a bad western.

'The shooter?'

I nodded. Tom shouted to a couple of uniforms to go down the street and called a car on his radio to reroute it in that direction. I was brushing snow off my coat as he turned back to face me. 'What are you doing out here?' he asked harshly.

'Dick thought it was my dad.'

'What?'

I told him how Dick had come to my apartment and what he'd said. I related the rest of the story without leaving anything out.

'So you decided to follow a guy who was shooting at you? What the hell do you have, a death wish?'

It still hadn't sunk in what I'd done, but hearing him say that made me start shivering. And it wasn't because the snow had soaked through my jeans. 'I thought if it was my father . . . ' My voice trailed off.

'You could help him,' Tom finished. He sighed. 'I can't fault you for that. But I don't think your father would shoot at you.' He paused. 'I saw you less when we were dating.'

Two figures were stomping through the snow back to us. By now the entire neighborhood had lit up like a goddamn Christmas tree, and I could see their faces, drawn and disappointed.

'We'll get him,' one of the officers said to me on their way back to their cruiser. Tom hadn't moved yet, which indicated that maybe he wasn't done with me, so I stood my ground.

'I'm going to put someone outside your building,' Tom said finally. 'You don't seem to see that you're in danger, and this way, maybe, we can keep you alive. Because if not, one of these times the bullet's going to hit you.'

I caught my breath.

He was nodding. 'This is real life, Annie. This isn't make-believe. And I won't let you die.'

Death. There it was, out in the open. Something that always happened to someone else, something I just wrote about. I'd never really contemplated my own death before. I guess I was just too stupid to do that. It was easier to get through life if you didn't think about it.

He was talking. 'I'll walk you back, but then I need to find out where Mac and Pete are and why someone would be lurking around their house with a gun.'

'Mac's at my mother's,' a familiar voice said behind us.

We turned to see Vinny standing in the snow, his hands in the pockets of his leather jacket. 'I don't know where Pete is,' he added.

Tom eyed Vinny for a second. 'Can you walk her back to her place and make sure she locks the door?'

'No problem.'

They were talking as if I weren't there, and I guess I wasn't in some way. It was all sinking in way too fast, everything that had happened during the day.

I let Vinny take my arm.

'See ya,' I said to Tom, but he was already gone. 'He's going to have someone watch me,' I told Vinny.

'Good idea.'

I looked around for Dick and spotted him talking to a cop near Mac's house. I walked over, with Vinny the Shadow right next to me.

'You okay?' I asked Dick.

His eyes were wide, and he was looking at me as if I were a stranger. 'You're really crazy,' he said again.

Tell me something I don't already know.

'I'm going home,' I said. 'Are you going to be okay?'

He was shaking his head. 'Just go already. I don't need your shit.'

Dick Whitfield swore at me. He was actually rude to me. I should write this date down for posterity. He was getting some balls. Go figure. I wanted to congratulate him, give him a high-five, for finally starting on the road to becoming a cynical reporter, but this wasn't exactly the time for that. I'd have to catch him at the paper tomorrow.

Vinny and I were quiet for a couple of minutes as we walked, but suddenly he stopped in the middle of the park. 'Dick thought he saw your father?'

'Yeah. Weird.'

Vinny looked around quickly, then ran a hand through his hair. I wasn't sure I was going to like what was coming.

'Remember, your father isn't the only one who came to town.'

I frowned.

'Your father's tall, dark, Italian. Dick thought that's who he saw — '

'Jesus Christ,' I interrupted. 'Who is it, Vinny?'

He shook his head. 'I'm not sure. All I know is, someone else is here. That's all your father would tell me. He asked me to keep an eye on you.'

A thought dawned. The guy who jumped

me. The one who told me to stop asking questions. I shivered under my puffy coat, and not because I was cold. 'But why would this guy shoot at me? I thought they wouldn't go after me like that; you said so.'

Vinny rubbed his forehead. 'I don't know. It's just speculation.'

'Why would someone with a gun be at Mac's?'

'He's looking for his money.' Vinny's voice was flat.

'It's good Mac's at your parents.' I looked back at the house behind us, the lights on the cop cars reflecting off the snow. 'Where's Pete?'

Vinny shrugged. 'Beats me.'

'Maybe we should go talk to Mac. She probably knows where he is. Pete might not be safe with a guy running around with a gun.'

But Vinny was one step ahead of me, and he'd already taken my arm and was walking me briskly across the park. 'Do we have to worry about Mac's restraining order against you?' he asked as we crossed Chapel and trotted over to Wooster Street.

'There's no restraining order. It was just a threat.'

We made our way down Wooster Street. Vinny's parents lived upstairs from their pizza place, which was down near Tre Scalini.

We slipped into the back near the kitchen and to the door to the upstairs. Vinny let me step into the hallway first, and he closed the door after me. He hit a switch, and a dim light went on up near another door at the top of the stairs. We climbed up, slowly. The day's events had taken a toll on both of us.

The kitchen was warm, lit only by a light over the stove. Vinny moved ahead of me.

'Hey, Mom,' he called out.

Mrs. DeLucia and Mac were sitting in the living room, Mrs. DeLucia in a rocking chair and Mac on the flower covered sofa.

'Hi,' I said quietly.

They glared at me.

'Mom, before you say anything, Annie was just over at Mac's house, and someone fired some shots at her over there, but he got away through the backyard. Do you know of any reason why someone would do that?'

Mac's face was blank, but I could see her eyes taking in Vinny's words. Mrs. DeLucia waited for her.

Surprisingly, Mac lifted her chin at me and patted the sofa next to her, as though she wanted me to sit down. So I did. She looked into my face. 'Annie, I know you've been doing your job, but why don't you just leave well enough alone?' Her voice was soft, calm.

Not at all like someone who just found out about a man with a gun outside her house.

Vinny noticed that, too. 'Mac, you heard what I said, didn't you?'

'You're mistaken, Vinny.' Mac looked at him now. 'Pete is at the house.'

'Well, you're going to have a couple of cops over here in a few minutes asking you a lot of questions about this,' Vinny said. 'Unless Pete is sleeping or sitting in the dark, he's not home.'

'Vinny, dear, Pete has been home all night.'

Vinny looked at me and shrugged.

Mrs. DeLucia got up. 'Why don't you two come into the kitchen and help me get some tea.' It wasn't a question; it was definitely an order. We followed her.

'Mac's doctor was here just a little while ago, and he gave her something to calm her down. She's been a wreck ever since the restaurant burned down, and then Sal and all . . . ' Mrs. DeLucia's eyes lingered on mine for a few seconds. 'Anyway, she's been staying with us the last two nights. Pete isn't being much help, unfortunately. He's been drinking a lot.'

'We're a little worried about Pete. Especially with that guy out there,' Vinny said.

His mother was quiet for a couple of seconds, then she looked from Vinny to me and back to Vinny. I could see in her face that she knew why we were worried, but all she said was, 'Pete's a big boy. He knows what to do.'

I stayed quiet. A very ugly thought was forming in my head, and I didn't like it. I knew for sure that no one in this house would like it, either. Vinny seemed oblivious, and this was the first time I actually wanted him to read my mind. So we could get the hell out of there and figure out what we were going to do.

'How close was Pete with LeeAnn?' I asked Mrs. DeLucia.

'I don't know about that,' she said, but she was playing with her cuticle and wouldn't meet my eyes.

I smiled, trying not to be condescending. 'Mrs. DeLucia, of course you do. It could be important.'

Her eyes moved up to my face. 'That's none of your business.'

Vinny took my arm. 'Okay, we have to get going. Sorry about this,' he said to his mother. But she pulled him back as we started down the hall.

'What are you doing with her?' Mrs. DeLucia's voice was a stage whisper; she wanted me to hear what she was saying.

Vinny glanced back at me and then looked

at his mother. 'It's just work, Ma.'

'Bullshit.'

I stared at a picture on the wall of two kids on ponies.

'Okay, maybe it's more than work,' Vinny was conceding. I bit my lip as I eavesdropped. 'I have to talk to Rosie first. Then you'll know what's going on.' He leaned over and kissed her cheek and came back to me.

We went back through the kitchen and down to the restaurant. I didn't want to ask him about what he'd said; he'd tell me in his own time. 'Who were the kids in the picture?' I asked instead.

'Me and my brother, Rocco. He's a writer, he's in Europe right now.'

I wanted to ask more about Rocco, but we had more pressing issues at the moment. I set the pace, and we hurried down the street and around to my building. At the door, I fumbled a second with my keys before fitting the right one in the lock.

As I turned the doorknob, Vinny put his fingers under my chin and turned my face toward him.

'What's up?' he asked.

I sighed. 'I know who it is. I know who killed LeeAnn.'

26

So what's up, Sherlock Holmes?' Vinny asked as I pulled my face away from his hand and went into my building.

He followed me all the way into my apartment, and it was killing him that I still hadn't told him anything else. I pulled two beers out of the fridge. I was going to get drunk if I wasn't careful, but I needed another one after getting shot at again.

'So are you going to tell me, Nancy Drew?' Vinny asked after taking a long drink from his bottle. I wondered how many literary detectives he would go through before I said anything.

'You're not going to like it,' I warned.

'So fucking tell me already.' He was getting pissed.

'Think about it, Vinny. Think about everything.'

He smiled weakly. 'It's been a long day, Annie, too long for riddles.'

'No, really, Vinny, think about what your mother said.'

He drank about half his beer in one swallow before answering, then put down the bottle and stared at me. 'No, Annie. That's ridiculous.'

'Why?'

'Because he wouldn't do that. He isn't like that.'

'He can get violent. You know that.'

Vinny's face was drawn. 'I've known him all my life.'

'So have I.'

'Why would Pete kill LeeAnn?' Vinny asked.

'I'm not sure why, but I think they were having an affair.'

Vinny shook his head. 'She wasn't having an affair with anyone. I told you that.'

'Not last summer. But before that? And after? You said yourself that you stopped trailing her after the farmers' market closed. And what about that kiss you saw him give her in Malone's?'

Vinny was quiet a second, then: 'Do you think he killed Sal, too?'

I shrugged. 'I don't know, but he was too broken up about LeeAnn, too quick to condemn Mickey.'

'What about Mickey? Say Pete and LeeAnn were having an affair. Mickey could've found out about the affair and killed her, like the cops think.' He was playing devil's advocate, but he was right about that. Maybe I was making this too complicated. 'And you forget there's an unidentified party out there,' Vinny reminded me. 'He could be the one who killed Sal, not Pete. And what about your theory that LeeAnn was killed because she was ripping off the Mob's money?'

'Maybe Pete found out, too. Maybe that was part of it. Maybe he didn't like it that she was ripping off his father, too.'

We both stared at each other for a few seconds, letting that sink in.

Vinny stared at me a second before asking, 'Where's your computer?'

My laptop was in the bedroom. He followed me as I went to get it. I grabbed it off the dresser, and we both turned to face the bed, which was unmade as usual. He hesitated for a second, grinning, before taking the laptop and going back into the living room with it. In minutes, he'd plugged it into the phone jack and was dialing up the Internet.

'You should get a cable modem,' Vinny complained as we waited for the server to boot up.

'Yeah, right. I don't need that here, I've got it at work. I don't make a lot of money, you know.' I sipped my beer as Vinny punched the keys. 'Jesus, don't pound on it. It's new,' I said.

'Don't worry,' he said absently as he stared at the screen.

I peered over his shoulder at the screen. Bank records for Prego. How the hell did he get in there?

'When Sal was missing, Mac gave me access to some of their documents,' Vinny said. 'I made sure I got passwords, just in case I might need them.'

'Just in case,' I repeated. 'And you committed them to memory. Just in case.'

He looked up at me and smiled, that slow, sexy smile I'd come to know so well. 'Yeah,' he drawled.

He stared at the screen, hit a few more keys. 'What the hell is this?' he muttered.

'What?'

'The money for those renovations went in and then it went right back out. Cash.'

That confirmed what Tom had told me.

'We know the Mob works with cash,' I reminded him. 'Anything else there?'

'I need to poke around a little more, and your computer's just too slow.' Vinny glanced at his watch at the same time I looked at the clock on the wall. Eleven o'clock.

'Where do you think Pete is?' I asked.

'I don't know.' I could see the worry etched into his forehead. 'I don't want to leave you here alone.'

Any other time I might think that was a maneuver to stay, but I knew better. 'Don't worry about me. Tom said someone would be watching the building.' I went to the window and looked down at the cop car parked in front of my building.

Vinny came up behind me. I could feel him, and he wasn't even touching me.

'Will *you* be okay?' I asked, turning to face him.

He smiled, but I could still see his concern. 'I've got a gun, remember?'

I could smell his aftershave. He had to leave. 'Call me in the morning,' I said.

'I remember you in high school,' he said quietly.

'Really?' I asked.

'I bet you don't remember me.'

'Sure I do.' Somewhere in the recesses of my memories, I saw him, an armload full of books, passing me in the hall.

Vinny chuckled. 'I was a geek.'

I smiled. 'Yeah.'

'And you, well, you . . . ' His voice trailed off as he put his hand on my cheek. It was warm.

'So you had a crush on me?' I asked quietly.

'Yeah, yeah, I guess so.'

'I wish I'd known.'

'You know now.'

'But it might be too late.'

He smiled and let his hand fall. 'It's never too late.' He grabbed his jacket from the chair and shrugged into it. 'I have a lot of work to do. I've got a fast modem. I'd be waiting hours for stuff to come up on your computer.'

After he left, I turned to stare at my empty apartment. I peered into my refrigerator and saw I had no beer left. I'd have to get to the supermarket tomorrow. I went into the bedroom and put my pajama bottoms back on, grabbed the comforter, went into the living room, and switched on the TV.

I fell asleep watching some stupid movie on HBO with Brad Pitt.

*   *   *

The sounds of gunshots rang through my head, and I lurched forward, my heart pounding. The TV was still on, and now it was an Al Pacino flick. Sunlight streamed through my windows and danced against my face, causing me to squint at the clock on the VCR: 8:00 A.M. The longest fucking day I'd ever lived had been followed by the shortest fucking night. And now I had to get myself put together, because Mickey Hayward was going to be arraigned and I'd be damned if I missed that.

The sunlight somehow made life seem a little more livable again. So did the long hot shower. As I pulled on a pair of wool slacks and a turtleneck, I wondered if Vinny had been successful with his computer. I itched to call him, but he might be sleeping now, and I didn't want to wake him. His day had been as long as mine.

He'd probably show at the arraignment, anyway.

The phone rang as I was putting on my coat.

'I need to see you.' It was my father.

'I'm heading to court, Mickey's arraignment,' I said.

'I need to see you,' he repeated, and I stopped digging in my pockets for my gloves. There was something funny about his voice.

'Are you okay?' I asked.

'Are you?'

'Sure.' I glanced out the window and saw that the cop car was still there. 'I've got the cops watching me.'

'Lose them,' he said. 'I need to see you.'

I glanced at the clock. I didn't have a helluva lot of time, but it sounded urgent. 'Okay. Where?'

'You can't lead the cops here.'

'I know, I know.' Although I wasn't exactly sure how I was going to ditch them.

'Remember when you were a kid and you were scared, and we had hot chocolate and I said it would make you invincible?'

'Like Wonder Woman.' If the FBI was listening in somehow, they would have no fucking clue. But I did. I remembered it as if it were yesterday.

'I'm where you lost the pink laces.' Still pretty cryptic, but I knew just where to go.

'I'll be there as soon as I can.'

Now I had to get rid of the cop. Tom wouldn't like that, but he wasn't liking much these days, so I didn't feel too bad about it.

As I bounded down the stairs, I met Amber on the landing. Her puffy coat could rival mine.

She stared at me coldly. 'Have any meat today?' she practically hissed.

I remembered the chicken and lamb at Tandoor and almost smiled, but somehow it didn't seem like it would go over that well. 'How's the picketing?'

She sighed. 'They're gone now anyway, killed in cold blood. But at least we got the TV stations out. Maybe that'll stop even more suffering.'

I tried to wrap my head around what she was saying, but it was so stupid, it was hard. 'I don't know that this'll keep people from eating chicken, Amber,' I said quietly.

Her eyes lit up with anger. 'It's not just eating chicken, Annie.' Her voice rose with each word. 'It's how they've exploited those poor harmless creatures.' She turned on her heel and went out the front door and down the steps.

This poultry business had gotten way out of hand.

'You've been upsetting her.' Walter the Pit Bull was coming up on my ass. Great.

'She's too sensitive,' I tried, but Walter glared.

'You should try being polite.' He swept past me.

I'd thought about moving a lot more lately, and maybe it was time. Maybe I needed to find a house, one that I could have all to myself and not have to worry about pesky neighbors.

I waited a few minutes before I went down the steps, since I didn't want any more confrontations. I needed to go meet my dad.

I walked up to the cruiser and smiled at the cop at the wheel. Usually they traveled in twos, but I guess Tom didn't think this job would take more than one. 'Hi,' I said. 'I have to go to court, Mickey Hayward's arraignment.'

The cop smiled back. I didn't know him, he must be new. 'I'll follow you there.'

I shook my head. 'No, you really don't have to. It's daylight, I'm getting right into my car, you can watch me, but I think I can make it to the courthouse okay on my own. You've been here all night, right?'

The cop shook his head. 'I'm not supposed to leave you until my relief gets here.'

'When's that?'

He glanced at his watch. 'He's late.'

'Why don't you call him, tell him I'm at the courthouse and he can catch me there.' This could give me a little window of opportunity. 'Then you can head home and get some sleep. This must have been pretty boring for you.'

He was struggling with this, but I could see I was winning out. 'Okay, sure. I'll have him wait for you there.'

I smiled again, thanked him for a job well done, and went to my car. Surprise, surprise, it turned over right away, despite the cold. I'd thought about getting a new car, but these old Hondas just keep going. It seemed silly to invest in a new car and payments when this one was just fine and had been paid off for five years now.

I pulled away from the curb and waved at the cop, who headed in the opposite direction. I put in a Rolling Stones tape and started singing along.

When the song was over, I was halfway there. And my thoughts pushed the music aside as I remembered that day so long ago, when I was about seven and my dad took me ice skating. I wasn't very good. But my dad had taken me out and gotten me new skates; they were white with bright pink laces. While my dad was renting a pair for himself, he left me alone on the bench. Big mistake. I was a scrawny kid, and quickly a band of bigger girls sat down a little too close to me, jostling me and teasing me about my pink laces.

Before I knew it, the laces were out of the skates and the girls were laughing as they ran out of the building and into the parking lot.

I can still remember the puzzled look on my dad's face. His eyes followed mine into the far parking lot, and he sighed as he sat next to me.

'I'm sorry,' he said quietly.

He unlaced his rental skates and put the laces into mine, and he hobbled out onto the ice in his dress shoes, holding my hand as I tried to steady myself on the slippery surface. Afterward, he took me to the diner for hot chocolate and told me that it was going to make me stronger, that I would be like Wonder Woman someday, that I would be big enough not to take shit from anyone.

Okay, so it was a silly story. But it was something I'd never forgotten, and every once in a while I did feel like Wonder Woman.

I pulled into the parking lot at the Ralph Walker Ice Rink on State Street, glancing around for any telltale cop cars or a black Cadillac, but I didn't see any. I pulled way in the back of the lot and got out. The rink was outside, but it had a big red roof. My dad was leaning against the back side corner.

'Hey, Dad, what's up?' I asked.

But before he could answer, a battered blue pickup truck careened through the parking lot and slid toward us. Pete Amato threw open the door, a gun in his hand. 'I had a feeling you'd lead me to him,' he snarled at me.

27

My father grabbed my arm and dragged me around to the entrance of the rink. I heard some shots as we turned the corner, crouching behind the four-foot wooden wall. I didn't think it would deflect any bullets, and neither did my dad, because he yanked a metal chair next to us and slid it on the ice in front of us, giving us a little more protection. My father moved to our side of the entrance, pulling out a gun and pointing it in Pete's general direction, then firing off some return shots.

On reflex, I shouted, 'Jesus, Pete, what the hell are you doing?'

'I didn't want to hurt you, too, Annie.' Pete's bodyless voice floated from somewhere to our right. He was crouched below the wall like we were. 'But your father killed my father. You should know that. He has to pay for that.'

I turned and raised my eyebrows at my father, hoping he could clear this up.

That's when I saw the blood on the ice.

I looked myself over, but it wasn't me. But before I could ask my father if he was hurt, I heard footsteps going around the rink. All Pete had to do was stand up and we were goddamn sitting ducks. I crab-walked over to my father, trying not to slide too much — the ice was fucking cold and hard — and took my father's arm. He saw what I was doing and we turned the corner, so now we were on the outside of the rink, below the wall. If Pete stood up now, he wouldn't see us.

'You have to get out of here,' my father said gruffly, and I could see a red stain spreading across the white shirt under his overcoat.

'I can't leave you here alone.' I was barely aware I was speaking. All I could see was the blood and my dad's face, suddenly very gray and old.

'Where the hell is he?' I muttered. My heart was pounding so hard, I could barely hear myself.

'You can't see him?' My father's voice was urgent, and I could hear the pain he was in, which pushed me past my fear for a second.

'Why the hell did he do this?' I asked.

My father coughed, a wet sound that made me look at him more carefully. The stain was a little thicker, and who knew where he was bleeding from?

But before he could answer me, I heard

tires on gravel. I glanced behind me to see a black Cadillac moving into the parking lot. Fuck.

My father saw it at the same time. 'Get out of here,' he said, more urgently this time, his hand jerking upward toward my head.

But I froze as I watched the car move past us and out of sight around the back of the rink. Where Pete was. Where my father had pointed with his index finger, probably hoping that I hadn't noticed.

'Go now, Annie,' my father repeated huskily.

But I couldn't move. A lump rose in my throat and my chest constricted as I huddled against the side of the ice rink. I didn't want to know what was going on back there, even though I could hear car doors slam, pounding feet on hard ground, then a grunt as something landed on the ice.

I buried my head in my knees as I tried to flatten myself even further against the wall of the rink. I heard more grunts, a hoarse scream, some scuffling, more car doors slamming. Then the car moved swiftly past us.

But it wasn't over. There were footsteps near us; someone was running. I didn't lift my head. I didn't want to see anything or anyone, then I wouldn't be lying when I told the cops that I didn't know what had happened.

Another car door, an engine roared and gravel spat out from under the tires as a vehicle squealed out of the lot. I looked up. Pete's truck was gone.

My father groaned and tossed a cell phone toward me with one hand, the other still gripping his gun. 'Call 911,' he growled.

I crawled on the cold ice toward the phone, picked it up, and dialed. When the dispatcher answered, I told her we needed an ambulance, there was a shooting.

After I hung up, my father dropped the gun and his hand clutched my wrist. 'No one else was here, Annie.' His eyes were cold, dark, and I nodded. I'd had to face too many things about my father in the last few days. Things that I'd suspected through the years, but things I'd hoped weren't true.

'Did you do it?' I hated asking him, but I had to. 'Did you really kill Sal like Pete said?'

His eyes flickered with pain. 'No, Annie, I didn't. I don't know who killed Sal.'

'Where are they taking Pete?' I whispered.

'Who?' he asked, and I knew I wouldn't get anything out of him on that score. It really was like no one had been there, that ghosts had carted Pete Amato off in a black

Cadillac. But then he surprised me. 'Pete killed LeeAnn.'

'Vinny and I thought of that, but we didn't know why.'

'They had an affair. LeeAnn found out about Pete's gambling problem and that he'd been stealing from his father's operation to cover his debts. Problem was, most of the money he was taking didn't belong to him or Sal.'

So Pete, not LeeAnn, had been taking the protection money.

Dad's face was tight and drawn. 'Sal didn't need LeeAnn to tell him what was going on. He'd noticed less money coming in from the chickens, and when he heard about Pete's problem, it made sense to him. He tried talking to him, but Pete wouldn't listen. Sal knew if the wrong people found out what Pete was doing, they'd kill him.'

Shit.

'Sal called me, wanted to see if I could help. He took out that loan to cover the debt. But before I could get out here, Pete told LeeAnn their relationship was over. He didn't think it was a big deal, it had run its course, but LeeAnn took it hard and she threatened to rat him out if he left her.' His voice was getting raspier, but he didn't stop. 'They were both drunk, and Pete knew he was a dead man if she opened her mouth. LeeAnn was on the inside. He didn't think he had any choice but to kill her.

'But as soon as he did, he knew he'd fucked up. He went home and woke Sal up, admitted everything. It was Sal's idea to torch the place, frame Mickey. Sal told him to hang loose, pretend like nothing had happened, his debt would be covered.'

'But what about Sal? Why did he disappear?'

My father took a deep breath and coughed once before answering. 'He wanted to deflect any guilt from Pete. Hell, he's his son. I would've done the same for you.'

But I wouldn't have killed anyone.

'Sal called me that morning. That's why I came out so soon. Dom and I were going to have a sit-down with the New York representative, intervene on Sal's behalf, try to settle everything.'

I didn't want to know all that.

I could hear sirens somewhere in the distance.

'But then Sal was murdered.' His voice was barely audible. 'I knew that Pete thought I was sent here to get the money and to kill Sal. That's why he came after us at Dom's yesterday, because he thinks I killed his father and I was after him next.'

'Christ, this is all my fault. He followed me here.' I remembered how Vinny had said I'd make a lousy private detective. No kidding.

'This isn't your fault.'

'Why did you leave your fingerprints in that house?'

He smiled weakly. 'Dom and I were heading over there to clean up the joint when we heard the cops were there. Some fucking kid saw Sal there. Put two and two together.'

'Whose house was it?'

'A friend's. He keeps it for anyone who needs it.'

I wasn't going to go there.

'So why was Sal at the restaurant that day, the day he was killed?' I asked.

My father shook his head. 'Jesus, he was so stubborn. He'd moved the chickens to the basement in the house, since he knew the restaurant would be closed on Thanksgiving and too cold for them with the weather the way it's been. But he knew it was all over after the fire, after LeeAnn, and the restaurant was going to be razed, so he told me he was going to take the chickens to the restaurant to kill them.'

'He killed the chickens?'

My father shrugged automatically, and I could see the pain sweep through his eyes. 'The birds were just a moneymaker. Hell, we

319

all raised chickens in the neighborhood when we were kids, we'd all slaughtered them when we needed to. It wasn't a big deal for Sal, and it was all over anyway. He didn't have any real attachment to those birds. They were just a reminder of what could go wrong.'

He moved slightly, and his eyes closed, his breathing got shallower. Hell, I needed to keep him talking. 'So why did you want to meet me?'

He opened his eyes, grimaced, and clenched his teeth. But he answered me. 'We heard about what happened at Sal's last night.'

When Dick and I got shot at.

'Do you know who it was?' I asked.

My father's eyes rested on mine, and I could see him mentally struggling with something. 'Pete was supposed to settle his debt last night. He'd sent his mother to the DeLucias and was waiting for the meet last night when you showed up unexpectedly. He panicked, thought he'd try to scare you off.'

Dick had thought it was my father. I had thought it was my father. But it was Pete. He was the one who shot at us.

'How do you know this?' I asked.

'We got word.' Which meant the guy Pete was supposed to meet must have been there, must have seen the whole thing.

'Vinny said the cops were watching you, so I knew you'd be okay overnight,' my father was saying. 'But I wanted to see you this morning.'

He took a deep breath. 'Just so you know, Annie, Pete really fucked up when he shot up Dom's house. Until then, I might have been able to help him. But you can't do that shit and get away with it. Dom's a respected member of the community.'

The cop cars swung into the parking lot as I digested that information. I recognized Tom's car, and when the ambulance turned the corner, I sighed with relief.

I glanced at my father's face, which had gotten even grayer. I pushed his hair back off his forehead. 'Are you doing okay, Dad? The ambulance is here.'

He closed his eyes, and he tried to catch his breath. It was as if a vise had clamped itself across my chest.

Tom's car door opened, and I saw him using it as a shield, his gun drawn.

'It's okay, Tom,' I shouted. 'He's gone, but my father's been shot.' I looked at my dad, and he stirred a little; he was way too quiet. His lips were colorless.

Tom jogged over with a few uniforms close behind and pulled me away from my dad, and I struggled for a minute before I saw the paramedics and their gurney.

'They have to take care of him. I'll take you to the hospital,' Tom said gently.

I let myself go limp then, and I felt Tom's arms around me, leading me away. 'Who shot him, Annie?'

'Pete Amato. But he's gone.' It wasn't a lie.

He frowned. 'Why?'

'He thought my dad killed Sal.' I tried to glance back, to see what was going on with my dad, but Tom steered me back. 'I should go with him,' I tried.

'We'll be there as soon as we can,' he said. He flipped his chin at another detective. 'I'll take her to the hospital, Dave. Can you handle this here?'

Dave nodded.

'Pete Amato,' Tom told him flatly. 'Find him.' He turned to me. 'What's he driving?'

I described the battered blue pickup, and Tom nodded at Dave, who was writing everything down in a small notebook.

The TV vans were lined up just outside the fence surrounding the rink on State Street. I glimpsed Dick Whitfield and Wesley Bell, his cameras dangling around his neck, but I let Tom put me in his car and turned the other way.

'I don't want anyone to see me,' I said.

'Don't worry. Just scootch down a little,'

Tom said as he got behind the wheel.

We drove out of the lot, Tom looking straight ahead and ignoring everything that was going on around us. I huddled on the floor like a fugitive. After a few minutes, Tom said I could get up.

'So tell me what's going on,' he said. 'Where did Pete go, and why did he think your father killed Sal Amato?'

I told him almost everything I knew, which was fairly substantial once I started telling it. When I was done, I started shaking so much that Tom pulled over, parked, and put his arms around me.

'It's okay. You're okay,' he whispered into my hair as I sobbed. His voice was so soothing, and I turned my face up toward him. Without thinking about it, I kissed him, but we both knew I didn't mean it. I just wanted to feel something.

It was too bad it didn't work.

'So who killed Sal Amato?' Tom asked, and I was thankful he was ignoring the kiss.

I shrugged, then told him how Sal was in the restaurant to kill the chickens.

'That's when I found out my neighbor's crazy,' I said, telling him about Amber's penchant for poultry.

Tom chuckled. 'We had a couple of uniforms over there making sure those picketers didn't get out of hand,' he said. 'What the hell's wrong with those people?'

'She keeps leaving those stupid tofu recipes under my door . . . ' My voice trailed off as I remembered our exchange this morning. Or, rather, what she was wearing when she left.

'It was her,' I said quietly.

'What?'

'Amber. She was wearing a big puffy coat with a hood this morning, just like the person I saw in the restaurant when I found Sal's body.' I stared at Tom.

The reality of what I was saying started to dawn on him. 'You can't mean that she killed Sal because he killed those chickens?'

I had no doubt that she would sacrifice a human for a stupid bird.

'We better find her, then, bring her in and talk to her,' Tom said, and I listened as he called headquarters and arranged to have a couple of uniforms go over to my building.

'I should call my mother,' I said, remembering then that my cell phone was in my purse, which was still in my car at the ice rink.

Tom handed me his phone, and I called my mother's office. Her secretary said she'd already heard about my father and was headed to the hospital. Without thinking, I dialed Vinny's office number.

The phone rang and rang, the machine didn't pick up. So I dialed his home number.

'Hello?' It was a female voice.

I wasn't in the mood to talk to Rosie, but I had to let Vinny know what was going on. 'Is Vinny there?' I asked.

'Who is this?'

'Annie Seymour. Listen, I need to talk to him. It's urgent.'

I heard a heavy sigh. 'He's not here. He hasn't been here since yesterday morning. I'm surprised you don't know where he is. Try his office.' She hung up.

Tom was watching me out of the corner of his eye as I dialed Vinny's cell phone. It rang and rang, just like his office phone.

Something wasn't right.

'Tom, Vinny was on to Pete last night, he was checking the computer, tracking the money. And now I can't find him.' I hated asking him this, but I had to. 'Can we stop at his office? That's where he told me he was going last night.'

I was asking a lot, I knew that. But a fear started growing in my gut that something awful had happened to Vinny, maybe worse than my dad. And in that instant when I heard Tom say, 'No problem,' I knew. I knew that it was completely over with Tom, even if Vinny never left Rosie.

Tom drove to Vinny's office on Trumbull Street, and we pulled up and got out. Cobb Doyle let us in, but Vinny's office door was locked. We could see through the frosted glass that it was dark inside.

'I just got in, but I don't think he's here,' Cobb told us.

'Vinny!' Tom called out, but only silence answered him. My mouth was too dry to say anything. Tom turned to me. 'It doesn't seem like he's here.'

'What if he's hurt or something?'

'Give me your scarf.'

I handed it to him, and he wrapped it around his hand and crashed it through the glass. He reached inside and turned the knob. I watched as he went in and quickly searched the office.

'He's not here,' he said, coming back out, and I took a deep breath, relieved on the one hand but still worried.

Tom's phone rang. After answering he nodded a couple of times and said, 'Yeah . . . okay . . . no problem,' before he hung up. 'Your father's in surgery. Your mother's at the hospital. What do you want to do?'

A thought dawned on me. 'Maybe Vinny went to Dominic Gaudio's looking for my father,' I suggested.

'I'll check that out,' Tom said, 'after I take

you to the hospital.'

I nodded mutely and followed him back to the car. I stared through the window but didn't see anything along the way. Tom pulled up in front of the hospital entrance.

'I'll let you off here,' he said.

'You're not coming in?'

'I'm going over to Gaudio's, and I have to find out if anyone's found Amber. You have to go see your mother.'

I smiled weakly. 'Thanks, Tom. I really mean it.'

He touched my chin gently and smiled. I got out of the car and went through the big automatic doors without looking back.

28

My mother's face was almost as gray as my dad's. She stood up, smoothing out the black wool skirt of her suit, and smiled weakly.

'He's in surgery.' Her voice was almost a whisper as she pulled me into her arms. I started to cry, and I felt her hand stroking my hair. 'He'll pull through this. He's tough, you know that.' Her words wrapped themselves around me as we sank into the stiff chairs in the waiting room.

I forced myself to stop crying and pulled a tissue out of my pocket. 'Who called you?'

'Your detective.'

'Tom?'

She nodded. 'I was at the courthouse, with Mickey. For the arraignment. One of my colleagues was there on another case, and he offered to take over for me.'

'Mickey'll be out soon,' I said, and I went into the whole story, reciting it the way I'd write it, without emotion, without judgment. She listened, frowning at times, especially when I told her about the shooting at Dominic Gaudio's, but didn't say anything and sighed when I finished with my father getting into the ambulance.

'Mickey thought LeeAnn was killed by the Mob.'

'Why?'

'Mickey found out in Boston that LeeAnn had been delivering Sal's payments. She made a payment when they were up there. He'd followed her, then confronted her. She told him it was no big deal, really downplayed it, but he knew better.'

So he wasn't stupid.

'They had a big fight, and she took off. When he got back and found out she was dead, he got nervous. He found out from Mac that your father was in town, and he tried to get him to tell him what was going on.'

I remembered how he'd found me that day after the diner and asked where my father was. 'Why would he talk to Dad?' As soon as I asked it, I mentally kicked myself. That was a stupid question.

My mother thought it was a stupid question, too, I could see that from the look on her face.

Another thought seeped into my head. 'Tom's looking for Vinny. He's not home and not at his office.'

'He was at the courthouse. I saw him when I got there.'

'He's not answering his cell phone.'

'That's odd. He was talking on his phone when I saw him.'

Pete was already following me to the ice rink when my mother saw Vinny at the courthouse. So Vinny must be okay. But where the hell was he?

'You didn't see him when you left to come here?' I asked my mother.

She shook her head. 'I don't think I noticed anyone on my way here. I just had to get here.'

I smiled involuntarily, and her eyes narrowed. 'Don't think it's because I'm still in love with your father, Annie. I do love him, but I'm not in love with him. I can't erase twenty years of marriage, raising a child with him. Of course I had to be here.'

'Did you call Suzette?'

'Yes. She's going to call when she gets a flight, and I'll get a car to pick her up in Hartford and bring her down here.'

Just then the door at the far end of the room slammed open, and I saw Paula walking toward us. Vinny was right behind her.

'Tom told us you were here,' Paula started, but before she could finish, I was standing with Vinny's arms wrapped around me.

'Are you okay?' he asked.

I nodded, then pulled back. 'Where the hell

have you been? I've been worried sick.'

He nodded his head at Paula. 'Blame her. She picked me up in front of the courthouse before I could even go in to Mickey's arraignment.'

Paula stared at the floor for a second, then looked up at me. 'We found out your father had been at Dominic Gaudio's, but no one was there when we got there this morning. We thought for sure Vinny knew where he was.'

'So you were going to try to strong-arm him into telling you?' I asked.

Her face turned pink. 'We had no idea what was going down.'

'I told them our suspicions about Pete,' Vinny said. 'I didn't find out too much from the computer, but there was a lot of money being deposited, then taken out in cash. I knew you'd come to the courthouse and we could figure out a game plan from there.'

'I tried to call your cell phone,' I said to Vinny.

He glanced at Paula. 'Blame her. They turned it off when they questioned me.'

'Where are the rest of your G-men?' I asked Paula.

She snorted. 'They said I could handle this. Yeah, now that they have egg all over their faces.' Her eyes darted around the room. 'I didn't say that.'

Vinny squeezed my hand. 'How's your father?'

'We haven't heard anything yet.'

'He's going to make it. He's strong,' Vinny said, echoing my mother's words. I knew that, I just needed to hear it.

I sat next to my mother and noticed for the first time the two cops on the other side of the room.

'They have to be here. They have to talk to him after the surgery,' my mother said.

I knew Tom would be back. This time he would be the one asking the questions, and I'd have to answer. I couldn't get away with 'No comment' in an official police investigation.

Which also meant, yes, there was Dick Whitfield loping through the doors toward us. He had no business being here.

But I wasn't in the mood for a fight. Or an interrogation from the boy wonder. This one I could say 'No comment' to. I braced myself, tightening my grip on Vinny's hand as Dick stood before me.

'Hey, Annie, I'm sorry,' he said.

I would've done the same thing. Play on the emotions, get those barriers to go down. He had to have known I knew all the tricks, all the ways to get the victims to talk.

'Tell Marty I don't have anything to say,

okay?' I said, my voice hard.

He shrugged. 'I'm not here to write a story, Annie.'

The look on my face and the fact that I couldn't say anything invited him to continue.

'Marty thinks I have a conflict. You know, because of the shooting last night and the restraining order threat and all. He's putting Renee on the story. I just wanted to let you know how sorry I am about your dad.'

I finally found my tongue. 'He's not dead, Dick. He's just in surgery. How the hell did you get up here, anyway?'

'I know someone at the desk downstairs.'

He knew someone? Oh, God, I didn't want to think about it. He actually had a source at the hospital. Which was a fucking smart thing.

'And what's this about Renee? Christ, she's good for the soup kitchen stories, but this? How the hell does Marty think she's going to be able to handle this?' I found myself standing face-to-face with Dick.

He shrugged again. 'I don't know, but he's got Kevin down at the courthouse dealing with the Mickey Hayward angle, and Renee's talking to the cops about Pete Amato.'

I was going to have to tell Marty what happened. The cops wouldn't tell Renee anything, and I didn't want the story fucked up.

Vinny's arm was around me. 'Annie, I think maybe you need to relax a little.'

I snorted. 'Relax?'

'Forget about the paper for a little while and be here with your mom. I have to get going.'

And with his words, I forgot about the paper, I forgot about Marty, and I forgot about Dick Whitfield, even though I could still smell the McDonald's French fries scent emanating from his person. I looked at Vinny. 'You have to go?'

He walked me away from everyone and to the doors that led back into the hallway. 'I have something that can't wait.' He put his fingers under my chin and lifted my face toward his. 'I'll be back.' His lips brushed mine, and he left me standing there.

★   ★   ★

My mother was touching my arm, asking me to wake up. I squinted and caught the blue scrubs of a masked doctor standing in front of us.

'He's still critical, but he'll pull out of this,' the doctor was telling my mother.

She nodded, smiling, tears in her eyes, and she pulled me up and hugged me.

'It's going to be a bit of a recuperation. I

understand he lives in Las Vegas?'

I didn't hear anything more. The doctor spoke softly to my mother, and I glanced around and saw Tom leaning against the wall across the room. I went over to him. 'Hey,' I said. 'Doctor says he's going to be okay.'

He nodded, smiling, but something was missing, something I'd gotten used to seeing and was gone for good now.

'Do you need my statement now?' I asked.

'We can go across the hall and do it there, okay? Paula's coming along.'

I noticed her then, still waiting, like the rest of us. 'Sure.'

Something else, or rather someone else, was missing, too. Vinny hadn't come back yet. Had he said he was going to?

The questions just kept coming and coming. I told them everything I knew. My father would have to fill in the holes when he woke up. I still couldn't believe that Pete Amato had tried to kill both of us. Had killed LeeAnn.

But then I remembered Amber.

'Did you find my neighbor, Tom?'

Tom and Paula exchanged a look.

'What?' I asked.

'This isn't the first time she's been involved in something criminal,' Tom said. 'Six years ago, she was living in Virginia and a farmer got killed. Seems he owned a chicken farm, but he wasn't looking to sell eggs. He was raising chickens to be slaughtered for one of those fast-food chains. They found him with his throat slit and the chickens were gone.' He paused. 'Amber's boyfriend is serving a life term. She was never charged. She testified against him, but he claims it was all her idea. So it's he said/she said. Jury bought her story and locked him up.'

'And she moved here,' Paula said. 'One of the cops down there called us when she moved, said we might want to keep an eye on her. He thought she had more to do with it but couldn't prove it. But she kept her nose clean here. She still protested the treatment of chickens, but the protests were uneventful. We stopped paying attention to her, especially after 9/11. We just didn't have time for someone like her.'

'So did you find her?' I asked.

Tom nodded. 'She admitted everything. I think she's trying to be some sort of martyr. It was her you saw in the restaurant. She'd been snooping around and saw Sal kill the chickens.'

'She just so happened to have a gun on her?' I asked.

'She's had a permit for years.'

'And she left when she heard me come in.'

Jesus. Amber. And I thought the worst thing she was doing was leaving me those stupid vegan recipes.

Tom had a funny look on his face.

'What?' I asked, not sure I really wanted to know.

'We found Pete Amato's body.'

Shit. 'Where?'

'In the woods in North Madison off Route Eighty.' He paused. 'We got a tip. Pretty damn accurate. Can't trace the call, though.'

My breath caught in my throat.

'We can't find the truck he was driving.'

And they probably never would. A chop shop would destroy any evidence that might have been lurking there.

'Did anything else happen out there at the ice rink, Annie?'

I wanted to tell him, I really did. But I couldn't. It was too fucking crazy anyway, and if I said anything, who knew who'd be after me? I just shook my head and shrugged. 'I told you all I know.'

Tom mulled that over and nodded slowly. 'Okay. I'll see what your father says when I can talk to him. And we've already got Dominic Gaudio at headquarters.'

I suppressed a smile. Tom didn't have a goddamn prayer.

They were finished with me, and I just

wanted to see my dad. But he was still in recovery, and it would be a while.

The rest of the day melted into the night. Suzette showed up, her usually bright green eyes dull.

'Have you seen him?' she asked.

I shook my head, and tears cascaded down her cheeks. I put my arm around her and was surprised to see my mother on the other side of her, helping her to a chair.

'He'll be okay,' she said.

'You must be Alexandra,' Suzette said.

'I'm sorry we have to meet like this,' my mother said, squeezing her hand.

I glanced at my watch and looked at the door. Where had five hours gone? And where was Vinny?

The doctor came out to tell us my father probably wouldn't be awake for another few hours, but we could go in one at a time to sit with him for a few minutes. Suzette glanced at my mother, who waved her off. Suzette got up and followed the doctor through the doors.

'Why don't you go home and get some rest?' my mother asked. 'You've had a difficult day.'

'But I want to be here.'

'He won't wake up for a few hours, you heard the doctor.'

'I don't have my car.' Not to mention my driver's license. But she didn't know that.

My mother produced her keys. 'Take mine. It's on the second level, row B.'

She pushed the keys into my hand, and they felt heavier than they should have. My shoulders sank with weariness, and the thought of my soft, warm bed was lulling me into saying yes.

'Okay,' I said, standing. I put on my puffy coat. The tape had come off partway, and some feathers floated by my face.

'I'll get you a new coat tomorrow,' my mother promised, always concerned about how I looked and not bothering to notice I didn't care too much.

I nodded mutely and walked toward the elevators.

He was waiting by the door, his hands stuffed into his pockets, his head wet with snow.

Oh, shit, it was snowing again.

'Come home with me,' Vinny said simply.

I held up my mother's keys. 'I need to get some sleep.'

He leaned toward me and kissed me. 'Come home with me,' he whispered.

I pulled back, suddenly wide awake.

'Okay, if it makes you uncomfortable to go to my place, we'll go to yours,' he said in response to my silence.

The butterflies started crashing into one another in my stomach.

'You broke up with Rosie?'

'She wouldn't give me the ring back.'

'Neither would I.'

He looked up at the ceiling. 'What the hell am I getting into?' he asked no one in particular before looking back at me.

'Are you sure?' I asked. I still hadn't smiled.

'Hell, Annie, I'm not sure about anything except that since I met you, I want to be with you.'

He leaned over and kissed me again. It was a long, slow kiss that made my toes curl.

When he pulled away, I smiled.

We do hope that you have enjoyed reading this large print book.

Did you know that all of our titles are available for purchase?

We publish a wide range of high quality large print books including:
Romances, Mysteries, Classics
General Fiction
Non Fiction and Westerns

Special interest titles available in large print are:
The Little Oxford Dictionary
Music Book
Song Book
Hymn Book
Service Book

Also available from us courtesy of Oxford University Press:
Young Readers' Dictionary
(large print edition)
Young Readers' Thesaurus
(large print edition)

For further information or a free brochure, please contact us at:
Ulverscroft Large Print Books Ltd.,
The Green, Bradgate Road, Anstey,
Leicester, LE7 7FU, England.
Tel: (00 44) 0116 236 4325
Fax: (00 44) 0116 234 0205

Other titles published by
The House of Ulverscroft:

LET ME DIE YESTERDAY

Theresa Murphy

When hired to trace a village girl who went missing in the 1960s, private investigator Gerry McCabe anticipates an early end to his assignment with the discovery of female remains. Instead, it plunges McCabe into the dark and hostile labyrinths of rural life. Intent on mending his broken marriage, he is distracted by the vivacious Beth Merrill — the missing girl's sister — and the alluring widow Sharee Bucholtz. Unwittingly causing a local tragedy, a distraught McCabe struggles to continue his investigation and resolve his own relationship difficulties. But can he succeed on either case?